DRAGON
WHISPERER

DRAGON WHISPERER

VANESSA RICCI-THODE

IGUANA

Copyright © 2013 Vanessa Ricci-Thode
Published by Iguana Books
720 Bathurst Street, Suite 303
Toronto, Ontario, Canada
M5V 2R4

Publisher: Greg Ioannou
Editor: Laura Lynn Foster, Stephanie Martin
Front cover design: Jane Awde Goodwin
Book layout design: Meghan Behse

Library and Archives Canada Cataloguing in Publication

Ricci-Thode, Vanessa, 1981-, author
     Dragon whisperer / Vanessa Ricci-Thode.

Issued in electronic formats.
ISBN 978-1-927403-65-5

     I. Title.

PS8635.I229D73 2013   C813'.6   C2013-902344-5

This is an original print edition of *Dragon Whisperer*.

To my daughter,

Sofia,

For helping me become the person I always knew I could be,

&

In loving memory of John Ricci: uncle, friend, artistic mentor, gone too soon.

PROLOGUE

THE Ovailens and the Joaseras sat at the dark barnboard table in the kitchen of the Ovailens' modest, one-and-a-half-storey farmhouse. From where they sat in the airy kitchen that opened out into the parlour on one side, they could see out the screened rear door to where their young children, Reiser and Vyranna, were playing in the expansive yard under an idyllic summer sky. The Ovailens' oldest, Loniesa, had gone into the city market with the neighbours.

Sivyla Ovailen cast a glance out the door to check on the children as she served her frequent guests chilled tea and fresh fruit, but her attention couldn't linger outside because there were other things to attend to. Today's visit by the Joaseras, although friendly, had a serious tone. Sivyla handed Draidel and Sharice Joasera each a cup and then the two families got down to business. The topic had been briefly discussed once before, but nothing had ever been decided.

"Now," Draidel began, "me and Sharice have thought over your suggestions from your visit in the winter. None of us are getting any younger and we need to see that the children will be cared for in the case of hardship or tragedy."

"As long as you're not rushing into the deal because of your illness," Lou Ovailen said to Draidel.

Draidel shifted slightly but shook his head. He was still gaunt and pale, still much thinner than he had been, with most of his black hair suddenly gone white, but his spirit had at least returned to normal.

"I'm better now," he insisted, "but it sure brought things into focus. It's hard to say what the lasting effects will be, but that's not the point. The kids need to be looked after and there's no reason not to go forward with this."

"They're still so young," Sivyla protested.

Lou gave his wife a stern look, annoyed over the comment, and then turned his attention back to Draidel, nodding solemnly.

"Now, Siv, it's not etched in stone," Sharice crooned, reaching across the table to give her friend's hand a reassuring pat. "Nothing is ever final in these matters. You know it's ultimately up to the children to decide once the time comes. A little nudge in the right direction never hurts."

"They're still only babies," Sivyla insisted.

"It's nothing final," Lou grumbled, echoing Sharice's sentiments.

Sivyla reluctantly subsided, but still wasn't entirely convinced it was a good idea. She wasn't against the idea of pre-arranging a marriage between her son, Reiser, and the Joaseras' daughter, but she felt that the children were far too young to be able to tell if they would be a good match. The Ovailens had waited until Loniesa was five before solidifying her match. Although Reiser Ovailen and Vyranna Joasera were only toddlers, they were cold towards each other and Vyranna, who was two years older than Reiser, often took to picking on him rather than playing contentedly like she did with her other playmates.

"We've been close since we were children," Sharice pointed out. "There's nothing wrong with continuing the bond shared by our families."

"Of course there isn't," Sivyla agreed. She peered outside to see that Vyranna was busy pushing Reiser away so she wouldn't have to share the bowl of berries Sivyla had given them. "It's just that our children don't seem to like each other."

She looked across the table to where Sharice was leaning back in her chair with her hands rested on her belly—swollen with the Joaseras' second child. Sharice insisted it would be another girl.

"I just don't think a nudge in the right direction will be enough for those two," Sivyla explained.

"The sooner we get this out of the way, the better," Draidel urged.

Lou caught his wife's train of thought. "If the young'un on the way is a girl, maybe we should include her in the final decision," he suggested.

The Joaseras exchanged a pensive glance and nodded. Vyranna was stubborn and defiant, and it was clear that she didn't like Reiser. It would be a great shame for the two families to go through the hard work of arranging the marriage, just to have the children reject each other in the end. Sharice was certain she would have another daughter by the end of the month, and she wanted to be sure that at least one of her children would be taken care of after she and Draidel were gone.

"All right," she agreed.

"Has the midwife been able to confirm the baby's health?" Lou asked.

"So far everything seems fine."

"The healer never found out what was wrong with Draidel," Lou said. "Is there any concern of his illness affecting the child?"

Sharice and Draidel exchanged another quick glance before Sharice spoke.

"The baby seems fine," she insisted. "But we'll have to wait and see. Assuming she's healthy, I see no reason not to include her."

Any further conversation was interrupted by an agonized squeal from the back of the house and Reiser came running up the steps crying, while Vyranna stood defiantly in the yard shouting about how he had deserved it. With dual exasperated sighs, Sivyla went out to comfort Reiser and Draidel was close behind to punish Vyranna. Lou and Sharice, meanwhile, started to iron out the details of their agreement.

CHAPTER 1

DIONELLE returned to the field with fresh waterskins slung over her shoulder and began handing them out to the groups of peasant children working the field. The sun was warm with the first traces of summer in the humid air, smelling of rich, fresh earth and new wildflowers. She gave the last of the water to Reiser and then stood watching the planting efforts, absently tucking the loose strands of her long white braid behind her ears.

"It's no use, love," Reiser said, pushing the windblown strands from her face and kissing her forehead. He was lost for a moment in her eyes, two blue pools rimmed in amber fire. He shook himself and smiled. "Fetch a hat next time you're up at the house, it's the only way you'll win."

She gave him a shy smile, but said nothing and continued to observe, doing her best to learn how to help her new husband run their farm. It had been only a week since the twenty-year-old had left the Joasera household to join Reiser on the ranch, so she was still getting used to farm life. Even the landscape was new to her. The farmland itself was something she was accustomed to, though the valley floor around Pasdale was perfectly flat whereas her home had been one gentle curve after another—a wide expanse, but not nearly so shapeless. And then there was the way the hills rose up at every horizon, some with a vertical climb that was most strange to her.

She bent over to help one of the smaller boys with a sack of seeds when they heard the first screeching cry. Reiser hadn't been entirely certain he'd heard anything, but Dionelle stood bolt upright and spun in the direction it had come from.

"Dragons," she whispered. "Get everyone to safety!"

She began running back toward the house before they heard the second cry that confirmed her fears—dragons were nearby and getting closer. Reiser gathered everyone and got them to help him move as much of the livestock as they could back to the barn so they could get to safety before the flight arrived. Dionelle came back out to join them with a brown cloak draped over her arm. Reiser had noticed it hanging by the doorway since she had unpacked her belongings a week ago, but this was the first time he'd seen her with it, even though they had been out in a heavy downpour.

"Fireproof," she said when she saw him looking at it. "To protect my clothes. Boidossen gave it to me."

"What do you mean to do with a fireproof cloak?"

"Whatever I need to. Get everyone inside, but leave me a horse."

"You're not going to come in?" he asked.

"I'll stay nearby, but I want to see where they go."

Reiser didn't know what she was up to so he got everyone into the house and brought his and Dionelle's swiftest horse with him, tethering it to the front porch. Dionelle was standing in the front lane, staring west, where the pine-covered slopes rose steeply, almost like a ragged mountainside. The dragoncries had become nearly deafening, but she hadn't spotted the creatures yet. She wore a determined expression but was less nervous about the dragons than she had been about the prospect of leaving her family behind before wedding Reiser after the deaths of his parents.

The dragons finally swooped over the hilltops on the western horizon, flying low and giving voice to another of their mighty cries. There were two of them—the larger one was a midnight black dragoness and the smaller one was a grey male. When the pair reached the farmland in the valley, the male swooped around, circling the fields while the female continued on toward the city.

"What would she want in the city?" Dionelle marvelled.

"To talk with our ruling lord, no doubt. He looks like he's intent on mischief though," Reiser commented, regarding the male.

"I'll see what I can do," Dionelle replied, taking the reins and leading the horse away from the house as she continued to watch the dragon.

He finally landed in a nearby field where the neighbour's cattle were grazing. Dionelle mounted up and galloped headlong toward the beast, and Reiser, who was terrified for her safety now as he fully understood her intentions, ran to the stable to find another horse to follow her. As he neared the field, he saw that Dionelle had dismounted a safe distance and left her horse to flee as it saw fit. Dionelle was running toward the dragon and trying to pull her cloak around her.

The dragon was diving and swooping, spewing dragonfire at the terrified herd, but hadn't mortally wounded any yet—enjoying the hunt before it moved in for a proper kill. It had one down and was preparing to move in when Dionelle got between the dragon and the cow.

"That's quite enough," she said calmly but loudly enough to be heard over the din.

Shocked and angry, the dragon landed in front of her and hit her with a fiery blast. Somewhere in the distance she heard Reiser cry out in terror, but she held her ground, squinting against the bright light and spreading her arms to make herself and her cloak as large a shield as possible as she tried to protect her neighbour's cow from the fury of the dragon.

The dragon recoiled, shuffling backward on all fours, when he realized she wasn't a charred, writhing mass. The dragons always reacted to her in surprise the first time they met her, as she wasn't a renowned sorceress and was unremarkable in her appearance, aside from being completely white. The dragon stood tall on his hind legs, spreading his silver-tinged wings to make himself as large and intimidating as possible, shrieking up at the sky. She barely came to his knee and he would have to lie flat on the ground to see her eye-to-eye, but she had conversed with dragons before, always under the same circumstances; she wasn't afraid of the display. It was a desperate dragon that would eat a human—most humans were all bone and hair and cumbersome clothing. Dionelle was scrawny as far as most humans went. Dragons were slow with their claws, especially when lying flat to converse with the humans in their presence, so she wasn't afraid of being torn to shreds—or she wouldn't be once she got the dragon to settle down.

As the dragon roared furiously at the sky, Dionelle nudged the cow and finally got it moving. It stampeded after the rest of the herd as they rushed from the dragon and back toward the homestead.

"That's quite enough," Dionelle repeated firmly, once the dragon quieted again.

"Who are you to command me!" he roared.

"These are my neighbour's livestock, and I will not permit you to destroy them. I know for a fact there is a man paid by the crown to raise oxen specifically for your appetites, so I suggest you take your mischief elsewhere."

The dragon finally spread out on the ground to look her in the eye. He blew another line of flame at her, testing.

"Oh, for heaven's sake! It didn't work the first time so just stop! I thought dragons were cleverer than this."

"You dare insult me?" he growled.

"You're the one behaving in a manner worthy of insult," she replied, still remaining calm. "I always expect dragons to be majestic beasts—like the mistress you travelled in with—but I must say your demeanour is incredibly disappointing."

Dionelle was surprised how this line of reasoning always worked with the males, but an angry dragoness was much more difficult to calm and bring to reason. The same trick always worked with the males, but it was always something different with the females. Boidossen, Dionelle's mentor and a powerful wizard, had been training her since she was a small child, and he had been schooling her about dragons from the beginning, but he was no expert and knew very little about their customs. Dionelle hoped that now that she was so close to such a large city, she could learn more.

"Why should I care about disappointing a white little twig like you?"

"Because I am one of the subjects of your world, whether you like it or not. If you would prefer I view you as a tyrant, then continue your present course. But these are human lands and it doesn't do your reputation any good to go about marauding like some kind of monster."

The dragon huffed, petulantly blowing more flame at her, before springing into the air and joining his companion in the city.

Dionelle sighed in relief as she removed the bulky cloak. Its sole purpose was to protect her clothing from the flames and it didn't even have a hood, though it draped on the ground around her feet to protect her boots. She glanced around to survey the damage, seeing scorch marks all over the field and some wounded cattle. She spotted Reiser leading the mare her way.

"What possessed you?" Reiser shouted, still panicking.

"They won't hurt me," she insisted.

"Just because they haven't yet doesn't mean they won't."

"Dragons are only a real threat to humans during times of war, or when they feel provoked, and the rest of the time they are only a threat to livestock and livelihood. As soon as they discover I can't be scorched, they tend to lose interest in harming me."

"What about those claws!"

7

"Dragons prefer to be eye-to-eye with those they converse with and will lie on the ground, usually on top of those claws," she explained. "The only real danger occurs before I can get them to settle down and talk to me, but at that point they're always more interested in using fire. When fire doesn't work, they become curious and usually abandon their mischief for a word with me. They're a highly inquisitive lot and would rather find out my trick than kill me once fire fails them."

"You do this often?"

"I didn't mean it the first time, but they were after Mamma's horse. I have no fear of their fire and jumped in to stop them. When it worked, Boidossen schooled me in their behaviours as best he could, and now I stop them whenever I can. They are just bullies, the lot of them—they think because they're so large they can forget their manners and behave like tired children."

"Please, I beg you, don't do that again!"

"Now that your neighbours know I'm immune to fire, I don't believe they will forgive me saving these cattle and not others. I've only had to deal with dragons a handful of times in my life. It's unlikely to happen again for years."

"Don't be so certain. Perhaps they don't maraud in your homeland very often, but they visit Pasdale several times a year to speak with Lord Dunham and Lady Karth."

"They really visit that often? What could they possibly want with a bunch of humans?"

"I know very little about the details, but they have treaties with the king and agreements with the wizards, and they come to the city frequently to discuss them. They don't always make such a display out of their arrival and don't always cause mischief, but they're here regularly and I don't want you risking your life for a couple of cows!"

"It will be all right," she tried to reassure him. "If he had landed much farther away, there wouldn't have been much I could have done anyway and I barely got here in time as it is. How often do they land in these fields?"

"That was the first time in years," Reiser admitted, shaking his head.

He didn't like it one bit, but it was clear there was nothing he could do to talk her out of it. Next time, he could likely restrain her and that was exactly what he intended to do. He would deal with the wrath of his neighbours if they lost livestock, but he wouldn't allow his wife to risk her life for a couple of animals or a barn that could easily be rebuilt.

He helped her up onto the mare and climbed up behind her, heading to find the steed she had abandoned, so they could get home and get the children back out into the field. They would have to watch for the dragons when they left the city again, but the dragons never left in the same direction they arrived from and never arrived from the same direction twice in a row. It made it nearly impossible to track them to their homes deep in the mountains and that was how they preferred it.

REISER had noticed a change in Dionelle's demeanour even before the dragons, but now she was even more put off. He was too flustered by the whole dragon ordeal to even say anything to her about it. He didn't know how to approach either topic. He still wasn't used to her fire immunity and seeing her being torched by a dragon had been a terrible shock. For what was neither the first nor the last time, he wondered what he'd got himself into—what his parents had gotten him into. There was still a lot of work left to do and he pushed his concerns to the edge of his mind and hefted another seed bag down from the wagon.

"Master Ovailen," a small voice interrupted. One of the field girls was trying to get his attention.

"Yes, Jinny?"

"Where's the water, sir?"

He looked around and realized for the first time that Dionelle hadn't returned, even though it had been over an hour since she went to refill the waterskins from the pump at the back of the house. One of the children, often Jinny herself, usually performed this chore, but it was the best way for Dionelle to make herself useful until she learned more about farming. Reiser became concerned and went to find her.

Reiser found her sitting at the kitchen table with a letter in front of her, her hands in her lap and her head hung, weeping. He entered cautiously and picked up the letter, not wanting to upset her any further by making her speak about it when he could easily find out for himself. She remained silent and still as he read.

The letter was from Cusec, her little brother, and it wasn't good news, though Reiser wasn't surprised by what the boy had to say. The Joasera household had become tumultuous in Dionelle's absence, with Vyranna and Sharice fighting constantly and the boy terrified and lonely. Vyranna's fits had become much worse and she occasionally became violent, throwing things or pounding her fists against the walls and kicking the furniture. Sharice was left with little choice but meeting Vyranna's tantrums with violence of her own and had made good on her promise to box her daughter's ears if she didn't keep her attitude in check.

"It's barely been a week," Dionelle whimpered, "and they're already falling apart."

"Your mother will make Vyranna leave if this keeps up."

"Cusec is still so scared. There must be something we can do."

"Tell him he can come help us in the fields for a week. If it's still this bad when he receives your next letter, then have him send for us and we'll bring him here for a little while."

Dionelle's face brightened. "You mean it?"

"The sofa is plenty large enough for him. Or we can find a new mattress for the other room."

She jumped up and threw her arms around him, hugging him fiercely for a moment before she pulled his face to hers and kissed him deeply. Though she hadn't quite found her place in her new home and missed her family intensely, she had adjusted well to the fact that she was now his wife. Making the space their own, after it had been his parents' for so long, had helped them both adjust to the change and set Dionelle at ease, though she alternated between wanting to help him in the fields and just wanting to be alone with a book or with the fire in the hearth.

Dionelle didn't know how to deal with the transition, but looked forward to the winter when she would be finished her apprenticeship and would be able to truly put her efforts into sorcery. Until then she felt in limbo and a little out of place. Reiser hoped that Cusec did come to visit because it would give Dionelle a little more purpose to her days until she could fill them with her studies.

"I'll write to him this evening," she said.

DIONELLE stayed up late responding to her brother's letter and trying to calm her thoughts after telling him the day's tale about confronting the dragon. She hastily washed up in the light of the moons, both full, their radiance pouring through the windows, and then she followed Reiser upstairs to bed. He had the lantern turned low, and the shadows seemed to swallow his already dark features with his olive skin appearing almost coffee-coloured in the dim light. His dark complexion, broad shoulders and strong build from years of farm work were a shocking contrast to her waiflike, snowy white appearance.

She sat at the edge of the bed to change into her night clothes and comb out her long, straight hair. She turned shyly, expecting to see Reiser watching her, as he always did, but he was staring straight up and looking inward. She gently leaned into bed beside him, but still couldn't get his attention.

"Is it because of the dragon?" she asked carefully.

"You could have been killed!"

She recoiled at the harshness.

"I'm sorry it frightened you," she apologized. "The dragons look far more frightening than they actually are."

"How can you know that?"

"I've done it before. And I've studied them for years. I've never felt like my life was threatened."

Reiser nodded, but she could see he still didn't agree.

"I just need to get used to the thing with the fire," he muttered. Seeing that she was curled in beside him, he turned out the lantern and rolled over to go to sleep.

His sudden coldness made her uneasy and she didn't know how to respond. While the intimacy of their fresh union still ran hot and cold, she certainly preferred the shy, awkward attempts to the anger she faced now. She thought to their wedding day, little more than a week ago now, and wondered if the decision hadn't been too hasty. She fingered the pendant around her neck, a wedding gift, and fell asleep pondering their decision to wed.

CHAPTER 2

DIONELLE was frantic as she tidied up and finished preparing dinner while waiting for her family to arrive. They were going to stay for three days—until it was time for Dionelle to leave for the foothills to continue apprenticing. Cusec had never ended up coming to visit them, so she hadn't seen any of them since she and Reiser had been married, over two months ago. She was nervous and it didn't help that Reiser's sister, Loniesa, was arriving with her husband, Braqin, and their children tomorrow and Dionelle hadn't seen her since they were children. Loniesa had had her second child recently and hadn't been fit to travel for the wedding, so now that the baby was bigger and she had recovered, she was coming with her whole family to stay for a week.

Reiser was looking forward to having someone around after Dionelle left for Boidossen's because it would be strange to be alone in the house again. It had taken him some time to adjust to losing his parents—first his mother, followed quickly by his father—and he expected to face much of the same loneliness with Dionelle away for most of the summer. He also looked forward to meeting his niece, Shaiz, for the first time. His nephew, Kieron, was almost five now and the two children would be certain to keep the house busy for the duration of their visit.

Dionelle had spent a great deal of time child-proofing the house and she was worried that she may have forgotten something.

"If your mother can't help you prepare for the others, then Loniesa will be quick to remove any dangers we've missed. It will be all right—we both grew up in this house and turned out just fine."

Dionelle ignored him and continued slicing a loaf of bread. She had gone to great lengths to prepare a large meal for her family, and she and Reiser hadn't eaten that well since their wedding feast. Part of the reason they hadn't eaten well was that neither Reiser nor Dionelle had had much skill in the kitchen. Until Reiser lost his parents, he'd never taken much interest in cooking, and after their deaths he usually got one of his workers to help. Dionelle had left most of the kitchen-work to her mother or Vyranna.

As Dionelle stirred the stew, Reiser took a quick peek at the roast in the oven and then peered over her shoulder at what looked like their first success.

"It smells excellent," he commented.

"It looks right," she said hopefully.

"You haven't tasted it?"

"No. Have you?"

They had suffered through over-spiced and under-spiced stew, watery stew, and in their last attempt the gravy had gone completely wrong. It had been watery with large clumps of thickener. They had always resorted to using home loaf to sop up the mess on their plates, as they'd mastered baking bread much quicker than everything else.

"I'm afraid to try it," he admitted.

Dionelle giggled, relieved to share his concern.

"The roast looks good this time," she said. "Maybe we finally got it all right."

Apprehensive, but grinning playfully, she spooned up some gravy and blew on it before giving it a cautious taste test. Her face lit up in victory and she handed the spoon to Reiser, who was equally delighted.

"Perfect!" he declared.

"And just in time," Dionelle added. "I don't think I could bear a lecture from Mamma or Loni about domestic work."

"Nor could I! If this hadn't turned out, I'd have begged something presentable from the neighbours," he said with a wink.

Reiser knew she wanted to impress her sister, who was no doubt going to find anything she could to complain about. Dionelle had always done everything she should to keep Vyranna's criticisms to a minimum.

Reiser still felt anxious when Dionelle opened the wood stove and shoved her hand in to check the temperature and make sure it hadn't gotten too hot or cold. She was trying to keep everything warm until her family arrived. She placed the bread in a basket, covered it, and set it on top of the stove. Then she began to pace, occasionally stopping in the pantry to take out any last minute items. On her most recent journey back she brought out a brick of cheese and began slicing some pieces off to serve with the bread and fruit.

"We're going to be eating this meal for a week. Please, love, just come sit with me until they arrive."

She ignored him and finished what she was doing before joining him on the sofa in front of the hearth. Reiser hadn't been paying attention to the fire and it had grown far too large so she scowled at it until it went cold.

"It's midsummer. Do we really need a fire at all?" she asked.

She rarely cared about the fire and how big or small it was, but he knew she was raising a fuss about every little thing—and then dealing with it—before Vyranna could.

"It's good ambience," Reiser protested, "and you know the evening will get cold quickly enough. Besides, I thought you liked having a fire going."

"You like it so you can watch it rise and fall with my mood," she teased.

"It makes it easier for me to read you," he admitted. "Not many men are lucky enough to know when to stay away from a troubled wife."

She grinned at him and turned her attention back to the now-cold embers, fidgeting and brooding.

"It will be fine," he repeated. "If Vyranna causes a scene, we'll make her sleep in the barn."

"She can still cause a scene from the barn. It would have been so much easier if your sister's visit hadn't overlapped with Mamma's."

"Love, you forget that we all grew up together. Loni isn't going to be surprised or shocked by Vyranna's attitude."

"Braqin might have some objections, and Vyranna is sure to frighten the children if she goes off the way she does sometimes."

"We'll make her sleep in the barn," he insisted.

"Mamma will likely cut the visit short if she acts up. And I'm sure Vyranna knows that and will use it to her advantage."

"It will be too late for them to leave tonight," he pointed out. "You'll get them at least until tomorrow morning, but we'll do our best to avoid a scene, and if we get one, we'll do our best to talk your mother into staying until you've left."

"You promise that we'll make her sleep in the barn?" Dionelle asked, a playful spark of fire dancing in her amber-blue eyes.

Reiser grinned. "I'll hog-tie her if I have to."

Dionelle chuckled but went on staring into the dark hearth, waiting and worrying. They both remembered all too well how their last encounter with Vyranna had gone.

DIONELLE pursed her lips and remained silent as she brought more of her things out to Reiser's wagon, preparing to start life anew as his wife. She was terrified and upset but there was nothing he could do to reassure her that the chaos they were leaving behind would settle down once they were gone. Her sister was shouting at her from the front door and he was glad there were no neighbours around to hear it—Sharice didn't need that kind of embarrassing hardship after everything else she had to endure.

Reiser wasn't paying attention to any of Vyranna's hate-filled tirades and wasn't sure what she said to set Dionelle off, but her eyes suddenly lit up like dragonfire and she spun around, trembling angrily and dropping her box on the ground.

"That's enough, you cow!" Dionelle screamed. "Your jealousy is your own problem so why don't you just deal with it like the adult you are?"

"I'm not anything close to jealous!" Vyranna snapped defensively.

"And I'm a warthog," Dionelle snapped back. "You've treated him like filth his whole life and doubled your efforts when you found out the deal Mamma and Da made with the Ovailens. You have no right to treat me like this. Would you rather we'd forsaken our families' wishes and had to go out on our own and find some rancher with too many sons, good enough to take on the daughters of strangers? I would have let you have him if you'd said you wanted him."

"Liar! You never let me have anything I want!"

"Don't be ridiculous! I've done nothing but sacrifice to please you—to try to keep the peace when you act like a spoiled harpy."

"Don't you dare call me spoiled! You're the one who's always had everything—everything I wanted whether I asked for it or not."

"If you want things you have to speak up because no one in this family is a seer! You had *years* to change your mind before Reiser and I ever made this decision. I always back down from you and you know it—you've been taking advantage of it all my life. So if you really wanted him, why didn't you say something this time?"

"What good would it have done?" Vyranna shot back. "They always wanted you to have him anyway! Why do you think they included you in the bargain before you were even born? Before you were even guaranteed a girl or healthy!"

"You act as though I planned this from the womb! You're the one who gave them a reason to include me in the first place."

"Oh, yes, you can't ever let me forget that I'm not good enough for this family—that they had to have two more children to make up for my inadequacies. Cusec the hero breadwinner and Dionelle the perfect angel who they can pawn off to a good man—her soulmate—and forget about me! Just let you run off and leave us alone, with me working at that awful inn until Cusec is old enough to work the fields."

"Don't try to give me a sob story about that job at the inn! You fought for that job and it's obvious to me just why. You let your stupid pride get in the way of having the one man you've always wanted, so you took that job to substitute any man you can charm in his place. You're nothing but a common whore and we all know it, whether or not anyone chooses to acknowledge it."

Vyranna cried out in incomprehensible rage. "I hate you!" she screamed so harshly her voice cracked. "I'm not fooled by all that beautiful white hair of yours. I'm not the real whore here because I know you're nothing but a freak and a bastard!"

"That's *more* than enough out of you!" Sharice cried out from the side of the house. She had been in the back yard, trying to comfort her son who was beside himself at the thought of losing his sister and confidante, but now she was storming straight for Vyranna, her face full of fury. "How *dare* you cause such grief for your sister at a time like this? And how *dare* you imply that I was anything but faithful to your father!"

Sharice finally reached her daughter and slapped her hard enough to bloody her nose and leave a mark that would last days.

"This is my house, and until you are wise enough to make a home of your own, you will obey me and the rules of my home! Now shut your mouth and go comfort your brother. I'll box your ears if I hear another bitter word out of your mouth for the rest of the week!"

Vyranna balled her hands into fists, but had the sense to keep quiet, mostly out of shock, but also because she knew she could never defend herself against her mother. For all her rage, Vyranna had a petite frame similar to her sister's and was no match for Sharice who wasn't much taller, but was certainly stronger and sturdier from the years of work that went with being the sole head of the house. Vyranna turned and disappeared inside. Sharice didn't particularly care if she ended up comforting Cusec or not, she just needed to get her away from Dionelle before they stopped throwing insults and started throwing fists. But now, Dionelle had collapsed to the ground, hugging her knees to her chest and sobbing. In order to give her a minute to calm down, Sharice picked up the box she had dropped and placed it in the wagon before she finally turned to her daughter.

"Come on, you've got a long journey ahead of you, so let's get it started."

"I don't want to leave," Dionelle sobbed. "Why can't you send Vyranna away and let Reiser stay in her stead?"

"That kind of thinking isn't going to help anything."

"We can stay here another day or two," Reiser interjected. "The field children can manage without me—they're good kids."

"Staying here won't help anything," Sharice insisted. "Vyranna will remain this bitter whether you're here or not and you may as well get away from it."

"But what about you and Cusec?" Dionelle asked.

"If your sister continues to overstep the boundaries, she will find herself out of a home," Sharice replied coldly. "She is a grown woman, and I am not obligated to continue to provide for her if all she can do is cause me grief. At this point I don't ever expect her to settle down with any one man, but she can find secure lodging somewhere else. If her tantrums don't subside with your departure, then that will likely be the case."

Dionelle was silent for a moment, thoughtful. "Mamma, she already feels that she's been wronged her whole life, don't give up on her so quickly."

"No one has ever wronged her but herself, and I don't think I should be punished for that any longer."

Dionelle sighed, "Just try. She didn't mean what she said."

"Oh, but she did," Sharice argued. "She doesn't believe you are your father's child. I don't know how you are so unlike anyone in the family, but I know you are his daughter. Now collect the rest of your things and go start your new life."

"Mamma, I don't want to leave."

"You heard the monk—you are starting anew, but your foundation will always be your family."

Sharice walked her daughter back into the house, and Reiser stood beside the wagon to wait. As they went back in, Reiser regarded mother and daughter with mild awe, Dionelle was a startling contrast to her mother—and her entire family. Her father and his family were primarily brunettes and, though there were a few people with blue eyes, there were no blondes as far back as anyone could remember. Sharice's family was much the same, as there had been only one redhead, and Sharice and her great aunt both had auburn hair and green eyes. Where Dionelle's physical characteristics came from, no one knew, and her odd appearance was as much a mystery as her talent for magic was. She had been born with it, but there hadn't ever been a wizard or sorceress on either side of the family, and while it wasn't unheard of for a family with no previous magic history to have a child with a bit of an ability, no one had heard of a child being born to a family such as Dionelle's and having the strong talent that she possessed.

She spent a lot of time away, deep in the forest with Boidossen, improving her methods and trying to understand the root of her ability and to discover where it had come from. She would leave for the mountains twice more before completing her apprenticeship. They could only speculate that her mysterious appearance was linked to her even more mysterious abilities.

Reiser knew he should go in and help the women carry the last of it out, but now he was contemplating whether he could get what was already packed out of his wagon and leave before either of them noticed.

"You're not going anywhere without her," Sharice said suddenly, coming out the door.

He was startled by the comment and looked at her, perplexed and ashamed.

"The anxiety and doubt is written all over your expression," Sharice said. "Today is not a good day and it's not a good way to start a marriage, but it will get better."

"She's so shy and a little afraid of me."

"It will pass. Take her home and keep her comfortable and, if you must, just go about your business like she isn't even there and let her do the same until you're used to each other's presence. She's due back to study under Boidossen at midsummer, so do your best to get acquainted until then and then you will get a reprieve until autumn. And above all else, remember that you're friends—that you've always been friends. Don't let marriage change that or you'll both be doomed to misery."

Reiser nodded and tried his best to compose himself.

"Has she got much left?" he asked Sharice.

"A trunk and a couple of bags."

"We shouldn't leave her alone to do the work herself."

When Reiser and Sharice reached the small room where the three children had grown up, they found Dionelle sitting at the edge of her bed, hugging a battered cloth doll that had been her favourite through childhood, and weeping silently. Sharice stood quietly at the door while Reiser went to Dionelle's side. He sat at the edge of her bed and gently rested his hand over hers, but she wouldn't look at him.

"We need to go soon," he said softly.

After a moment's silence, she sighed wearily and began to stand, reaching out to leave the doll on the straw mattress of her bed, which had already been stripped of blankets that she would take to her new home. Reiser caught the doll and placed it in the trunk with the rest of her belongings.

"I'm a grown woman, I don't need that anymore," she protested, though her tone suggested otherwise.

"You may be a woman and a wife now, but that doesn't mean you should be denied the occasional comforts of childhood or the familiarity of where you grew up," Reiser replied, standing as well. He made sure the trunk was latched properly and then heaved it up and headed back down the stairs, leaving Sharice and Dionelle with the few remaining things.

"I know you don't want to leave, and I know you're going to want to come straight home as soon as you get there, but I want you to promise to stay with him for at least a month before you consider a trip home to visit."

"Why so long?" Dionelle lamented.

"You can still write to us as often as you like, and I'm sure Cusec will write to you daily. You need time in a world of your own—just the two of you—if you hope to learn to be happy. You need that time to adjust. And forget any expectations, real or imagined, that you think anyone might have about what it means to be married. Remember that you've always been friends and the rest will come naturally. Now off you go."

Sharice gave her daughter a nudge toward the door, and then they headed out to Reiser's wagon, packing in the last of Dionelle's things. Sharice wouldn't allow Dionelle to drag out the goodbye and quickly helped her into the front beside Reiser.

"I'll bring your brother to come see you before midsummer."

Sharice retreated to the doorway, where Cusec was standing uncertainly. There was no sign of Vyranna. Cusec gave a little wave as Reiser started the wagon moving, but quickly buried his face at his mother's side, unable to bear the sight of his sister leaving. Dionelle returned the wave and watched her family for a moment as the horse pulled her down the lane, farther and farther from her home, but she finally turned away from them and faced the journey ahead. All of her previous excitement about the trip to Pasdale had melted away under Vyranna's cruelty.

DIONELLE pushed the memory aside and couldn't sit still, so she got up again to check on their dinner, still fretting that something would go wrong and that her sister would cause trouble. It wasn't long before they heard the clatter of the Joasera family's wagon in the front lane and Dionelle ran out to meet them, excited despite her concerns.

But only Sharice and Cusec were in the wagon.

"Mamma! Where's Vyranna?"

"Don't worry about that right now, dear. It's so good to see you! You look wonderful!" Sharice called, jumping down from the wagon and rushing across the lane to greet her daughter with a strong embrace. "It's been so long since I've been here and it's been far too long since I've seen you two!"

"Di, can we go to the city while we're here?" Cusec asked, tethering the horse.

In her letters home, Dionelle had gone to great lengths to describe the wonders of the city to her brother, especially the marketplace full of the exotic and strangely mundane. None of the Joasera children had ever been to a city before and, now that she'd had time to grow accustomed to it, Dionelle loved the occasional adventure into the stone walls of Pasdale. The cobblestone streets had taken her by surprise more than anything else, even more than all of the unusual items being peddled in the marketplace, from brightly coloured clothing, to new spices, to dragon skin.

"I'm sure we can find some time to at least visit the market before I have to leave for the foothills," Dionelle replied, hugging her brother. "Have you grown?" she asked him.

"Maybe a little," he said shyly, giving her a sly grin.

"You'll be in the fields before long, won't you?"

"Mamma sure hopes so!"

"Have you been giving her grief?"

"Not nearly as much as Vyranna."

"Hush now," Sharice interrupted. "We don't need to worry about that right now."

Dionelle wondered again what her sister's absence meant, but knew her mother wouldn't speak of it if she brought it up again.

"Would you like a hand bringing your things in?" Reiser offered.

"Yes, thank you, dear."

"The house is so small!" Cusec commented. "Will there be room for everyone?"

"There's the sofa and a cozy straw mat that will make plenty of room for you and Mamma in the front room," Dionelle replied. "And we have an extra room upstairs where Reiser's sister and her family can stay. If Vyranna isn't coming, then that's just more room for you," she continued, ruffling his unruly brown hair.

"Lots more room!"

"I can't wait to see the baby!" Sharice cooed. "Have you two thought about starting a family yet?"

Dionelle blushed. "Mamma!"

"Oh, come now, you're married! Well?"

"We talked a little, but not right now. This is enough adjusting. I'd like to get some more studying done and get established as a sorceress first."

"You've got plenty of time, and I'll just enjoy Loni's little ones until then," Sharice grinned. "Now, have you got some dinner for us?"

"She made enough for the whole kingdom," Reiser commented.

"I could use a good feast!"

While Cusec, Sharice and Reiser got settled at the kitchen table, Dionelle left the plate of cheese and fruit and the basket of warm bread on the table for them to whet their appetites, while she got the rest of their dinner ready. She had made a roast chicken as well as a hearty rabbit stew, thick with gravy and spring vegetables. Plus, she had a large bowl full of fresh greens from the garden near the barn. She placed the greens on the table and then went to retrieve everything else from the hot stove. She had already taken care to set each place before her family had arrived and they were able to tuck in to dinner immediately.

The empty place meant for Vyranna still troubled her, but Dionelle had been smelling the cooking all afternoon and she was famished, so she was too busy enjoying the fruits of her labour to give it much thought.

As they finished their meal in peace, Dionelle didn't want to admit that she was relieved her sister wasn't there, but it was hard to deny. She hadn't realized just how concerned she had been until she had seen Vyranna wasn't present and the weight of the anxiety had lifted from her shoulders and the tension knot in her chest had eased, leaving her feeling taller and lighter. There would be no scenes, no leaving early, and no worrying about temper tantrums frightening the small children. No one would have to sleep in the barn unless they wanted to.

"All right then," Dionelle demanded, as she set out a strawberry cake with cream for dessert. "Where is Vyranna? Why didn't she come?"

"I don't know where she is," Sharice replied, her voice cracking. "Please, just let me enjoy this cake because it looks far too good to let your sister spoil my appetite now."

Dionelle shrugged and sat down in front of her own plate, relieved that everything had turned out as well as she had hoped. They finally finished eating and Cusec helped her clean up. Dionelle was surprised by the gesture because she'd never seen him wash the dinner dishes before in her life. She wondered just how much had changed since she had left. Their letters had made things seem like life was carrying on as usual, but Cusec had clearly become more helpful and something was going on with Vyranna. Her mother seemed upset and Dionelle finally got her talking once they were sitting in front of the hearth. It had begun to grow cold in the house, so Dionelle reignited the coals to have them properly warmed again.

"You know, we all had to learn to build a fire again after you left?" Sharice commented. "It's a good thing you didn't move out in the winter!"

"Oh, Mamma, don't be silly!"

"No, I mean it. I didn't realize just how much you tended to the fire until you were gone and it needed to be done. For nearly twenty years I didn't have to worry about keeping the house warm and I'd forgotten about all the work that goes into it, especially when I can't coax every last bit of warmth out of the dying embers the way you can. We use so much more wood now!"

"I'm sure you're doing fine and you've got plenty of time to get used to it before winter. The three of you will manage."

"Oh, it's just the two of us now," Sharice said gravely.

"Will you tell me what's happened? Did you finally hold to your word and send Vyranna away?"

"Yes, I did. She lost her temper with your brother and hurt him quite badly not too long ago. He's only just starting to feel better now, but could barely walk for a while and tending to him really cut into my work. The minute she touched him, I made her leave. I even packed up her things and left them on the porch."

"It sounds like it was for the best," Reiser said. "Your letters indicated a growing level of violence, and she is a grown woman. If she wants to live as a spinster, that's her choice, but she's old enough to do it on her own now."

"Yes, I agree. But it's worse than just that," Sharice replied, taking a deep shaky breath. "I don't know where she is at all now. She went to the inn and was living there for a while. Someone told me she started living with one of the men who frequented there, but that only lasted for a few days, because now she's gone entirely. Not even a week ago, we had several travellers come through—all different sorts of characters from charlatans to businessmen and nobles—and they were all coming from the same place—some festival in the west, and were all headed back to the king's lands in Golden Hill. When they cleared out of town at last, Vyranna was gone too."

"Oh, Mamma! You haven't even received a letter from her? She didn't tell you she was leaving or where she was going?"

"I've heard nothing from her. I don't believe she planned to leave, I think she just met someone who struck her fancy and left with him on impulse. Most of her things were left behind, but she took just enough that I don't believe she's in any specific danger. I think that when she realized they were all leaving at the same time and going to essentially the same place, she packed a few things and fell in with them. It's likely she hasn't arrived where she's going to end up yet—maybe she never will—but I hope to hear from her once she gets some kind of idea."

"Have you spoken to her at all since you made her leave?" Dionelle asked.

"No, I'm afraid I haven't. It's likely I'll never hear from her again, unless her manipulations land her some good fortune and then she'll want to rub that in my face."

"At least you'll hear from her then," Dionelle said, understanding now why her mother was so upset. Vyranna had always been difficult, but she was still her daughter and Sharice would worry herself to her grave unless she heard some scrap of news regarding Vyranna's whereabouts and well-being. Dionelle was strangely relieved by the news though.

"Maybe now you can find some good fortune of your own," Dionelle continued. "Your life has been greatly unburdened recently, with me and Vyranna both out of the house. And Cusec is growing up. It must mean more money for you, if not a little more time to yourself and maybe even some romance?"

Sharice laughed, "Romance at my age? Don't be foolish!"

"Have it your way," Dionelle said with a grin. "But you must have at least more time to yourself."

"Your brother is still a handful," Sharice replied, tousling Cusec's hair.

"Mamma just isn't used to all the quiet and time to herself," Cusec said. "Rastov, the man who sells eggs in the market, really likes her but she says she has no time for anything like that, but she gets all her mending done before dinner now and then just sits at the fire until bedtime."

"See?" Sharice protested, good-natured. "He's still young enough not to know when to keep certain observations to himself. And Rastov isn't interested in me," she insisted, absently rubbing at the diagonal widow's tattoo on her wrist.

"He always says how pretty your hair is, or that he likes your scarf, or asks how Di is doing. None of the other men at the market say those kinds of things and Rastov isn't the only one without a wife," Cusec countered.

"Oh, you kids," she laughed, waving her hands. "Maybe I like the new-found quiet just a little too much to worry about a man right now."

"You still shouldn't ignore this man from the market," Dionelle said, moving to sit at the edge of the hearth where she could more easily tend the fire. "That quiet could turn to loneliness. Cusec will be a man before you know it! Then what will you do with yourself?"

Sharice chuckled. "You think I should run off and marry every man in the market who fancies me? I can have divorce tattoos halfway up to my elbow, like some sort of eccentric noble."

"Oh, Mamma! Don't be foolish."

"I'm not going to live with you forever," Cusec pointed out. "I like Rastov. He's nice to us."

"Yes, dear, but there's plenty of time to think about that later. I've got plenty of other things to get used to first."

"Do you still miss Da?" Cusec asked.

"Yes, my darling, I do."

"What happened to him?" Reiser questioned. "He seemed so healthy, and far too young. Was it an accident?"

"He was unwell before Dionelle was born—he was quite sick actually and it took a lot out of him," Sharice explained, nestling deeper into the sofa as if she were trying to sink out of sight. "Perhaps it took years off his life because he was never quite the same after that. Then, one day, he just wouldn't wake up."

"I don't remember him anymore," Cusec said, suddenly distraught. He turned in his seat to face her more directly.

"You were very young when he died," Sharice replied.

"Tell us about him," Dionelle requested. "I remember very little of him now. How did you and Da meet? Were you always friends too?"

"No, I didn't meet him until I was almost a woman, only a handful of years before we were married. My brothers had had marriages arranged for them, but your grandparents didn't know anyone with sons my age and so I had to find your father on my own."

"Was it hard? Were you scared?"

"It wasn't that hard, but it's not as easy as just accepting something someone else has already decided. He was friends with one of my friends' brothers and that was how I met him. I wasn't very interested in him, but he took a shine to me right away and was very persistent and eventually charmed me."

"You loved him?"

"Yes, I did," she replied with a reminiscent smile.

25

"What did you love about him?" Cusec asked. "Did you think Da was handsome?"

"Not at first, but he had been slovenly—like a vagabond or something—until he was determined to court me. He started combing his hair and keeping his clothing neat. He was always polite and I think that hooked me in more than anything. So many of the young men I knew were crude and without manners."

She told them of how he had stepped in when some of the local girls she knew had been teasing her about not yet having been matched. That he had stood up for her enabled her to fully appreciate him and it was that particular act of kindness that had drawn her to him. She talked well into the night about his unique sense of humour and how much he loved the animals they had raised. Sharice had had to sell the animals after his death because she couldn't look after them as well as the children.

Cusec had her convinced that they should start raising animals again and insisted they start with a puppy.

"Maybe we can find a puppy in the market!" he whooped.

Sharice talked until even Dionelle couldn't coax anymore warmth out of the embers and conversation ended; the spell of Sharice's words broke when Reiser finally got up to put fresh wood on the coals. It was late and Loniesa would be there early with her family.

CHAPTER 3

CUSEC was standing impatiently on the front porch, urging Dionelle to hurry as she gathered her things to take him to the market. It was mid-morning and the early summer sun was warm. The boy was eager and had been awake since dawn, and now called to his sister through the open front door.

"Do you really need all of that?" he insisted, bursting at the seams in anticipation.

She was hastily trying to pack some essentials into a large shoulder bag. The day was damp and, despite the current sunshine, she knew a rain shower or storm could roll over the hills with little warning. She wanted to be sure they had some rain gear, as well as a bag large enough to fit the treasures they were likely to find that day. As she was grabbing her money purse off its shelf, she heard the clatter of a wagon in the lane and rushed out to join her brother as he watched Loniesa and her family approach.

"Trying to sneak off?" Loniesa teased when she saw Dionelle's bag.

"I'm taking Cusec to the market. He's never been there before and has been nagging me since he arrived. Would you like to join us?"

Beside her, Cusec sighed impatiently, knowing that bringing anyone else with them would only hold them up even longer. They would have to wait for Loniesa and her family to settle in before heading into the city.

"I can see the market any day," Loniesa commented. She lived just outside of Pasdale, but on the other side of the sprawling valley. "And I would like to settle in and feed Shaiz. But perhaps Kieron would like to join you?"

The young boy's expression, bored from the travel, finally showed some signs of life. "Mamma, can I go?"

"Do you want to take them both?" Loniesa asked.

"I'm sure they won't be a problem," Dionelle said. "Are you ready now, Kie? Cusec has been waiting all morning to leave."

Kieron jumped down out of the wagon, not waiting for either of his parents to help him, and darted over to Dionelle and Cusec. He flung his arms around Dionelle's thighs in a quick hug of greeting and then bounded off down the lane back the way they had come, while Cusec chased after him.

Dionelle moved to call them back, but Loniesa urged her to go.

"They won't wait for you. We'll get settled in with Reiser and your mother and see you for dinner. We have plenty of time to catch up this evening," she commented, ushering Dionelle after the boys.

Dionelle was secretly relieved that her role of hostess would be delayed until that evening and she sprinted to catch her brother and nephew.

"Thanks, Auntie Di! I love the market!"

She was delighted that the boy was calling her auntie already and was pleased to have the chance to spend time with him and her brother. She was excited to visit with Loniesa later on, but knew that the presence of the newborn, Shaiz, would only lead to more questions about when she and Reiser planned on starting their family. All Dionelle wanted to do was enjoy the family she already had and a trip to the market with the boys was an excellent opportunity to do just that.

"What's your favourite part of the market?" Cusec asked as she reached them.

"I love visiting all the vendors. They have such unique wares for sale and there are so many wonderful book tents as well."

Kieron wrinkled his nose. "Books are so boring! Just smelly pages and black squiggles."

"They're better once you learn how to read the squiggles," Cusec promised. "Di gets her spells from books."

"That's right, and there are some very wonderful and unusual spells to be found in the books at the market here. Kie, what's your favourite part of the market?"

"All the pastries! Mamma can't ever make them that good. I like the market treats."

"The dragon eyes are my favourite treats," Dionelle said and laughed when Cusec's face turned white. "Don't worry," she assured him, "they're not made of real dragon eyes. They're brightly coloured like the dragons are and come in so many different flavours. They're so sweet!"

"Can we get some?" Kieron begged.

"I insist," Dionelle said with a wink. "We'll stop for dragon eyes first."

Skipping along at her side, Kieron took her hand and babbled on about the things he loved about going to the market, while Cusec listened earnestly. Dionelle kept her word and they stopped at the first table selling dragon eyes. They were round, sugary balls in every colour of the rainbow with a piece of candied fruit in the centre. She bought them each one to start and Cusec was sceptical at first, unable to get over the name, but soon discovered his sister hadn't lied. She bought them each two more, and Kieron was a sticky rainbow by the time they moved on. He washed up quickly at a fountain and then dashed off in the direction of nearby music.

"Minstrels, Auntie Di! Let's go!"

Cusec trotted along after him and Dionelle found him standing at the edge of the crowd gathered for the show. He was spellbound as the trio of minstrels played. There were no minstrels in the market of their small town and certainly none of the same quality that played regularly in Pasdale. Kieron had already joined many of the other children in the centre of the crowd, in the area directly in front of the show, dancing and laughing.

When Kieron saw that Dionelle had finally joined them, he pranced over and grabbed her hand, insisting she dance. She caught her brother by the arm and insisted he join. The three of them held hands and skipped in a circle in time with the jig that was playing. She bowed out when the song ended, but watched from the edge as the two boys continued to dance and cheer. There was a book vendor not far from the minstrels and she was able to watch the boys play while she perused some spellbooks and finally picked out one she thought might be helpful during her summer studies. She was constantly on the lookout for some of the books Boidossen had suggested in the past or that she'd observed him using frequently.

As she paid for her book and tucked it into her bag, the boys came bolting over to her, bursting with excitement.

"One of the girls says there's a vendor on the east end selling dragon skin!" Cusec said. "Is it real skin? From a real dragon?"

"Likely," Dionelle replied. "There are a handful of vendors who travel the cities selling it and I've seen one here before."

"Why aren't there more?"

"Dragon skin is difficult to get and even more difficult to work with. Hunting dragons is dangerous and can lead to wars with them, which humans always lose. The only real way to get it is to find a dragon that has died recently, or get permission from one to use its skin once it has died and then hope to be around once it actually does."

"Wow! Why would anyone go through the trouble?"

"Because it's very expensive and can fetch a fortune if sold. Let's see if we can find the seller and I'll show you."

At the eastern edge of the market, they easily found the tent, made entirely out of dragon skins, all of which were for sale. Dionelle could only laugh at Cusec's shocked expression when he found out how many gold coins it would take to buy even the smallest swatch of dragon skin.

"Di, have you ever seen that many gold coins in your whole life?"

"No, I haven't. Mostly it's the very wealthy who purchase dragon skin. It's just as hard to make anything out of it as it is to get it in the first place. See how this man is using clamps to hold his ropes to the edges of the skins making the tent? Everyone else just punches holes in the tarpaulins for rope to weave through."

"I haven't the time, patience or tools to put enough holes in these skins for the ropes," the vendor said. "It would devalue them anyway."

"Why's that?" Cusec asked.

"Those with the fortunes to afford these often make cloaks or clothing out of them. The skins are no good to them full of holes."

"Why would they make clothes out of it if it's so hard to work with?"

"Here, feel this, lad." The vendor spread out one of the smaller skins, one that was a vibrant purple flecked with silver.

Cusec ran his hand over it, surprised by how luxuriously soft it was, noting that the skin moved as gracefully as the finest silks they'd passed at other booths.

"Now, watch this," the vendor said, a mischievous twinkle in his eye. He pulled out a hatchet and smashed it down into the centre of the skin. The blade sank deep into the wood plank of the table, the skin wedged into the gash, but when the man yanked the blade out and worked the skin out again, Cusec could see that there wasn't a mark on it.

"Oh wow!"

"Ye won't find a tougher fabric in all the lands. Once it's pulled taut, the blades just bounce right off. Takes very special tools, or a certain kind of wizard to be able to cut and sew these skins into clothing. It makes the most beautiful and impenetrable armour for the elite."

"How does someone learn how to do this?" Cusec asked.

"Mostly it's wizards calling the elemental demons from their realms. Dangerous work, ye can be sure. The wizards often call to be possessed by the demons to get the work done. Regular folks can buy special tools that have been charmed by the demons, but that will cost ye plenty."

Both boys were mesmerized, but Cusec's curiosity hadn't been fully satiated yet.

"Which elements do they call for help?" he asked.

"Oh, I reckon it's the earth and the fire demons they need to make the tools."

He looked to Dionelle, worried he was being misled—a country bumpkin on the receiving end of a city man's joke—but she nodded and he grinned in wonder.

Cusec had been dazzled by their entire trip to the market and couldn't stop talking about the dragon skin as they headed home again. When Dionelle stopped outside the lane to one of the farms they passed and pointed out a crude, hand-painted sign advertising puppies for sale, she thought he just might burst with delight.

CUSEC and Kieron chased the puppy around the yard while the adults watched from the front porch. They had picked up a golden herder on their way back from the market the day before, and the puppy, named Fuzzy by the boys, had been an instant source of entertainment for the children. Sharice had already begun to show Cusec how to properly care for and train the dog, but it was still young and more interested in play.

The boys had convinced Dionelle and Reiser to join them in their game of chase, but Reiser had since gone out to the fields to check on the field children and Dionelle was cradling Shaiz against her, almost afraid of dropping the fussy baby, while Loniesa went in to get a fresh diaper. When she came back out, Dionelle went out with her to a patch of cool grass on the side of the house, under some trees, to change the baby while Braqin and Sharice remained on the porch chatting about Braqin's growing farming business.

Dionelle watched on curiously as Loniesa fussed over the baby, as she had been doing for their entire stay. She always liked to learn about the new things in her life and she had been too young to help much with Cusec when he had been an infant—that task had gone to Vyranna instead. She never thought that a child as tiny as Shaiz could be so much work. Loniesa was definitely relieved to be in the presence of other women to help her tend to her children.

"It's so much work!" Dionelle finally commented. "Do you find any time for yourself?"

"A bit of time in the evenings, once Braqin comes in from the fields and Kieron has gone to bed. Braqin looks after her then so I can do a bit of reading or weaving."

"That's good, at least."

"Braqin's mother helps with the chores, but I will be glad when this one is a little older and in school. Then I'll really get time to myself and not have to worry about others helping me keep my house in order."

Dionelle nodded, relieved it wasn't something she had to worry about.

"When will you and Reiser have your first? It would be great if you had one soon and Shaiz had a little playmate."

"There are no other babies in your circle of friends?" Dionelle asked, somewhat surprised by the thought and also getting annoyed by that question. It came up more than she cared to hear.

If she'd had the luxury of studying her craft and becoming established as a sorceress before marrying Reiser, the question probably would have been less irritating, but she still felt like a child herself and needed direction in her life before she could even consider having a family to chase after. She could tell that Loniesa was exaggerating the amount of free time she actually got, because even in the presence of so many extra hands—as a guest at someone else's home—she still had hardly any leisure time to herself. There was no way Dionelle would be able to pursue her interests with small children around.

As soon as good manners would allow, Dionelle removed herself from her sister-in-law's company and caring for her niece, and went back into the house to start preparing dinner and packing up the last of her things for her journey the next day. She was looking forward to getting into the foothills and practicing her craft, even if it meant sleeping on that hard, creaky cot and doing all that work for Boidossen. This year would be especially difficult because her lessons, usually spread over a few weeks each season, were being condensed into two months each during the summer and winter in order to accommodate her wedding and new station in life.

She looked forward to getting away from the baby question and Reiser giving her a hard time about the dragon—there had been more of them, though they hadn't landed anywhere near their fields, but Reiser had tried to keep her in the house. She knew he had wanted to physically hold her down and had stood in front of the doorway blocking her path as it was. She had to dart away from him and go out the back door, leaving her cloak behind.

When she had returned to the house after seeing that the dragons were far beyond her sphere of influence, there had been a drawn-out argument and she realized that Reiser knew very little about the dragons. He thought she was in far more danger than she actually was and his over-protectiveness only made her feel like he thought she was some foolish child. She had expected him to respect her more than he did and she looked forward to getting away from all of it for a few weeks. He had initially been encouraging of her desire to ply her craft, and she recalled the conversation they had had about it on the journey from her home after they had been married.

DIONELLE was exhausted by her sister's words and the stress of leaving her family, but was determined to stay awake for the trip to Pasdale. She hadn't travelled to Pasdale in years—not since before her father died—and she'd never stayed awake for the entire journey before. The long hours ahead would give her the opportunity to properly consider her new life and to talk to her husband beyond the anger of her sister and the fears of her brother. Despite her concerns, exhaustion won and she dozed off until after midday and awoke to the lush greenery at the edge of the prairie she had always called home.

Though the plant life had changed, the land was still largely flat with a shallow valley carved by a gentle river as the only break in the landscape. They still weren't far from Dionelle's home and the area was familiar to her because her family had often come this way to visit a friend of her father's.

The nap had helped her feel more relaxed and her mind was less muddled with anxieties. She glanced back at all of her possessions packed into the wagon, amazed she had accumulated so many things and even more amazed that it had all managed to fit comfortably into the house and the small room she shared with her siblings. A good portion of the things they brought with them were wedding gifts and leftovers from the wedding feast.

"Mamma packed us a lot of food," Dionelle commented. "Does that mean we won't get home before dark?"

"We should get home in time for dinner, actually. I think she just wanted to get rid of some of the leftovers from the feast. Your neighbours brought so much, and I think they were a little too generous. If your mother had kept it all it would have surely spoiled before they could have eaten all of it. I don't think we will have to worry about cooking for a couple of days."

"Do you expect me to cook? What chores do you expect me to carry out?"

Reiser was startled by the questions, turning suddenly to face her. "I hadn't actually considered it. I don't have any expectations right now, I guess. I've been keeping house on my own since my father died. Sometimes I'll get one of the field children to help me if it's more than I can manage."

"What am I going to do then?"

"What would you like to do?"

"Well, I sure don't want to spend my life cleaning up after you."

"Who would?" he chuckled.

She smiled at that. "But all I've done is help take care of Cusec so Mamma could work to provide for us. She's been doing mending for pretty much the entire village since Da died, and it was my job to keep Cusec out of trouble and focussed on his schoolwork and other chores. Since I finished school, my life has revolved around looking after him when I wasn't apprenticing. But you're a grown man and can look after yourself. So what will I do?"

"There aren't many chores for us to share," he admitted. "You can fill your days however you please. You can join me in the fields if you like. Do you study your craft much when you're away from the wizard?"

"No, I was always so busy with Cusec and keeping the peace with Vyranna." She looked at him with a sudden spark of excitement in her eyes. "I can study magic? Is that what you suggest I do in Pasdale?"

"If that would please you."

"I think it would, but shouldn't I put my efforts into something more practical?"

"There are plenty of opportunities for a sorceress, especially one with talents as unusual as yours. Pasdale is much larger than your town and our ruling lord is the king's nephew, so he's well connected with a vast court. Would you like to work? You could be a working member of the court—no working in an inn for you!"

"They would let me into the court? A lowly commoner—a peasant and the wife of a simple rancher?"

"You finish your apprenticeship this winter, don't you?"

"Yes."

"Then you will be a full-fledged sorceress and likely admitted to the Guild. All Guild members are eligible to work for the royal courts, regardless of their origins," Reiser explained.

"That's wonderful! I've never considered the possibility of making a career as a sorceress. I wouldn't have thought it even possible, other than to teach the craft to others, as Boidossen does."

"He's not just a teacher. You must know that!"

"Well, he's mentioned helping the courts, but never what he does specifically."

"When you see him at midsummer, you should ask him how he puts his talents to use. Find out what books we need to find so you can continue to study at home. But with your talents for taming fire as you see fit, you could be very vital in Pasdale. You've never been there during a drought, but the surrounding forests become one giant tinderbox and fires are a terrible threat."

As the possibilities began unfolding before her, she felt strangely liberated and hadn't realized until then just how limiting her family had been. She immediately felt ashamed for even considering the possibility that her family had somehow been a burden to her.

"This is why they made the arrangement with my family," Reiser said, reading her guilt. "If your father was still alive, your mother would be chasing after Cusec and you and Vyranna would have had more freedom to have dreams and chase them."

"But what are Cusec and Vyranna going to do without me to help?"

"With one less mouth for your mother to feed, things will get a little easier. It will be difficult for them for a while, but we will be perfectly secure on the farm and anything you make as a sorceress can go to helping your family."

"All that simply because we got married? Why didn't we do this sooner?"

Reiser smiled at her and stroked the long silk rope of her braid, relieved that she didn't shy away from his touch this time.

"I'm sure it won't be as easy as that," he replied, not wanting to get her hopes up too high. "But it's certainly not going to be the disaster you feared last night, or even this morning while listening to your sister's tirade."

Dionelle was far too pleased by the prospect of making a living as a sorceress to care much about the difficulties they were likely to face in the coming months. She missed her family already and was still uncertain of the idea of calling a strange house her home, but at the same time there was all this new-found freedom and opportunities in the future to help her family. She grinned at the image of herself sitting in front of a warm hearth and practicing from one of Boidossen's dusty old books—comfortably at home and at her own pace. She couldn't even call Reiser's home hers yet, but she was already dreading the thought of leaving it over the summer to spend weeks on a cot in the cramped back room of the wizard's cabin, slaving away at his chores to earn a few scraps of knowledge. Her family couldn't afford to pay him in coin, so they paid him with the sweat of her brow instead.

"Maybe I can shorten my apprenticeship this summer," she mused. "Do you think we can afford to pay him for a few proper lessons and maybe a book or two, so that I can spend more time at home?"

"We can certainly consider it," he replied. "We can discuss it further as your summer lessons near and see how you feel about it then, once things have had the chance to calm down."

He smiled at the fact that she had called it home and that she already wanted to spend more time there, even though she hadn't set foot in it as his wife. She was grinning broadly, and it brought him the warm feeling of the light from their wedding and a peaceful certainty that everything would be just fine. She reached out and touched the side of his face, still grinning, and then leaned in to kiss him quickly, before turning away shyly.

DIONELLE had lost a lot of that sense of independence since confronting the dragon. Reiser seemed to have forgotten his promises and she wasn't sure how to remind him or reassure him of her safety. Working for the royal courts would be much safer than chasing marauding dragons through farmland, and she couldn't understand why he wasn't supportive of that.

She thought someone as educated as Loniesa would be more sensitive to her need to establish her own path. She knew Reiser had told his sister about how resistant Dionelle initially was to married life, and it bothered her how much of their personal life he shared with his sister. Dionelle certainly hadn't told Cusec nearly as much.

Reiser came in not long afterward to finish with the supper chores so Dionelle could pack.

"Are you nervous about leaving?" he asked her.

"No, it's just like always. I'm looking forward to asking him about finding actual work as a sorceress."

"Will it help you feel more settled into life with me?"

"Yes, definitely. You have your place in the fields as a rancher, but you have enough field children that you don't need my help and it's not a strong desire of mine—not when I can work flame for a living."

He nodded but didn't say anything. He didn't want her to leave, but had stopped saying so and she was glad. He didn't seem convinced of how important it was for her to learn just a little more and get started learning at home. He would see when she returned and was able to settle properly into their life's rhythm. She continued packing in silence and soon her mother joined her, collecting Cusec's things that had been scattered throughout the house as he'd played with Kieron, and now with Fuzzy. Her mother and brother were also leaving tomorrow and needed to be ready when the morning came. They both wanted to leave the evening open for visiting just a little more.

"How are you doing?" Sharice finally asked. "Really—don't just tell me everything is fine."

"It's hard," she replied hesitantly. "A lot of the time it's not hard. Most of the time it's just chores, and farming, and reading together in the evenings and trying not to burn supper, and enough of the time I really like it. When we're not trying to avoid problems—when we just don't talk about them because we're just not thinking about them—then we have fun. It's like being friends when we were younger. He helped me

37

get comfortable with the city, we took an afternoon trip to a waterfall in the hills, and we sit and watch the stars. But then Reiser changes and gets controlling. He wants to start a family right now and doesn't seem to want me to work. He doesn't like that I interfered with the dragon."

"It has its dangers. But you know that and Boidossen has done well to prepare you."

"I'm a beautiful maiden," she added with a wry grin. "And a strange-looking beauty at that. They'd all rather stop their rampages to speak with me, even if it means going without dinner. Dragons are strange creatures."

"They are oddly preoccupied with beauty. I've heard stories—when I was younger and used to go to the inn with your Da—that dragons will even sit and watch artists creating their work. Especially if the artists are beautiful too," Sharice said with a wink.

"Yes. So I really don't feel in any danger. One day my beauty will fade to something different—something less appealing to the dragons, but by then I'm sure I will not have the adventure in me to chase after them anymore anyway. Why doesn't he understand that?"

"Darling, he loves you and he's always ever seen dragons as a threat. He's afraid they'll hurt you. His fears aren't completely unfounded, but I think he has a lot to learn about dragons. You could stand to learn more too, and I think that both of you learning a bit more together might reassure you both."

"Maybe I'll have to find him a book while I'm at Boidossen's. I'd like to set his mind at ease because he infuriates me when he gets like this. Now he doesn't want me to go to the foothills at all because he's worried I'll run into danger on the way, even though I've been going there by myself for the last six years."

"He's still young and needs to learn how to let you be independent. Your father was the same way when we were younger. I was never as adventurous as you, but he still found reasons to fuss over me. It will pass."

"It had better," Dionelle grumbled.

"He's going to miss you, too. You're going to have company, even if it is a cranky old wizard, but Reiser is going to be alone here."

"That still doesn't give him the right to try to get me to stay. It would be one thing if he was just going to miss me, but he tries to actually convince me not to go."

"He'll get used to it. He has to. And it will be better when you get back and have something you love to keep you busy while he's in the fields."

"I can't be idle, not the way I have been, and I need this. My family has been my whole life, and now that my life can be something different, I feel trapped as I wait for the change to take hold."

"Change will come for you tomorrow morning," Sharice promised. "It will give you more opportunity to build on your new desires. When you return in the winter, your transformation will be well underway and things will look more promising."

"I sure hope you're right. This has been trying for me in a way that Vyranna's wrath never was."

Dionelle had most of her things ready for the journey and joined her family downstairs again. Cusec was trying to teach Fuzzy to sit on command, but it wasn't working very well as the puppy was more intent on scampering after Kieron. Cusec and Sharice had most of their things packed up again and waiting near the door, and Dionelle left her bags there as well before she joined her family at the fireplace.

REISER stood with his sister and her family on the front porch as they watched the Joaseras prepare to leave. Dionelle was helping her family load the last of their things into the wagon. She was sad, but Reiser was certain it was because her family was leaving her and not because she was leaving home. He had overheard her talking with her mother about what a relief it would be to get to the peace of the foothills.

He knew she needed to see the wizard at least one more time to get set on the proper path to establishing herself as a sorceress, but he was going to miss her. He hoped she would be less temperamental once she returned. She was heading out to find some purpose and he hoped that was all she needed to settle down. If she was a sorceress for the court, she would likely spend more of her time in the city and he wouldn't have to worry quite so much about her chasing dragons through the fields.

He was shocked when Sharice tried to assure him that getting in the path of a dragon wasn't as dangerous as one would intuit, especially not for someone like Dionelle. Reiser no longer cringed when Dionelle dug her hands into the blazing hearth or reached into the oven to retrieve hot food without so much as a tea towel for protection, but it was still hard for him to think of her facing down a dragon. He knew the fire wouldn't hurt her, but there were so many other ways for dragons to be dangerous.

As her mother's wagon trundled down the lane, Dionelle came to say goodbye to Reiser. She gave him a quick kiss and a long embrace before she finished securing the last of her things to the mare and headed off after her mother. They would be travelling together for a short time until Dionelle turned west and her mother continued northward. At least Dionelle would only be away for a few weeks this time. Reiser had sent a sack of coins with her so she could buy proper lessons and some books and start practicing at home. With any luck, that would shorten the length of her next two visits to the wizard.

"Uncle Reiser, why don't you get a puppy? I miss Fuzzy!" Kieron chirped, watching the Joaseras disappear with their dog in tow.

"I'm afraid I spend too much time in the fields to properly care for a puppy," Reiser replied.

"You should get one when Auntie Di comes back. She can look after it and bring it in the fields to see you. Do dogs know how to plant seeds?"

"I don't think that they do. Maybe we can get a smart one to help the field children."

"Do you think Fuzzy will learn to help in the fields?"

"I don't know. Sharice isn't a farmer and doesn't have large fields to tend. Maybe they will teach him to clean the house instead."

Kieron giggled at the thought of the puppy cleaning the supper dishes.

"I want to be a field boy when I'm big, but Mamma won't let me."

Reiser gave his sister an enquiring look.

"I would prefer if he followed in his father's footsteps," Loniesa replied, glancing at her husband. "But I'm sure he'll start as a field boy—all of you do."

"I'm sure learning to understand the dirty side of the business will be an advantage to him as a businessman," Reiser replied.

"Business is boring!" Kieron protested. "I want to play in the fields!"

"Well, there's your answer," Braqin said with a laugh.

By now, Dionelle and her family were well out of sight and Reiser and the others headed inside. Reiser was glad to have them around to help ease him into Dionelle's absence. He couldn't help but wonder if maybe some of Vyranna's independence had rubbed off on Dionelle after all, as she had no qualms with being married as long as she didn't feel like it held her back. She had been excited to discover the possibilities it offered her and now she would settle for no less.

As long as she didn't run off the way her sister had then he was sure he would eventually learn to cope with whatever she chose to do with her life but watching Braqin with Kieron and Shaiz made him wish she wouldn't bristle every time someone mentioned starting a family. Ever since Kieron was born and Reiser had held him for the first time, he had wanted to be a father, to experience the delight that Braqin and Loniesa did. It would be trying, particularly at first, but children grew and it was its own kind of magic to watch them develop their own character.

"She'll settle down," Loniesa said, reading his troubled expression. "She's not taking well to the change just yet, but once she's a practicing sorceress and has her own little corner of the world carved out, then she will settle down. Give her time—you're both still young."

Reiser nodded, "There is just a lot of uncertainty right now and I look forward to life finding some kind of routine. It could take until the spring for her to really be happy with her place in life and certainly longer than that for her to properly establish herself."

"It will come. The first year is never easy, but you'll manage."

Reiser nodded, but didn't respond. As his sister got her children ready for bed, Reiser sat at the hearth and recalled how he and Dionelle had worked so hard to make the house theirs.

EARLY in the evening, after Dionelle dozed off in the wagon, Reiser shook her awake as they crested a hill and the shadowy forests spread out below them. In the eventide, the lush green forest was rich and dark, giving it a strange air of beauty and mystery as they descended the hill and into the trees. The air was close and still with a pleasantly pungent smell of damp earth and bark, wildflowers, and crisp grass.

"Are we home?" she asked sleepily.

"Another hour at most. We pass between those two hills and Pasdale is on the other side."

Dionelle was surprised by how much the landscape had changed in such a short time. She had grown up on the plains, surrounded by low, rolling hills and endless blue skies, but now the land rose and fell suddenly and felt more like the foothills where she apprenticed. The forest was thicker than in the foothills, with dense underbrush that looked impenetrable in the late-day light, with only the small ribbon of road winding between the tall, sturdy pine trees. She could see how fires could be a problem during a dry spell.

Now that they were near the end of the trip and the surroundings had become so different, Dionelle was growing nervous again as she wondered what to expect. Reiser tried his best to reassure her—letting her know there would be a couple of field children left to help them unload the wagon, and that one of them was supposed to have tidied up the house in anticipation of their arrival.

It wasn't the prospect of having to deal with chores that had her concerned though, so she remained nervous as they passed through the forest and between the two hills. The wagon descended into the wide, flat valley that was a patchwork quilt of bountiful green and yellow farmland hemmed in by piney green foothills with the beginning of the Great Mountains a hazy blue in the distance. A narrow blue stripe of river cut through the valley and the city itself sat in the centre of it all and sprawled southward, away from them, and seemed to stretch on forever. Reiser's farm was one of many at the northern side of the valley and Dionelle was relieved that they wouldn't have to pass through the intimidating city, whose size she had never before realized.

As they approached the farmhouse, she could see that there were lamps lit inside and two boys, not much older than Cusec, were lounging on the front porch, awaiting their master's return.

"Here we are," Reiser announced, finally halting the wagon.

One of the boys immediately began tending the horses, while the other went straight around the wagon to start unloading. Reiser left them to their tasks for a moment, and brought Dionelle into the simple log house. The mudroom opened up into the middle of the house with the kitchen on the left and the parlour on the right, with a massive stone fireplace as the centrepiece. There was a loft with two bedrooms, and the pantry and washing room were separate rooms at the back of the house, one at either side of the back door.

As soon as Dionelle entered the house, Reiser became acutely aware of the fact that he hadn't changed a thing—hadn't moved or thrown out a single item—since his parents had died. He had simply gone about his days in familiar surroundings, and it was her presence that made him realize the place seemed like a shrine to Lou and Sivyla.

"Perhaps once you're settled in properly, we can start making this home our own," he suggested.

"Have you been living with their ghosts all this time?" she asked.

"I hadn't even noticed until now," he admitted.

"I'm sure the change will be good for us both."

Dionelle hoped Reiser kept to his word about making the house their own because she felt terribly awkward and half expected to see Lou sitting at the hearth smoking a pipe and Sivyla bustling around in the kitchen. It was strange to be in that house without their parents present and it made her miss the Ovailens as much as she missed her own family. She also felt like a guest—like she was intruding—and was concerned Reiser might treat her as such.

They helped the boys unload everything from the wagon and get it into the house and then, once the help had gone home for the evening, they picked at the food Sharice had sent with them. They were both too anxious to eat properly. Dionelle still felt out of place and more like a guest—she was having a hard time feeling at home—and wanted to stay up all night to remove the strong presence his parents still had in the house. Finally, realizing neither of them was going to eat anymore, he got her to help him bring everything into the pantry and the cold cellar underneath it so she could get used to where to find things.

She was exhausted and decided to go to bed with most of her possessions still in a pile in the main room. Reiser brought her up to the loft and to the room he had once shared with his sister, who had long ago married and moved out. Across the hall, his parents' room seemed almost eerie with the skeletal bed frame as the only real piece of furniture in there because Lou had died in his sleep and had been carted to his pyre on the straw mattress.

Dionelle stared uncertainly into the half empty room for a moment.

"We'll change things, I promise," Reiser said, closing the door to that room and ushering her into the room they would share. "Leave your things wherever you want for now and we'll make a proper place for you here tomorrow. Just get some rest."

"What about you?"

"I slept much better than you did last night, and I have some chores I'd like to tend to tonight. I'll join you later."

Reiser left her to herself, suspecting she needed the privacy and solitude—the tomb-like state of the house throwing off the carefree joy she had shown on the journey. If she wanted him to stay, she was again too shy to speak up, so he went back downstairs and paced restlessly between the kitchen and the parlour, unsure of where to begin. He wanted to start clearing away his parents' ghosts immediately, but didn't want to make too much noise and couldn't decide where to start. Finally, he removed everything from every shelf in the parlour and every cupboard in the kitchen, leaving every last dish, pot, book and ornament neatly piled on the wood floors so that he and Dionelle could sort through it together and decide what to keep and where to keep it. He silently went upstairs and emptied his parents' dresser and wardrobe in the same fashion.

Finally, feeling exhausted but strangely liberated, he crept back into his room where a solitary candle was still lit and slowly brightened and dimmed with the rise and fall of Dionelle's gentle breathing as she slept. She was curled uncertainly at the edge of the bed, and Reiser hoped she would be more at ease tomorrow once they made the house theirs.

He was cautious as he changed, trying not to make any sound that might disturb her, but when he slipped into bed beside her, she gave a start and sat up for a moment until she remembered where she was. Reiser was relieved when she saw him and smiled. She slid across the bed so that she was lying beside him and draped her arm over him. He slipped both his arms around her and kissed the top of her head as she settled against him. She extinguished the flame without so much as a glance at it.

DIONELLE stood in the middle of the strange house, still in her white and yellow nightgown, and stared at the chaos that surrounded her. She'd had a head start the night before and Reiser was still asleep, but she felt refreshed and was feeling calm until she came downstairs to wash up. She finally decided to ignore the mess Reiser had made, knowing there had to be a good reason for it, and she carefully stepped over and around the piles to the washing room. She pumped cool water into the wash tub and then more of it into the kettle she found in the middle of the kitchen floor. She heated the water on the wood stove in the kitchen and added it to the tub before cautiously peeling off her nightgown so she could wash away yesterday's road dust.

She rarely poured herself a bath in the spring and summer, no matter how filthy she managed to get, usually making do with a basin and washcloth because she preferred to use the bath to warm herself on a cold wintry day, but today she needed to relax a little more. Sleep had helped, but she was still in a strange house and hadn't yet been able to ease all of the tension caused by the wedding, the move and her sister. She scrubbed away some stubborn dirt and rinsed her hair, then just lay back with her head resting against the wall, focussing on each deep breath.

Dionelle felt like she might drift back to sleep when she heard a creak from upstairs and the thud of Reiser's feet hitting the floor. In a panic, she rushed out of the tub, cursing as she sloshed water everywhere, and began to wring the water out of her hair and searched in vain for a towel as Reiser clomped down the rickety stairs, calling for her.

"In here," she said, desperately pulling her nightgown back on, despite still being soaking wet. She was standing awkwardly in a puddle on the cold stone floor when Reiser pushed the door open.

"Good morning," he said, smiling.

"I couldn't find a towel," she said, still feeling out of place and painfully aware of how the wet nightgown clung to every curve.

Reiser smiled and dipped back out into the hall, retrieving a towel from a small cupboard beside the door. Graciously and silently, she accepted the towel and quickly picked her way back across the piles of kitchenware and up the stairs to their room, leaving Reiser alone to wash up so she could dry off and dress. She sat on one of the large, soft chairs in the parlour, her knees drawn up to her chest, and waited for Reiser to bathe and dress.

"What have you done?" she asked, gesturing to the mess.

"I just thought I'd get a head start on making this place ours," he explained.

"By turning it upside down?"

"Everything had to come out before we could put it back or get rid of it. Let's start in the kitchen, because I could certainly use some breakfast."

Dionelle rummaged through the mess to find plates, a mixing bowl, cups, the teakettle, utensils and a couple of skillets. She made pan biscuits while Reiser made ham and eggs. At first they kept bumping into each other, but quickly found a rhythm and gracefully moved around each other, almost like dancing, as they prepared their meal in the small space.

"These skillets are getting old," Reiser commented, as he worked to scrape their breakfast from the pan to their waiting plates.

"We received a new one as a gift," Dionelle said.

"We'll have to unpack our gifts and the rest of your things to see what we have new to replace the old. That will certainly help get rid of some of the clutter."

They finished eating at the corner of the large table Reiser had left clear and then cleaned up their breakfast dishes so they could begin reclaiming the house from the ghosts. They unpacked their wedding gifts first, replacing old linens, pots, skillets, and cups. Some of the items were returned to where Sivyla had always kept them, while others found new homes that better suited the new couple.

Dionelle wouldn't let Reiser get rid of his mother's teakettle though, because it was in perfect condition and she liked the antique look.

"It's cozy," she explained. "We can't wipe your parents from this house entirely."

So Reiser let her keep the antique and brought the new kettle out to the front porch to the growing pile of cast-offs. He told his workers they could take what they wanted home to their wives and mothers, or peddle them in the market if they chose. No one had come looking on his porch yet, but he expected most of it to be gone when they left at the end of the day. All of his workers—adults and children alike—were peasants with little to their name, and he suspected they would keep most of what he and Dionelle discarded.

Dionelle argued they keep most of the old blankets, insisting that in a harsh winter they could never have too many. Plus, they had received a large blanket box as a gift and it would easily hold both the old and the new with plenty of room to spare.

Cleaning the kitchen hadn't taken much time at all, as they kept almost everything that was still in good working order, whether new or old, and there wasn't much left that was kept out of sentiment, except the old kettle. Reiser knew organizing the rest of the house would be another matter.

"What should we do next?" he asked her.

"Get some fresh air!" she laughed.

They took a break from the chaos inside and Reiser took her out to the fields so they could enjoy the warm sun and spring breeze. He showed her around the property and introduced her to his field workers, most of whom were close to Cusec's age and all came from poor families in the city, or families like Dionelle's. Dionelle and Reiser returned to the house after midday and had a quick lunch from the wedding feast leftovers before Dionelle suggested they get the bedroom in order next.

"I'm starting to wonder if we'll finish this before nightfall," she said, "and I know I will sleep better if our room has been reclaimed by tonight."

They moved the emptied wardrobe and dresser from the room across the hall so that Dionelle could unpack more of her belongings. They put their brand new linens on the bed and covered it with the old quilt Reiser's grandmother had made—Dionelle agreeing the heirloom must be kept. She rested her doll on her pillow and they hung a gift mirror over Dionelle's dresser. Reiser moved some of his keepsakes to the top of his dresser, while Dionelle unpacked her jewellery box and other ornaments and spread them on top of hers. Since Reiser had cleared out both pieces of furniture the night before and nothing in the other room needed to be dealt with immediately, making the bedroom a shared sanctuary hadn't taken long at all.

It was late afternoon when Dionelle finally sat on the edge of the bed to admire the new space.

"It was alarming to walk into this tomb at first," she said, "but now I'm glad you left it as it was. It would have been harder for me to carve my own place out of something you'd already put your stamp on."

"Some of these things have been in the same place my whole life and I didn't even realize I was a stranger here too. I think it's better for both of us this way."

"Does it help you let them go?"

"I think so. Keeping the house theirs eased my loneliness, but with you here now, it only feels strange to have their strong presence around."

"And not everything has to go," she said, running her hand over the soft and worn quilt that had once been his grandmother's. "We will build our new life on their foundation."

Reiser leaned into her for a quick, gentle kiss before sitting back on the bed and enjoying the new peace they had brought to the room.

"The parlour now?" he finally asked.

The parlour took much longer to go through as every piece in there came with its own little history. There was the carved wooden bear that had always sat on the mantle. It was Lou's and he had loved the old thing, even though Reiser thought it barely looked like a bear at all.

"It was a gift from a friend, a man who died before I ever met him, and I think Father saw it as a connection to his lost comrade. I can't stand the sight of it really," Reiser admitted with a sheepish grin, "but it meant so much to him."

Dionelle paused and then stood, picking her way across piles of books, embroidery, and Sivyla's knickknacks to retrieve the old but sturdy trunk that most of her possessions had come in.

"We'll use this for sentimental value," she said. "You won't have to look at that ugly old thing, but don't have to get rid of it either. We can leave the trunk against the wall between the two rooms upstairs."

Reiser was relieved and the ugly bear was the first of many objects to find a new home in the trunk, along with a plain piece of embroidery Sivyla had been so proud of—it had been her first successful attempt—and a couple of his parents' favourite books. Some pieces, like the new teakettle, were even brought back in from the porch to reside in the trunk until their use was needed.

They returned the books to the shelves, including Dionelle's few, re-hung some of the tapestries they both liked, and put Dionelle's wrought-iron dragon on the mantle as its new centrepiece. They shared stories about everything they kept and most of what they discarded, learning more about their shared history and each other. Once there was room to move freely again, Dionelle moved one of the big chairs closer to the fire, where she liked to sit and read or practice her craft.

"Oh, this is breathtaking!" Dionelle said, marvelling over a large crystal vase that had been on the floor beside the sofa.

"Another heirloom," Reiser said. "It belonged to my great-grandparents and was a wedding gift from one of the lords in the city. My great-grandmother was a seamstress for the court, I think."

"We're keeping it," she insisted, and placed it in the middle of the low wooden table in front of them. "I'll keep it full of fresh flowers all summer long."

It glimmered in the firelight and Reiser noticed the light had grown much brighter when Dionelle found the vase. Whenever she laughed, the flames would erupt and when something they came across brought on a brief melancholy, the flames would ebb, nearly to embers. He was learning to read her emotions as much through her demeanour and body language as through nearby flames.

Reiser took a glance around the room, noting that there were still some piles, mostly of books and a stack of his mother's needlepoint, left to sort through, but they had put away Dionelle's things, and moved some of Reiser's from the storage shed. They had rearranged some of the furniture and the small stacks left did little to reduce the feeling that this was a new, different house from the one Lou and Sivyla had made together.

It was well after dark and the workers were long gone, taking much of the treasures from the porch home with them, as Reiser had known they would. He suggested to Dionelle that they leave it alone for now and they both went to sit on the back stairs to watch the distant glow of the city and the starlight over the spring fields, before finally going to bed.

CHAPTER 4

IT was late in the evening when the knock came at Reiser's door. It was after dark, more than a week after his sister had left, and he was surprised to have guests, and even more surprised when he opened the door to see who it was—Lady Karth Dunham herself, with her military escort and personal aides. He rarely interacted with the nobles since he wasn't a member of the court, but the lady kept a high profile and was easily recognized by almost everyone in the region. Most had learned from her infamy to recognize her in order to stay away from her—she was renowned for having a cruel streak and often struck without warning. Her husband, the king's nephew, wasn't much better and his popularity sank even further after marrying the haughty woman.

Reiser couldn't fathom what she was doing on his doorstep at this hour and why she hadn't simply sent a messenger to set an appointment for tomorrow. Her straight red locks were pulled severely away from her creamy face, erupting into a bizarre plume at the back of her head. Her grey eyes were cold, a pair of steel daggers, and she watched him closely with the hint of a cruel smirk playing at the corners of her blood red lips.

"Reiser Ovailen?" she asked, when his shock and growing fear left him speechless.

"Yes, m'lady," he replied with a bow, finally remembering to speak.

"I have heard rumours of a simple rancher with a most unusual wife and those rumours have led me to your door," she replied tersely. "I must speak with her."

It wasn't a request. She pushed past him and into his house, her black feathered cloak swishing along the floor behind her. She took a quick, scrutinizing look around, sniffing the air as if the house held some old corpse, and finally took a seat on the sofa, her white legs crossed and her hands folded on the hem of her short black dress, her gaudy but expensive jewels sparkling in the firelight. The smirk hadn't left her expression for an instant and she now regarded him with a sharp, knowing gaze.

"Dionelle?" he sputtered. "What would you want with my wife?"

"I understand she has special talents, particularly regarding fire."

"Yes, m'lady, she is immune."

Lady Karth arched an eyebrow. "Fully immune? The rumours said only that she worked with fire exclusively."

"She can control it as well—at least, she is learning. But she was born with the immunity."

"This changes everything. Where is she? I must speak with her at once."

"I'm afraid she's in the foothills, apprenticing."

"That will never do. Fetch her home at once."

"I'm not certain of how to reach her," Reiser stammered, stumbling over his words and trying to maintain polite calmness in the presence of such a powerful woman.

"In the foothills? She's studying under Boidossen then—that old fool. I shall have a messenger retrieve her immediately, and I will return when she is due home."

"M'lady, please, what is going on?"

"My husband has lost our only dragon whisperer—killed in a ridiculous bar fight—and the dragons have been particularly unhappy these past months. I need your wife to act as our new dragon whisperer."

"M'lady, she's hardly trained!"

Lady Karth cackled, truly amused, even if at his expense. "I understand she is beautiful, as well as being immune to fire. She will not need any training."

"There are still grave dangers and she is not prepared for them!"

"Our kingdom needs a new dragon whisperer and it would be unwise to refuse," the lady said threateningly. "I will return for her once she is home."

Reiser could only watch helplessly as the woman bustled out of his house again, vanishing as abruptly as she had appeared, leaving him feeling lightheaded and jittery. He wasn't sure how Dionelle would react to being called away early, or how she would like being thrust into the position, though it seemed like there was little they could do. Dealing with dragons wasn't new to her, but stopping them from eating a few cows and stopping them from demolishing an entire kingdom were entirely different realms. She was eager to join the courts as a sorceress, but he didn't think dragon whispering was like anything she had considered.

REISER stood at the window, watching into the dusk for Dionelle and the messenger, intending to rush out to greet her and to try to prepare her the moment she arrived. He was also using it as an excuse not to interact with Lady Karth, who he found rude and unnerving as she sat on his sofa with her entourage surrounding her, scrutinizing every corner of his humble farmhouse. She was incredibly intimidating and impatient and Reiser knew his wife wasn't going to take well to the woman, or to the intrusion. He wondered how long Lady Karth would give Dionelle to prepare before she thrust her into the realm of dragon-work.

Lady Karth had arrived at his house at the precise time the messenger was expected back with Dionelle, and when she arrived to find that Dionelle hadn't returned yet, she became indignant, acting as though it was Reiser's fault the messenger was running late. But Reiser finally spotted the carriage pulling up, Dionelle's mare in tow, and he rushed out the door to greet Dionelle before she'd even got fully out.

"Love, we've got a bit—" he began.

"Reiser! Look, he gave me some books!" Dionelle gushed, pulling her bag out of the back of the carriage and opening it to show him the books resting at the top.

"That's great, I'm sure you'll put them to good use. But we haven't got a lot of time—"

"What's going on? The messenger said it was urgent, but everything looks fine to me. Mamma isn't hurt, is she?"

"No, love, your family is fine. I'm really sorry, I tried to get her to give you some time, but she's so persistent."

"Who?"

"Lady Karth. I wanted to—"

"That is quite enough chatter," Lady Karth snapped from the doorway, striding toward them. "We have work to do."

"What's going on?"

"They didn't give us a choice," Reiser tried to apologize.

"Come along, dear, we need you now."

"What! What's going on?" Dionelle demanded, looking to Reiser, who was cut off as he opened his mouth to explain.

"You are the kingdom's new dragon whisperer and we need you to get whispering," Lady Karth snarled, grabbing Dionelle by the arm and thrusting her back toward the carriage.

"Right now?" Reiser protested. "She only just got home!"

"And you weren't expecting her for another two weeks, so it does not matter. I shall have her returned by morning if they haven't killed her."

"Stop!" Reiser shouted. "You can't thrust her into danger completely unprepared."

"Rancher, you cannot dictate to me what I shall and shall not do. We will brief her, but the dragons are waiting."

Dionelle's eyes were wide and fearful, but she was too terrified to speak or even to struggle as the lady's men forced Dionelle back into the carriage. The lady climbed in after her and the carriage sped away, with Reiser chasing it down the road and shouting empty threats at them. He stood in the darkness at the end of his lane, wondering what he could do—if anything. Forgetting that the lady had left the door to his house wide open, or that Dionelle's things were strewn in the lane with the abandoned mare, left behind by the uncaring noblewoman, Reiser continued down the lane and jogged all the way to his neighbours' house to seek their counsel.

DIONELLE shook with rage and fear as she listened in disbelief to the Lord and Lady Dunham give her instructions on how they wanted her to deal with the dragons. Standing behind them in the arched tunnel that was separated from the main dragon chamber by a piece of tactless fireproof glass, were their advisors whispering information about what other kingdoms had done to minimize their responsibilities to the dragons. There were two advisors and four men-at-arms, bringing the total number of idiots to eight, and not one of them would listen to a scrap of what Dionelle had to say.

She couldn't believe they were so arrogant and knew so little about dragons. They kept calling it a negotiation, but there was nothing to negotiate. Dionelle was simply expected to tell the dragons that the kingdom would no longer provide oxen for the flight.

"M'lady, this is an insult to them," Dionelle insisted.

"Insult! Do not patronize me, girl. Beasts do not have sensibilities that can be insulted," Lady Karth snapped.

"We have better uses for our oxen, and all you have to do is make them understand that," Lord Dunham said.

"M'lord, that explanation will sound thin to them and I am simply trying to do what you insist I must. If I am to keep peace with them, there needs to be a better explanation to break part of your accord with them."

"Nonsense," Lord Dunham insisted. "Many kingdoms have successfully reduced their involvement with dragons and trimmed the provisions of their various accords."

"Those changes were made because of hardships to the kingdoms. What hardships befall Pasdale?"

"Hardship? Why, I need a new wardrobe!" the lady quipped with great mirth. The others laughed as if it was the cleverest thing they'd ever heard.

Dionelle stood before them gravely, not joining them in the joke. Her life was on the line and she couldn't make them see or care.

When the ruckus quieted, Dionelle hotly asked, "Is it your intent that tonight I shall die and a dragon war be started?"

The lady's eyes flashed and she seized Dionelle by the arm.

"Get out there and do your job!" she barked, shoving Dionelle out into the dragon chamber.

Dionelle stopped for a moment, flabbergasted by the ugly room—all stone in the massive circular domed chamber, grey and unending rock, broken only by the wide slat near the distant ceiling where the dragons came and went. She couldn't believe anyone would be ignorant enough to host dragons in such a boring place.

"Who is this, then?" a crackling voice boomed, and Dionelle started, realizing for the first time that there were three dragons in the room. It was a stunning black dragoness who addressed her, and in a quick assessment, Dionelle realized she must be the flight's leader. The two other dragons were males, one green with silver-tipped wings, horns and claws, and the other a mottled grey and scarlet.

Most dragons had markings in a different shade or colour from the rest of their body, often with different coloured horns, spikes or wings, but this dragoness was entirely black, her features discernible only by the darkening shadows or a shimmer of light. Her claws and horns were impossibly black, shards of obsidian against her dark scales, and Dionelle had never seen anything like it before.

"I beg your pardon, Mistress," Dionelle said with a mock curtsey, since she wasn't wearing any skirts. "I was taken aback by the hostility of this room's aesthetics and have forgotten my manners. My name is Dionelle and I am to be Pasdale's new dragon whisperer, should your flight choose to accept me. And if I may be so bold, you have the most beautiful markings—or perhaps the utter lack of them—that I have ever seen. You are like midnight come alive."

"Thank you my dear; I shall overlook your unflattering entrance. This room is a blight, as anyone who has sense can see."

Dionelle smirked, glad that her back was to the nobles, but she still heard the lady sniff indignantly. She desperately wanted to agree with the dragoness, but knew it would be gravely unwise to mock her leaders and employers. She remained silent, but didn't let the smirk go unnoticed by the dragons. It would be a difficult balancing act to keep from enraging either party.

"We have tried to negotiate more appealing chambers," the dragoness explained, "but our requests have been ignored."

"My apologies, Mistress. I am sure the Dunhams have a good reason for not being able to provide you with prettier accommodations."

"They have given us a more beautiful dragon whisperer with you, and that at least is a good start. Your manners are quite good and that also pleases me. Have you always been so white?"

"White like the snow since the day I was born," Dionelle replied tentatively. She could feel the Dunhams' impatience growing, it radiated from the room behind her, but she knew she had to entertain these niceties with the dragons if she hoped to have them accept her as a whisperer.

"Most unusual! I must say, if you survive this negotiation, then we happily accept you as our new whisperer."

"This pleases me," Dionelle said, feeling awkward. "I do hope I survive, then, and have further opportunities to speak to you."

"Very well. Now please explain this new business. Recently one of my superiors stopped at the oxen farm to feast, as is our agreement, only to be turned away by lancers. She was already famished and exhausted from a long journey over desert wastelands in her trip from the southern seas and then was denied the meal she needed and forced to defend herself in a most shameful retreat. One of my comrades was able to hunt for her until she was rested enough to fully tend to her own matters, but

55

this was a dreadful inconvenience and a clear breach of Mountain Dragons' Pasdale Accord."

"Mistress, please give my sincerest apologies to your superior, and it pleases me to hear that she did recover from her physical distress. It is difficult for me to discuss policies that were decided upon before my arrival here tonight, but I assure you it was a mere oversight that the ruling nobles did not provide you with warning over their need to put their oxen to other uses."

"Indeed," the dragoness said in a testy tone.

When she said nothing more, Dionelle grew nervous. The dragoness had not settled in to properly converse, still sitting on her haunches with her head at nearly full height, nearing the ceiling, and looking down at Dionelle, who was only a little taller than her clawed foot. Until the dragoness relaxed and lay down to speak with her, Dionelle couldn't let her guard down. She hadn't offended the dragons in any way, but hadn't won them over yet either.

"Mistress, my ruling lord and lady regret that they must withdraw from this section of the accord, but they must use the oxen that the kingdom raises for other uses."

"What uses are more pressing?" the dragoness asked, her tone rising and her body becoming more rigid.

Dionelle floundered, lacking any answer other than the nobles' spite, greed and ignorance, the admittance of which would doom her to death by one party if not the other. She didn't actually know what else the nobles had planned for the oxen and hadn't thought to ask. Before she could say as much, there was a brilliant flash and roaring filled her ears. She was knocked backward and then slid partway across the floor from the blast of the dragoness's fires.

She hadn't been afforded the opportunity to grab her fire cloak before leaving home and she huddled into a ball, trying to protect as much of her clothing as she could, but as the flames died, Dionelle realized that most of what she wore had been incinerated before she even hit the floor. Even her boots had been destroyed and she kicked off their remainders, as she felt the soles beginning to melt. She'd never been flamed by a dragoness before and hadn't known the true depths of their fury.

Dionelle frantically tried to pat out the flames from the small swatches of fabric clinging to her, ignoring the snickering from the nobles, but once she'd put out all the fires, there was nothing left but a few charred rags in a heap at her feet. She pawed through them quickly, desperately, but nothing was big enough to offer her any protection at all. The continued tittering from the nobles indicated they would offer her no support.

"What devilry is this?" the dragoness demanded.

Dionelle was startled, forgetting the situation in her embarrassment, but was also relieved to see that the dragoness had leaned forward, resting her chin on the floor to be as close to eye level with Dionelle as she could.

"I'm immune to fire," Dionelle whispered, her voice choked with shame as she furiously blinked back tears.

"More of the Dunhams' scheming, is this?"

"They could not find an experienced replacement for the previous whisperer, and so chose me since I had the best chance of surviving any lapses in etiquette."

"How did you achieve your immunity? You are too young to have learned it already. Who has enchanted you? Did they call on elemental demons?"

"I don't know who or how I was enchanted, but I have been this way since birth."

"White as the snow and immune to fire. You are very unusual."

"Thank you, Mistress."

"Stand up then and face me."

"Mistress, if you will forgive me, I would prefer to hold what dignity I might have left and remain sitting."

The dragoness grunted and gave her head a brief shake. The nobles, safe behind their repulsive fireproof glass, continued to laugh and taunt. Dionelle caught a snatch of a comment about having the backside of a newborn babe before she shut her ears to the nobles and did her best to focus on the dragoness.

Dionelle stood slowly and cautiously, clasping her hands behind her to try to block some of the view. She didn't care what the dragons saw, suspecting the dragoness simply wanted to study her form for aesthetic value, but she refused to let the nobles see her so vulnerable.

"Will you turn?" the dragoness requested.

Dionelle bit her lip and started to form as eloquent a refusal as she could, but howls of laughter rose from the noble gallery and the dragoness scowled in their direction, quickly silencing them.

"No, of course, that's enough for now," the dragoness replied. "You may sit and retain some dignity."

"Thank you, Mistress. You show immense kindness to such an ignorant stranger as myself."

"You are not wholly ignorant, my dear, and neither am I."

Dionelle carefully sat on the cold stone, letting the floor hide her bottom while she pulled her knees up to her chest to hide the rest. It didn't take long for her to begin to shiver, though she wasn't entirely aware of the chill of the stone, only her anger and humiliation. She fought back as many of the tears as she could and chose to ignore the ones that fell. The dragoness was kind enough to do the same.

"Now then, shall you answer me?" the dragoness demanded.

"Yes, Mistress. As best I can."

"You know better than to lie?"

"Certainly. I would only tell you the truth—or as much of it as I am party to."

"So you don't have an answer about what our oxen will be doing? Or why we must hunt abroad rather than be shown hospitality?"

"I'm afraid I didn't think to ask what the other use was for the oxen and the information wasn't volunteered. I am new to this land, the new bride of a simple rancher, and until this night I had no use for the wider kingdom's politics. I know little about the current state of the kingdom or its wealth, but when I have time to confer with my lord and lady, I can find the answers you seek."

The dragoness snorted, annoyed but placated for the time being.

"Very well. I must bring this news—this breaking of the accord—to my superiors and await further instructions, but I suspect that some other form of compensation will be required."

"Yes, naturally," Dionelle replied quickly. "Once I am able to discuss details with the Dunhams, I can help you come to a new agreement."

Dionelle heard an angry hiss from behind the glass—Lady Karth, no doubt—but couldn't fathom what she had done wrong. She had done just as they had asked. She had convinced the dragons to accept a major break from a longstanding accord and hadn't even been killed in the process. At least, not yet.

Dionelle bowed her head and then looked enquiringly to the dragoness.

"Does my mistress have any further concerns for this evening?"

"We have many, but I believe you need time to be fully briefed on recent activities in the kingdom. We have sufficient explanation for now. I bid you goodnight, Dionelle."

"May the winds that carry you be blessed," Dionelle replied.

It was the customary leave-taking phrase amongst dragons, but the dragoness seemed charmed that Dionelle had used it, smiling briefly—a quick twitch at the corners of her vast mouth—before leading her flight out of the ugly room.

Dionelle remained on the floor, stunned and relieved, and was oblivious to the sound of booted feet stomping across the stone tiles until a coarse, threadbare blanket was thrust rudely over her shoulders by one of the guards. She startled and looked about in time to see Lady Karth reaching for her. The noblewoman caught Dionelle by the hair and wrenched her to her feet.

"We did not authorize you to make a new deal with them!" Lady Karth screamed. "Now they're going to expect something else to replace the oxen."

She shook Dionelle as she berated her and the thin old blanket began to slip loose. Dionelle was too confused to fight back or try to break the woman's hold and all she could think to do was grasp the blanket before it fell to the floor and left her exposed. Lady Karth dug the fingers of her free hand into Dionelle's shoulder and turned the poor girl to face her, relishing in Dionelle's distress when she cried out in pain.

"Do you really believe a daft little waif like you can walk in here and undo all that my lord and I have worked so hard to achieve? You are a peasant! You will remember your place or I will see to it that the dragons feast on your frail flesh. Remember your place, because if you raise that tone of contempt against me again, I will rip you to shreds in a manner to rival that dragoness!"

The lady let go of Dionelle's hair, and she felt a moment of relief until she realized that the horrible woman had only released her to unsheathe her blade. Still digging her fingers so hard into Dionelle's shoulder that Dionelle was certain they would pierce the flesh, the lady pressed a broad-bladed dagger under Dionelle's chin.

"Do not believe that you have knowledge," Lady Karth snarled. "You are nothing but a poor fool and not in the league of my advisors who have studied with great men and travelled to locales you could never even imagine!"

Dionelle realized that the woman was completely mad and she held her tongue against any retort that came to mind, knowing that any answer would result in death.

"That's enough, my dear," Lord Dunham said in an even and serene tone, easily breaking his wife's hold. "She has staved off war with those beasts, so we mustn't harm her so long as she keeps them happy."

Lady Karth was spinning the blade in her palm, eyeing Dionelle with pure malice, looking for a place to maim her.

"We must keep her whole," the lord continued. "The dragons are placated as much by her appearance as by what she says."

When the lady sheathed her blade, Lord Dunham smiled winningly.

"I believe this calls for a celebration! Wine!" he said, gesturing to one of his advisors, who scuttled off to fetch wine, before turning back to his wife. "Shall we finalize the design on your new chariot tonight or wait for the morrow?"

"Tonight," Lady Karth purred lustily, brushing Dionelle aside as they exited the chamber.

"Get this wretch out of my sight," Lord Dunham said to a guard as he nudged Dionelle in their direction.

BY the time the moon was high, a handful of ranchers had gathered to hear Reiser's plight, but it seemed there was nothing any of them could do against the power of the ruling lord or the king. Dionelle was a sorceress and could use the sway of the Wizards Guild to petition the nobles for fairer treatment, but that was the best they could hope for— and that was only if she survived the night. It would take every last farmer and rancher in protest together to have any kind of say over how the ruling nobles conducted themselves. It was unlikely they'd even get half those kinds of numbers when most of them were treated decently or just flat out ignored by the ruling class, except when it was time to collect taxes.

They needed a dragon whisperer, no matter how unfair the situation seemed, and Reiser returned to his empty house, finally gathering his wife's possessions from the dooryard and stabling the mare. He sat in front of the hearth with Dionelle's things in a pile in front of him, lamenting his inability to start a proper blaze and worrying about Dionelle's fate. He had begun to doze off in his chair when he heard the clatter of a carriage near dawn.

He jumped from his chair and rushed out the door to find Dionelle walking gingerly toward him across the gravel lane and the carriage already making a quick retreat. Dionelle was barefoot and wearing only an old blanket that she had pulled tightly around her shoulders trying to cover herself as best she could. Reiser became furious when he realized what had happened.

"You couldn't even give her proper robes!" he screamed after the fleeing carriage. He turned to his wife and saw that her eyes were puffy and red—she had been crying.

"They didn't even let you grab your fire cloak," he said, furious. "What happened?"

"The dragoness lost her temper with me," Dionelle whimpered. "And the *diplomats* all just laughed at me when my clothing burned away," she hissed, glaring back the way the carriage had vanished. "They left me in that room full of dragons, completely naked, for the duration of the meeting. I have half a mind to let the dragons feast on this entire cursed kingdom!"

"Come inside and let's get you cleaned up. You can head back to Boidossen's tomorrow and I'll tell them you went back to your mother's. I won't let them do this to you again."

"Why did you let them do it in the first place!" she snapped.

"Lady Karth left me with little choice. She barged in here with her men-at-arms and wasn't open to negotiations. Surely you noticed that about her."

Dionelle only glowered.

"I went to the neighbours, but could only find a handful of ranchers willing to stand against this tyranny. The taxes haven't yet become bad enough for them to revolt. What else could I do? I had hoped you would get home before she came and I could hide you until I could negotiate with her."

"What could you possibly have hoped to negotiate with her? You said yourself it's pointless!"

"I had hoped to buy at least an afternoon to get you out of here—back to your mother where she can't do this to you."

"You didn't even consider that maybe I just needed some time to prepare for it, did you?" Dionelle spat. "Every kingdom has dragon whisperers, and the ones who have had some training never die at the claws of a dragon. Just like the gent I'm replacing—killed by his own stupidity rather than a dragon. You never even considered that I might enjoy this with some time to prepare."

"Don't be ridiculous! Working for that woman, with dragons lurking over you?"

"That woman terrifies me far more than even the dragoness when she's lost her temper!"

"Lady Karth won't eat you alive!"

"But she would! You didn't see her tonight—a raving lunatic! Dragons don't eat humans, so don't be ridiculous. I'm not a child and I've been learning about dragons almost as long as I've been learning to control fire. I'm your wife and an adult and you need to start treating me as such. There are far more dangerous things in this kingdom than dragon whispering. It's far less dangerous than stopping their cow raids. I will not have you dictating my life to me!"

"Dionelle, be reasonable. I'm not dictating anything, I'm just stating my concerns and trying to keep you safe."

"The last time the dragons came you would have restrained me, I know you would have, but by then you knew well enough that I would quit you if you did. You haven't quite learned enough yet and I'll quit you still if you don't stop this! I've got some books from the wizard and some proper instruction and a list of even more books that will help me with dragons and as a sorceress."

"You're not really considering this," he said, horrified.

"I am! I need to have something in my life!"

"What about me? Do I not matter? Do my concerns not matter?"

"I barely know you. As friends, you wouldn't have tried to manage my life like this. You get angry that I resent you, but you won't let me have a life outside of this marriage and it's maddening! Your concerns are largely unfounded. You know very little of dragons, except that they burn down your forests and eat your cows. Outside of war, when was the last time you heard of a dragon killing a human?"

"Novice dragon whisperers are always quick to meet their deaths!"

"That's why I need time to study. I am lucky to be immune to their fire and that's what that horrible woman was counting on. It has distracted them for now and I think their curiosity will be enough to hold them interested until I learn more of their ways and in the art of diplomacy with dragons."

"You're really thinking about this."

"Yes! For the love of the stars would you just listen to me!" She reached into one of her bags and produced a heavy tome bound in fire-orange leather. "Read this. All of it, front to back because Boidossen sent *this* book for you. I will not discuss this with you a moment longer until after you've read the book."

"What is this?"

"Just read it!" she cried, turning from him and heading up the stairs. She stormed straight into the spare room, still clad in nothing but the tattered old blanket Lady Karth had been *kind* enough to send her home in, slamming the door behind her.

Reiser looked down at the thick hardcover she had practically thrown at him, and opened it. It was a book of dragon lore—their ways and their customs. He sighed and sat down at the hearth, skimming over it in the dim firelight and growing dawn light. He had no concentration left and felt even more wretched than he had when Lady Karth had carted Dionelle away, or when his lovely wife had returned home again, naked and in tears—humiliated. He finally went to bed to sleep for a miserable hour until it was time to meet the children out in the fields.

Dionelle was dressed and in the kitchen when he came back into the house at lunchtime. She had put all of her things away and seemed in a better mood. She had made some chilled tea and was nibbling at some cheese as she finished up her meal. She made enough for Reiser and left it on the table for him when he came through the door, but she left the kitchen and went to the hearth to read, clearly not interested in talking to him yet.

He finished his meal in silence and then went into the parlour to try to coax a better mood out of her.

"Will you come out to the fields with me and tell me what you've learned?"

"I'd prefer to stay inside," she replied flatly.

"If you change your mind, I welcome your company. I've missed you in your absence and we didn't get the chance for a proper greeting when you returned."

"Yes, that wasn't ideal, but I need to study a lot more now that I know what I've been dealt. Whether you like it or not, Lady Karth isn't giving me a choice on this so I need to be prepared for the next encounter."

"Is she going to find someone more willing to take over for you?"

"Maybe I don't want someone to take over for me."

"All right," he surrendered, not interested in a repeat of the previous night's argument. "I will be out in the fields if you change your mind. Otherwise, I'll see you this evening. Thank you for the lunch."

She kept her gaze directed firmly at the pages in front of her, though Reiser could tell she wasn't actually reading anything, and just trying to avoid further conversation with him. Her return had been marred by the lady's intrusion and now things remained icy. Reiser was concerned and hoped that a couple of days in the comfort of home with her books would improve Dionelle's outlook. He hoped Lady Karth and the dragons would leave her be for a few days to get her bearings and really consider how she felt about the prospect of being a permanent dragon whisperer. Reiser desperately hoped it would be a temporary thing.

That very afternoon, as the sun arched back down toward the horizon, the air was shrill with dragoncries and Dionelle came running out into the field again, both terrified and in awe as three of them landed just outside the house where she was standing. The midnight black dragoness was in charge, landing gracefully with nothing more than a plume of dust kicked up around her claws as she touched down. She scratched at the ground as she crouched down on all fours to bring herself to Dionelle's eye level, resting her chin on the ground. She was accompanied by two males—one blue and one orange—and they had come specifically to see Dionelle.

"Please, just leave her be!" Reiser begged.

"Oh, stop it!" Dionelle snapped. "Go read that book like I asked you to." She ignored him and turned her attention back to the dragons. "What brings you to my home?"

"We prefer to give counsel away from the influence of the nobles," the black dragoness replied, her voice like a roaring hearth-fire.

"Why is that?"

"You may not outright lie to us—we know you are clever enough to understand the consequences of lies—but you choose your words more carefully in the presence of your mistress."

"She's hardly my mistress," Dionelle said hotly.

"See? We are getting more truth out of you already. She is not a kind woman, even when your lord manages to rein her in, and we prefer not to deal with whisperers in her presence. Sometimes it is necessary, but certainly not ideal. I do apologize for what happened with your garments last night, I am sure you understand that I meant to kill you, not embarrass you."

"The real embarrassment was at the treatment afterward."

"I intend to speak to the lady about that," the dragoness replied. "Leaving you shivering and exposed in that manner was utterly unacceptable. And I apologize that I did not think to keep breathing fire on you to keep you warm. I am not used to dealing with those completely immune to dragonfire and in the future I won't forget my manners."

"Thank you," Dionelle replied with a little bow. "But in the future, I would appreciate it if you remember that your fire will only harm my clothes."

"Yes, it's fascinating. You are beautiful and mysterious," the dragoness sighed, her rapture echoed by the other two males who had accompanied her. Their sighs were like steam hissing from a kettle. "Do you know what caused this? Do you have many magic folk in your family?"

"I am the first and my family is a clan of brunettes. Boidossen was helping me try to understand the origin of my strange appearance and talents when the lady pulled me away from my studies."

"I apologize that she interrupted your education on our behalf, but if it is any consolation, we will not impose that incorrigible woman or any of the lord's staff on you unless it is necessary. If you do not think it will frighten your neighbours badly, then we will take counsel with you here."

"That would be all right—just no more raids on the neighbours' cattle! There are plenty of beasts in the wild, likely fatter and more fun to hunt, so I will not tolerate any marauding in these fields."

"Your request is reasonable."

"Very well, you may take counsel with me here if you promise to maintain the peace."

"Dionelle, don't encourage this madness!" Reiser begged.

Dionelle cast him an angry glance to silence him before quickly turning her attention back to the dragoness.

"Please forgive my husband," she pleaded, stepping in front of him in anticipation of some kind of attack. "His rudeness is the result of ignorance, not insolence, and I will make sure he remembers his manners on your next visit."

"Yes, I would appreciate it if you tame his outbursts."

"If it is your will, he will remain in the fields, tending to his business the next time you arrive."

"He may do as he pleases, so long as he does it politely," the dragoness replied, glaring at Reiser.

"You have my word, he will remain polite from now on."

"That would be most excellent. Do you have chores to tend to now?"

"Not any specifically."

The dragoness furrowed her brow, silent for a moment. "My companion can make the loveliest melodies with his wings. If he shows you one, will you dance for us?"

Dionelle glanced at the brilliantly coloured cerulean dragon next to the dragoness, with his indigo claws and horns, and sky-blue-tinged wings, and then back at her mistress. "I have little talent for dancing, but I will oblige you as best I can. Would you like Reiser to join me?"

The dragoness narrowed her eyes at him for a moment, studying him, before finally replying dismissively, "That is not necessary. He may return to his work in the fields."

Dionelle nodded toward Reiser and was relieved when he didn't protest and hurried back to where the field children were huddled in terrified awe. The blue dragon had been standing alertly on his hind legs, his underbelly shimmering in the late day sun, watching their surroundings and wary of Reiser and the help. When the dragoness indicated that he should play, he leaned down onto all four legs, circled around to the other side of Dionelle, while the orange dragon, like a living fire with crimson markings, took up his place in the vigil. The blue dragon began to rub the smooth leather of his tail over the membrane of his wings, producing a humming sound like a field of wildflowers alive with bees on a gentle summer afternoon.

Dionelle was surprised by the honour—few people ever heard dragonsong and it was something that often took years to earn—and she stood entranced by it until he worked it into a proper melody. It was a slow one and she had hoped for some kind of jig, but understood that they were less interested in her actual dancing and more in the way she moved her body. Many people considered her scrawny, but the dragons likely thought she was elegant and so she did her best to sway and twirl in tune as gracefully as she could, knowing any clumsy missteps could earn her a scorching.

Curious neighbours began looking on, and the dragons became shy, finally flying off silently. The large dragoness spread her great wings and they seemed to span the whole of Reiser's acreage, bringing a gale down with each mighty flap, until she had climbed skyward and disappeared. When they were gone, Reiser rushed over to her.

"What on earth was that! You're not serious about letting them come back, are you?"

"You try telling them they can't!" she replied, trying not to let her frustrations with him overshadow the honour she had just received. "They are no danger! They will take counsel peacefully, because it would be rude of them not to. Dragons are terrible egoists but pride themselves on their manners—you would know that if you would read the book I gave you!"

"How was burning your clothes away *not* rude?"

"It was! And she apologized for it. But I provoked her because I was guarding what I said far more than I should have. She was right—Lady Karth is a terrible influence to be around when dealing with dragons. Dragons hate to be deceived above all else. Please, just read that book so you understand this a little more."

"There must be someone who can take over this nonsense for you."

"It's not nonsense and I like it. Today was amazing! Did you hear— do you have any idea what an honour that was? Please, don't ruin that for me."

Reiser opened his mouth to argue, but she only glared and he quickly subsided.

"Dragons love beautiful things! They would no sooner hurt me than tear their own eyes out, especially now that they know me. They played *dragonsong* for me! Humans are rarely given the honour! They're prone to mischief but are not mindless beasts and if you would take some time to learn about them, you'll see that they are quite intelligent with a great deal of integrity. Their ways are very different from ours, but when we learn their customs and mind our manners in their presence, then they become powerful allies."

Reiser wanted to argue, to tell her it was dangerous, but the dragons really had been entranced by her and he was hard pressed to find any danger in a bit of music and song. He would have to read that book to understand her point of view if he truly hoped to talk her out of it.

CHAPTER 5

"I'M going to the market for the afternoon," Dionelle informed Reiser when he came in for lunch. "Shall I fetch you anything?"

"We have everything we need," he said. "You were there four days ago, why are you going back so soon?"

He tried to keep his question as neutral as possible, not wanting her to think he was interrogating or accusing her of something. She had been on edge since the dragons came to visit, and they were both careful of what they said, because neither of them wanted to ignite a new argument.

"I heard there was a new caravan of traders in the market," she said. She kept to herself that most of the vendors in the caravan specialized in all things dragon.

"Will you be home for dinner?" he asked.

"I expect so."

Reiser nodded and took his lunch to the porch to eat and enjoy the beautiful day. It barely mattered when she was home because she spent most of her free time buried in her studies. She wanted to include Reiser in what she was learning as a sorceress, but the only time she had tried it had led to an argument about her desire to keep being a dragon whisperer. That had ended quite badly, and she'd spent the night in the spare room, too angry to be in the same room as him.

When Reiser was in the fields she often went into the city, now that she didn't find it as intimidating, to scour the markets for tools of the trade and books that could help her. Boidossen had sent her home with a list of books that would help her but that he didn't have, and there was a wealth of knowledge about dragon whispering too and she wanted to tap into it. The more she knew, the better she would do at her job and the less chance of getting shredded to pieces.

As soon as Reiser went back into the fields, she set out for the market. She'd packed everything she needed and was waiting only for him to come back to the house so she could let him know she would be gone.

It was a warm, pleasant day and the smell of baked dirt rose up from the road as her sandals kicked up small plumes of dust. The smells changed as she got closer to the city, more pungent—the smell of too many people living too close. Sour sweat, waste, garbage, penned animals, stagnant water—all baking under the heat of the late-summer sun. As a lifelong resident of the countryside, she noticed the smell even more than most.

The market was kept a little cleaner than many other quarters of the city, and the fresh water, fresh produce and open square surrounded by trees, helped make the air easier to breathe. The dominating scent was from the kitchen fires of the food vendors.

She found the new caravan and wasn't disappointed by what they had to offer. There was a dragon skin vendor with large hides, nearly full size, as well as teeth and claws to be used for ornamentation and weapons.

"I've never seen such an expansive collection!" Dionelle told her.

The woman smiled. "My brother whispers for a kingdom near Golden Hill, and he gets a lot of contracts for me with dragons, that I can use their skins when they die. My sister is a huntress and tracker and watches the dragons I have contracts with as they reach the ends of their lives."

"You are very fortunate," Dionelle said.

The woman smiled modestly, but Dionelle wondered at the kind of fortunes she must have waiting for her upon her return home.

What Dionelle had specifically come for though was the academic tent, laden with books and scrolls, some very old and very pricey. There was another woman perusing the selection when Dionelle arrived. Many of the older scrolls were framed in glass to keep them protected yet legible, and Dionelle picked one up to inspect its content. It spoke of a dragon city in the sky.

"The shimmering city," the other woman commented, reading over Dionelle's shoulder.

"This is the first time I've heard of it," Dionelle said, skimming the contents before setting it back down.

The other woman ran her finger along the frame, longingly, before turning her attention back to Dionelle.

"I've seen descriptions of it in other books of lore," the woman explained, "but I think that's the original account. It was made by a wizard who made it to their hallowed mountain ranges and learned of the city from dragons he had befriended."

"It's one of five copies of the original," the vendor corrected. He was a bespectacled man in his middle years with greying brown hair and a pleasant round face. "The original hangs in the library of the Wizards Guild. This copy is the only one I have—one hundred gold pieces."

The woman sighed. She was cleanly dressed but her simple garb was that of a peasant.

"No one has ever seen the dragon city," the woman finally said. "The dragons won't let any humans—not even whisperers or wizards—see where they live. I don't think any human has even seen the home of a living dragon."

The vendor only shrugged at this.

"There are certainly details of their homes in the mountains," he said, "but I think most of them are visited after the residing dragons have passed. I think Muina's sister has seen some of their homes," he said, gesturing to the woman selling the skins, "but not until after the dragons have died and she goes to collect their pelts."

"Do you know why they keep so private?" Dionelle asked. "Is it more of their conceit?"

"They don't like to be bothered by rude neighbours, particularly unschooled humans," the scholar replied. "And they don't want lancers finding where they live."

"I think it's more than just that," the woman said. "They perform their strongest magic when they are gathered together. The more of them there are in one place, the stronger their magic. I would expect they would keep those places sacred, like our temples where we perform our most solemn rituals."

"Dragons have magic?" Dionelle asked.

"Oh yes, their very being is an act of magic, I'm sure," the woman said. "But they don't build their grand fortresses in the mountains, or that beautiful city, just through fire and sheer strength. I know little of the extent of the enchantments they're capable of, but they possess deep and ancient magic that grows stronger with their numbers."

"Are you a scholar too?" Dionelle asked the woman. She seemed to know almost as much as the man selling the dragon lore.

"I'm still apprenticing," she replied. "My mistress says she doesn't know if I'll ever be admitted to the Guild because I spend far more time on dragon lore than on my spellwork. I'm more interested in dragons than sorcery, but there isn't much proper apprenticing to be done in that area. I had hoped to learn enough to be the kingdom's next dragon whisperer, but I haven't gained enough experience yet and didn't expect Ishin would have perished the way he did—so abruptly and so young. And now they've replaced him, so my chance for the position has likely passed."

Dionelle's ears grew hot but she nodded and kept quiet.

"Besides, I'm a little too plain to be a dragon whisperer," she sighed glumly. Dionelle wanted to argue the point out of politeness, but the woman was right—she was plain. Not ugly, but lacking the sorts of features that lured a dragon in. She was short and broad and not terribly graceful, with muddy hazel eyes and a mottled complexion.

"You have got very lovely hair," Dionelle commented. It was true— her red hair glimmered and cascaded to the middle of her back like a tumbling wave of dragonfire.

"Oh, but that's not enough."

Dionelle shrugged. "Are you sure? It doesn't take much to catch their initial attention and you know enough of their ways to impress them with your manners."

"Maybe. Maybe one day. You seem to know enough about their ways yourself," she commented. "Do you have experience with them?"

"A little," Dionelle said vaguely. "I've had to stop a few from eating livestock, so I learned some of their lore while apprenticing."

"Ah, you're a sorceress and an aspiring dragon scholar too?" she said excitedly.

"Yes, I'm a sorceress. Becoming a dragon scholar has been more a necessity than a choice though. I'm immune to fire, and once people found out, they started to expect me to help when dragons were causing mischief."

"Immune? Fully immune?" the woman said sceptically. She stopped short and studied Dionelle carefully for a moment, really noticing her for the first time. She gasped. "Oh my! Are you Dionelle?"

"Er... Yes."

"Ha! I knew it—young and immune to fire. Well, I certainly won't ever get that dragon whisperer position in this kingdom—you'll be set until I'm too old to catch even a desperate dragon's attention. It's wonderful to meet you, though! I'm Ondias."

"You knew I was the new dragon whisperer just because I'm immune to fire?"

"Oh, not just that. Being entirely white is what really gave it away."

Dionelle sighed, "Yes, there's that." She had hoped that the size of the city would afford her some anonymity despite her appearance.

"How long have you been studying dragon lore?" Ondias asked.

"Since the first time I stopped a marauding dragon after my mother's livestock. My master started training me then. He figured I may as well put my immunity to good use. His knowledge is limited though, so I've come here to find some more books."

Ondias was beaming. "I've been trying to learn more about fire and fire spells. There's little dragon lore left for me to learn."

Both women turned their attention back to the books on the table, painstakingly narrowing their searches down to the books that contained the most information for the smallest sum of money. As they scoured the selection, Dionelle made Ondias an offer.

"It seems we both have plenty of knowledge that the other needs or wants. Why don't you teach me about dragons and I will teach you about working with fire."

Ondias was positively glowing with delight at the suggestion. Dionelle grinned back. It had been a long time since she had made a new friend and she almost felt bad about taking a job the girl wanted so badly. She hadn't even wanted to be a dragon whisperer before she had been forced into it.

She had collected her first pay as the new whisperer on her last trip to the market and hadn't told Reiser about it yet, because she was worried it would start another fight. It had been exactly one hundred gold pieces—a start up fee on top of her regular wage—and she had planned on sending most of it to her mother. Now, she decided her mother could have her next wage. She gave the sack of coins to the vendor in exchange for the scroll about the dragon city.

Ondias's mouth fell open as Dionelle handed the scroll to her.

"I can't take this!"

"Yes, you can. Tell me everything you know about the city and I'll consider it a fair trade."

Ondias sputtered and kept trying to decline, but Dionelle insisted. She had a few coins left in her regular coin purse and she used every last one of them to buy three more books: one on dragon lore and two on spellcraft. Ondias was still flabbergasted by Dionelle's gift and couldn't concentrate enough to pick any books. She decided to return another day and as Dionelle turned for home, Ondias followed her, clutching the scroll to her chest.

"You just spent all your money!"

"Not all of it," Dionelle said. "Just what I brought with me to the market."

"I just really don't think I can take this."

"Yes, you can. I don't think I've ever met anyone with such a genuine love for dragons before. Even the academic selling those books isn't nearly as passionate about his knowledge as you are."

"I can never repay this."

"I told you, you can repay me in knowledge. Have you ever seen a dragon den in the mountains?"

"I saw a drawing once," Ondias admitted sheepishly. "It was drawn by someone who had actually been there. Not an artist, but someone good with a sketch. Their homes in the mountains are quite impressive, but I understand that it's their tunnelling ability that's far more impressive and the outside of their homes is fairly unremarkable. Until you're right up to it, it's designed to blend in with the rest of the mountain. You have to see it from just the right angle to see the towers for what they are and to discern the perches and spires as anything but piles of mountain rubble."

"That is fairly impressive. Their city sounds far more spectacular."

"It's meant to be seen, but only by them. It's in the heart of a mountain range so treacherous that flight is the only way to reach the city, so they can make their city as grand as they like and well, you know how much the dragons like to show off."

"A shimmering city in the sky," Dionelle mused. "I wonder what it looks like, more specifically. I wonder if I can get the dragoness to say."

"The black one?"

"Yes. Have you spoken to her?"

"No, I wouldn't dare. I've seen her coming and going from the Dunhams' fortress. She always seems to have different companions each time. There's a blue male who I've seen with her a couple of times, but that's it. I don't see her every time though, so who knows."

"I've met the blue one. If it's the same one I'm thinking of."

"Probably. Blue is rare in dragons, particularly all blue."

"I didn't realize."

"Oh yes. Blue markings aren't unusual, but to be entirely blue—that's something."

"Must be the same dragon then."

"Do you think she'll tell you about the city?" Ondias asked.

"I hope so. She might. She took to me much quicker than I ever could have expected. They always get curious when I won't burn, but the novelty usually wears off quickly. This time it was different. She even got the blue one to play dragonsong for me."

Ondias grinned. "She likes you! That's wonderful. What did it sound like?"

"Like a field of wildflowers humming full of bees."

"Oh!" Ondias swooned. "Yes, I'm going to have to take this scroll. It's the only way I'm going to be able to control my envy!" Ondias cast her a sly grin to show she was kidding. Mostly kidding.

Dionelle smiled in return, dumbstruck that she had formed such a quick friendship with the woman.

"Why don't you come with me? I'm heading home for dinner," Dionelle said. "We can talk more on the way."

"That would be wonderful! Do you live far?"

"It's a bit of a walk. My husband's ranch is one of the northernmost, but I like how quiet it is there."

"I guess the city is noisy if you're not used to it."

Dionelle explained how she had grown up in a small farming village on the neighbouring prairie. Ondias was two years Dionelle's junior and had lived in Pasdale all her life. Like Dionelle, Ondias had never had much money, so she'd always worked through her apprenticeship. But she had been lucky, because her mistress had travelled quite a bit and would often bring Ondias with her. She had even been to the Wizards Guild twice.

"Their dragon hall is stunning," Ondias gushed.

"The one is Pasdale is hideous," Dionelle said, with complete disdain. She wasn't surprised the dragons would rather visit her at home.

Ondias was shocked and pleased to discover that the dragons were going to her house.

"They never visited Ishin," Ondias said. "But then again, he lived in the city."

"Ishin?"

"The whisperer you've replaced. He was a fine specimen of a man. Well, visually speaking. His personality was a good match for the

Dunhams though. I suspect his narcissism was his downfall, but I haven't been able to find out what caused the fight that cost him his life. I know it was a foreigner, someone from the southern sea region, who delivered the fatal stab. They held a special execution and he was executed the next morning, along with Ishin's family."

"Why on earth would they execute the dead man's family?" Dionelle was shocked and horrified.

"The Dunhams were furious about losing their whisperer," Ondias explained. "I don't know if they were trying to punish Ishin's family for not keeping him out of the bar full of foreigners, or if punishing the murderer alone wasn't enough to satiate their rage."

Dionelle was stunned. Knowledge of the Dunhams' cruelty had reached as far as her hometown, but she'd never heard specific examples of their madness until arriving in Pasdale. The extent of their fury was both astounding and terrifying, but Dionelle was glad to know what was at stake. She would have to be very careful.

"How do you know so much?" Dionelle asked.

"I listen. And my mistress is a terrible gossip," Ondias said with a wink. "I'm well matched with her because she passes on anything she hears that's even remotely dragon related and she's well connected within the noble court. I can barely remember my letters some days and I'm completely lost with my numbers most days, but tell me something about a dragon and I'll never forget it."

"It sounds like dragons are your destiny."

Ondias smiled at the thought. "Perhaps meeting you today was part of it then."

"I will gladly pass on any new information the dragoness gives me. I'd like to know what makes the city shimmer. Gems, perhaps?"

"They love gems, so it could be. Maybe gold? I hope she tells you!"

"If they have such a beautiful city so far away and safe from humans, why do they live in mountains so near to us?"

"That's something I can't answer. They are all spread out too, which I find odd, considering how close they are to each other. There are only a few hundred dragons and they all know each other quite intimately. I know they return to the city regularly, for festivals and their Dragoness Superior summons them back in a crisis."

"What counts as a crisis for dragons?"

"War, specifically with humans. No human army has won against a dragon because the dragon sends a distress call to the others. That one dragon will often retreat only until the others have gathered, and then they strike back in one devastating blow. Other crises usually include the death of one of their kind. They gather to mourn. But they don't gather just in times of hardship. They celebrate festivals to mark the seasons and they celebrate new hatchlings."

"That must happen often enough."

"I don't think so. Maybe a couple of new broods a year. A dragoness can only spawn once in her lifetime. They don't celebrate until the hatchlings have survived their first year, as I think nearly half of them don't. I don't understand why though."

"If I can find a way to bring it up politely, I will try to find out for you," Dionelle offered. The more she learned, the more interested she was. They were nearing the Ovailen homestead and Dionelle became a little nervous. She didn't want Ondias's unbridled love of dragons to set Reiser off.

"Ondias, can you keep it to yourself how much that scroll cost? Downplay its importance around my husband."

"Would he be angry at you for spending the money?"

"He might. His farming is successful enough that we are not without, but he doesn't understand about dragons. We've been fighting about my job as the whisperer."

"Oh, I'm sorry. Should I not talk about the dragons at all?"

"Is that even possible for you?" Dionelle said with a wink. "It might do him some good to learn more about them from someone other than me. He won't take my word for it."

Ondias nodded but said nothing.

As the two women approached the house, Reiser rounded the corner from the other direction, coming in to prepare dinner.

"Dionelle! I didn't expect you back already. And you've brought company."

"Reiser, this is Ondias," she said, introducing them. "She's going to teach me about dragons and I'm going to teach her about managing fire."

Reiser nodded. "That sounds like a good arrangement."

"We can make dinner, if you'd like to stay in the field a little longer."

He shook his head. "My work is done for the day."

"Are your conversations always this strained?" Ondias blurted. "You need to sort this dragon business out."

Ondias immediately flushed with embarrassment, but Reiser actually laughed. It was the first genuine laugh Dionelle had heard from him in over a week.

"Don't worry, my dear, you didn't say anything untrue," Reiser reassured her. "We do need to talk about Dionelle's job, although I think I need to learn far more about her clients before I could hold up my end of the conversation."

"Well, it's a good thing you've got me now!" Ondias said cheerfully.

"Have you started to read that book?" Dionelle asked him.

They moved inside and began to make dinner, Ondias insisting she help.

"I have started to read the book," Reiser said. "I haven't read much, but it's a start. Tell me, are all of the dragons so vain?"

"Oh my stars, yes!" Ondias said, with a giggle. "They are incredible egomaniacs. But calling them on it, or trying to argue with them about it, is the best way to have yourself reduced to a pile of ashes."

Reiser was alarmed.

"This is why humans and dragons don't get along," Ondias said gently. "Humans are quite willful and headstrong and don't like how illogical the dragons can be about their own self-worth. But dragons really are phenomenal creatures, so I think they're entitled to at least some of their conceit. So let them have it. Accept their arrogance and to some degree ignore it. Move on and remain polite. Once you get around the arrogance, you get to learn so much more about them. They really are quite fascinating, but first you have to stop viewing them as monsters, and you have to get around their ego."

"They seem so hung up on manners, and yet consider the strangest things to not be rude," Reiser said. "How can they value manners so much, and then eat our cattle?"

"It's a double-standard. That's just another thing you have to accept. Sometimes they get carried away—they can be terribly emotional and quick to rage—and they feel entitled to it. Or maybe they don't even notice. Anyway, it's okay for them to be rude, but not for you. You can never point out their rudeness, but can demand an apology if they admit to rudeness on their own."

"You saw that with the dragoness," Dionelle said. "She apologized for burning my clothes away, but during the meeting, she didn't think there was anything wrong with it."

Reiser nodded, but only half understood.

"You have to remember, that for all their human mannerisms—their ability to speak our language, their love of some of our culture and art, their similar emotions—they are not human. In some ways, it's obvious. Most humans call the dragons monsters. But then they talk and act so much like humans and part of you forgets how different they are. You have to get around that too before you can fully and safely deal with them."

"You insist it can be done safely though," Reiser said.

"Oh yes. If a dragon whisperer is in any kind of danger, it's usually during the first encounter. After that, trust and understanding is either gained or it isn't. When a dragon whisperer survives that first test, it usually takes a gross misstep to draw the wrath of a dragon afterward."

Both women could see that Reiser was grappling with the new information. He was conflicted, starting to believe Dionelle was safe but not wanting to believe. Ondias felt like Reiser had enough dragon lore to digest for one evening, and managed to turn the conversation away from dragons, asking the pair about their courtship and about their families. She didn't stay long after dinner because she had a curfew at the house where she stayed—a residence for apprentices—and wasn't allowed out past dark without gaining permission.

"She's so enthusiastic," Reiser commented, once Ondias had left.

"It's fantastic!" Dionelle was giddy and Reiser hadn't seen her so happy since her family had come to visit. Reiser smiled, happy to be rid of the tension for an evening. He sat down in the parlour, intending to read until dark, expecting Dionelle would be studying again all evening, but she plunked down beside him, turned so that her elbow rested on the back of the sofa, with one leg folded under her, her knee touching his thigh.

"No books tonight?" he asked.

"I learned more from one afternoon with Ondias than I could with a week reading my books."

"Am I going to be able to enjoy your company for the rest of this week then?"

"Yes," she said immediately. "Yes, I'll only study when you're reading or in the fields. For the rest of the week."

"But you're not going to give up the studying completely," he tried not to sound too disappointed, not wanting to cause any more tension when it had only just dissipated.

"It's like Ondias said—I survived the first test, but it's still possible to misstep. I need to learn as much as I can as quickly as I can to ensure I remain safe. My safety is your concern, isn't it?"

"Yes, but—" he paused, stopping himself from saying the same things over again. He knew where it would lead, and Ondias was right; they needed to talk about the dragons. "The truth is, I feel neglected. Aside from my concerns about your safety, which, admittedly, are dwindling, I feel like the least important aspect of your life. I've watched you put so many other things ahead of me."

"You're jealous of the dragons?"

He was silent for a moment, contemplating. "Yes, in a way. And not just the dragons. Your family, despite their distance, still occupies more of your thoughts than I seem to."

Dionelle looked down at her knee, thinking. She realized he was right and felt guilty for it, trying to search through her actions for her intentions. Lately, she had been avoiding him to avoid confrontation, but it hadn't started that way.

"I don't do it intentionally. I wasn't before things got so tense, anyway. I lost all sense of freedom and opportunity when my father died, and I'm only just beginning to regain some of that. I need to be able to enjoy it for a while before I can consider what you want from me— before I can try to settle down the way you want. I want the things you said I could have when we were first married. It seems almost like you've changed your mind."

"I want you to be happy."

"You want me to be happy for the reasons *you* think I should be."

He wanted to argue, but wisely checked himself.

"Marriage has been much easier for you," she continued. "Little has changed for you and you forget that I have some catching up to do. That's all I'm doing. I'm catching up so that we can both have what we want from this marriage. I want the things you do—I'm not opposed to us having a family. I've told you that before. I just don't want that now. I want some time to recapture the life and opportunities that died with my father."

"So it's not always going to be like this?"

"Heavens no! I'm facing so much change so quickly and there are so many opportunities that I'm trying to gain all at once. I want to get my apprenticeship over with so that I can join the Guild within the year, and I need to learn a great deal more about dragons and politics to manage this job. I'm putting you last right now so that I can get all of that out of the way and put our marriage first for the rest of our lives. I promise you that all of this madness is me trying to build a life in which I can be content, independent and myself, and also be a wife and, eventually, a mother."

Reiser nodded, trying to take in everything she had said. It was promising, but a lot for him to process at once, especially in light of all the new dragon information Ondias had given him.

When he didn't reply, but seemed content with what she'd said, Dionelle smiled and leaned forward, cupping his face in her hands and pulling him into her kiss. He responded immediately, wrapping his arm around her and turning to face her. She slid across him, straddling his hips and pressing her body tight against his. It was passion he hadn't seen since their first encounter on their journey from her home to Pasdale.

IT was nearing midday and Reiser steered the wagon off to the side of the road, tethering the horse not far from the river. It was a spot where his parents had often stopped on their way to visit the Joaseras and he wanted to share it with his new wife. They grabbed a crate of food and a blanket and walked to the riverside, under the shade of a cluster of trees, to rest and share a meal.

"This is so beautiful," Dionelle said, watching the sun glitter on the surface of the gently rolling water.

"There are rapids farther down the road and they're beautiful too— exciting. It's private and quiet here."

Neither of them had found their appetite yet and they sat on the blanket, taking in the quiet beauty of the river, still wrapped in the warmth of their new-found joy. They were on a gentle, grassy slope, and the vibrant green trees stretched out over the water, bending down to touch it in some places, and also blocked the road from their view. There were high reeds along the water's edge, but they were far enough back to give a clear view of the sparkling river and its rocky opposite shore.

Reiser was enjoying the gentle beauty of his new wife even more than the picturesque scene before them, and he reached out, brushing some of her loose strands of hair away from her face. She smiled at him, still shy, but welcoming his touch. He ran his hand over her cheek and down her neck, pushing the collar of her shirt back and leaning in to place a gentle kiss at the curve where her neck met her shoulder.

She giggled nervously, shying away from him, but met him with a playful gaze before leaning back into him and taking his face in her hands to hold him close while she kissed him deeply, longingly. He untied the ribbon in her hair and deftly unplaited her long braid, running his fingers through her hair as it streamed out beside her in the spring breeze. She smiled at him as she watched him enjoy her snowy white locks for a moment, and then she took hold of his collar with both hands and pulled him back into her kiss.

He eased her down onto her back and propped himself on his elbow beside her, his forearm cradling her head, and continued to kiss her while his other hand untucked her shirt and slid up her side, finally feeling the unusual heat of her soft skin.

"You're so warm," he whispered.

"Mamma says the fire in my eyes courses through my entire being," she replied, still smiling. She took a nervous glance around, but seeing they were still perfectly alone, her playfulness returned. "The world is ours, don't stop now," she whispered.

She touched his face and brought him back down to her, kissing the side of his neck. Her hot breath made him shiver. They helped each other out of their clothes, and Reiser felt the true fires of her body and the searing heat of her skin on his.

She was still too shy to let him admire her afterward, and quickly wrapped herself in her riding cloak as she continued to lie at his side under the warm spring sun. Reiser hated to disturb the tranquility of the afternoon, but they needed to press on soon or they wouldn't reach Pasdale before dark. He kissed her gently and sat up to get dressed. He left her at the riverside while he went to check on the horse, giving her a bit of privacy to dress again. He desperately wanted to see her, but knew it was a trust he would have to earn over time.

When she finally called him back, she had even plaited her hair again, and was layering cheese and smoked meat onto a slice of her mother's homeloaf. She smiled at him sleepily and they enjoyed a brief picnic at the riverside before they moved on again.

REISER pulled a blanket around himself and Dionelle as she drifted to sleep with her arms wrapped around him, marvelling at how quickly their relationship had changed since that first day. They had known each other only as children, and had had to fill the missing years—a decade of maintaining a relationship through only letters had made their reunion awkward. It had seemed like Dionelle's shyness would never subside, but now there was nothing but passion where the awkwardness of old friends had once been.

CHAPTER 6

DIONELLE remained more affectionate towards Reiser after making a friend. He knew she needed a confidante outside of their marriage and he was glad she had found someone. She hadn't been able to connect with the other ranchers' wives, though she was on friendly terms with them, but making a friend had done her outlook wonders.

Ondias became a regular fixture at their house, spending as much of her free time as she could practising with Dionelle. The dragons came around occasionally, but not on official business since the night they had met Dionelle. Reiser almost wanted to call it a friendship though it was hard to believe something so intimate could occur between a human and such beasts.

Reiser had been in the barn and the two women practising at the hearth one afternoon when the dragons came for another visit. They hadn't announced their visit with any of the usual dragoncries because Dionelle had mentioned to them that it frightened the field children, so they had arrived silently. The dragoness tapped at the front door with one long obsidian claw and waited patiently.

"Hello, Mistress!" Dionelle gasped, quickly grabbing her cloak and heading out onto the front porch. "I thank you for taking my suggestion."

"The children are still frightened," she replied.

"Oh, I'm sorry about that. Maybe I should get my friend to school them. She's been working on my husband already."

"Your friend?" the dragoness said inquisitively, looking behind Dionelle to where Ondias stood timidly in the doorway.

"Mistress, this is my friend Ondias. She's an admirer of your kind and has been schooling me and Reiser in your ways."

"Mistress," Ondias said with a bow.

"If you're not here on business, may she join us?" Dionelle asked.

"It's always business," the dragoness replied mischievously.

"Dragon business or noble business?"

"I've had a lifetime's worth of noble business and would prefer it if they were just a little fatter so I could make a meal out of the lot of them."

This earned an appreciative giggle out of Ondias who hadn't had the misfortune of dealing with nobles, but had heard plenty from Dionelle, not to mention all the gossip around the city.

"It's no wonder they need dragon whisperers with manners like that!" Ondias commented.

"Fools are easily parted with their money," the dragoness replied. "Who am I to interfere if it benefits Dionelle?"

"It seems absurd that they pay me what they do simply to talk to dragons. If they bothered to read a little, or even learn some manners by human standards, they could easily talk with the dragons without my aid."

"I was still a hatchling the last time I encountered a noble who was both beautiful and well-mannered. It does not bode well for your kind that they are the representatives we must deal with, but we are quite pleased that they found you for us."

"She is pleasing to look at," Ondias agreed. "You haven't answered whether I may join you today. I know that I am a blight on humanity compared to Dionelle, but I rarely get the opportunity to put my education to good use."

The dragoness studied Ondias with a shrewd, open gaze, drinking her full appearance. She reached out one long black claw and brushed Ondias's fiery locks from her shoulder with surprising grace. Ondias, knowing that if the dragoness saw fit she would kill her regardless of anything she said or did, only stood patiently and didn't flinch when the claw came so near. Flinching would indicate mistrust and dragons disliked mistrust almost as much as lies.

"You have a frumpy appearance and a plain face, but your hair is remarkable," the dragoness finally said.

"Thank you, Mistress." Ondias gathered her hair over the front of one shoulder where the dragons could see it easily but still maintain eye contact with her. "Shall I braid it?"

"Yes, that would be quite pleasing. Your lovely hair makes up what you lack in beauty elsewhere, and you are not without your charm. You do know our customs and that will help you, as manners go further than beauty when we consider human companions."

Ondias was surprised, "You believe I could be a dragon whisperer?"

"Not in place of Dionelle, as I'm sure you understand, but if you were to travel to other lands you could take up the practice. Learning new and ornate braids will help you and braid it over your shoulder as you have it now on your first encounter with the dragons you meet, and you will succeed. Your hair has enough beauty to captivate until your manners prove your worth."

Ondias tried not to smile too broadly and distracted herself by stroking her locks and letting the sun catch them to maximize their beauty and keep the dragons interested in her. She was nervous, but wouldn't let it show. She was also excited about what the dragoness had said, though she wouldn't show that either. She knew she could bask in the joy with Dionelle once the dragons left. For now, she just wanted to keep them interested in her so she could watch and listen.

Dionelle wrapped her cloak around Ondias, since the dragons had allowed her to join them, and they moved to the side of the house to sit under the trees. Ondias spread the fabric of the cloak out around her in the most pleasing manner she could think of and remained close to Dionelle. The cloak could only protect against fire and not the heat, so she wanted to be near enough that Dionelle could help shield her if it was necessary. They were careful to be subtle about what they were doing, not wanting to offend the dragons, but also needing to keep Ondias safe.

Dionelle was confident that Ondias wouldn't say anything to upset them. They were interested in her hair, but had otherwise come to talk to Dionelle, and Ondias understood that—she knew better than to interrupt, something Reiser had quickly learned. He applied basic human manners when the dragons were around, but the more he talked with Ondias, the more he discovered about the complexities of what the dragons considered polite and impolite.

Ondias sat quietly, only speaking when spoken to, and just observing. The dragons never spoke of their world or their lives when they weren't on official business and were mostly discussing aesthetics and the rudeness of the nobility.

"I've learned that Lady Karth has a new cloak of dragon skin," the dragoness said. "It was an unsolicited skin as well, and we suspect that the dragon in question did not die of natural causes."

"Was she foolish enough to have a dragon killed to satisfy her outlandish tastes?" Dionelle asked in horror.

"The comrade in question lived and died a great distance from here, so that is unlikely, but I know there is a profitable trade in illegally obtained skins such as the one the lady now has."

"That's revolting. If she tries to wear it in your presence, I'll tear it from her shoulders and damn the consequences."

"That I would like to see," the dragoness said with a smirk, "though I don't wish for you to forfeit your life because of that woman. It is curious that she can afford such luxury—an illegal dragon skin cloak after purchasing that ridiculous gold chariot—when the kingdom can no longer afford to provide a few oxen to guests."

Dionelle winced.

"Don't let the actions of an ignorant madwoman insult you, Mistress. They are the foolish actions of a fool of a human. View them with the contempt they deserve, but try to ignore her, unless she does something truly worthy of war."

"She is bordering on it," the dragoness said gravely.

"I wish I had more sway, Mistress," Dionelle lamented. "She pays her inner circle too well and they tell her whatever she wants to hear. They find her vague scraps of information from distant and impoverished lands and then bend the information to suit her will. She and Lord Dunham tax the life out of their subjects and forsake ancient accords with allies to pay for her foolish trinkets and to line the coffers of the men who stroke their egos. If the Dunhams push our kingdom into war with your kind, I hope you will remember where the true blame lies."

"War seldom goes well for humans, but we are learning to distinguish foolish leaders from their helpless subjects."

They turned the conversation to lighter subjects and spoke at great length about Dionelle's family, as she had recently discovered that her sister had made it all the way to the king's city. This dragoness had never met the king, but heard a great deal about him from the Dragoness Superior who did talk to the king.

"I should tell her to come meet you," the dragoness commented. "My Mistress Superior would love your eyes. I've heard the king's dragon whisperer has lovely eyes, dark and rich like the night. But yours hold a flame only dragons can appreciate."

"Thank you, Mistress. I would be honoured to host your superiors, though I would not suggest she come here before I have worked on my husband's manners and perhaps convince the workers of their safety."

"Perhaps you are correct. My mistress can be quite fickle and unforgiving."

The dragons finally left and Reiser, who always maintained a safe distance when they were around, came over to the women to see what had gone on. He didn't get much out of them though because Ondias was far too excited about being allowed to sit in and about the encouragement the dragoness had given her. There was a time Reiser would have argued with her for being so encouraged, but he knew better now. He knew that dragons didn't lie because they felt it was a waste of time simply to spare someone from the truth. They were firm believers in the truth, even if it was hurtful, though they only dished out the truth however they saw fit and didn't appreciate not having the truth delivered eloquently—bluntly, but eloquently. He thought it was a ridiculous double-standard, but it was their way and he wasn't about to argue with them on it, not yet at least.

"Oh, Di! I can't believe she let me stay and said my hair is beautiful! I will certainly practice different braids now. Do you think they will let me listen in again?"

"If you're here when they visit, I don't see why they would turn you away."

"I can't believe they've played dragonsong for you! The blue one you said? He's very quiet, it's unusual."

"He says very little and tends to remain vigilant when they're here. He puts a lot of his effort into the melodies though. I hope you get to hear it some day. It's incredible."

Reiser turned and went back out to the fields, not interested in hearing the finer points on the art of dragonsong or the two of them giggling and chatting excitedly about the fact that the dragons hadn't tried to eat Ondias. He was far too intimidated by the beasts to have any sort of appreciation for their crafts, but he was still learning and, though their ways were rife with contradictions, it was certainly an interesting study.

Ondias stayed for dinner that night and they were still marvelling over the dragons when he returned.

"You know, Reiser, we wouldn't sound so daft to you if you'd take a little more appreciation in their ways," Ondias commented. "I could have read that book you have, cover to cover, four times over in the amount of time it's taken you to get through the first three chapters. You would understand why it's such an honour that your wife has heard dragonsong at all!"

"I'm sure you're going to enlighten me," he said ruefully, sitting down to dinner.

"Humans have little appreciation for true beauty," she began, "and are more interested in money and power and cattle and crops. It's hard for most humans to understand the beauty of simple things and to truly appreciate it, but dragons have little use for the things humans hold dearest, so they focus on aesthetics. Dragons are most mesmerized by visual beauty, but they put the most effort into their songs."

Reiser nodded, but said nothing.

That night, when Ondias had gone home and they were alone, Dionelle broached the subject again.

"You are moving rather slowly through that book," she commented. "I know you think it's dangerous work that I do and would rather the whole thing went away, but it won't. I like the dragons and I like this work. It hardly seems like work to me!"

"Just wait until they're angry."

"They won't be angry with me though, and if I feel their anger is justified I will let them tear the Lord and Lady Dunham apart."

"That's not helpful. Why not let Ondias do the job for you?" he suggested. "They like her well enough and she's so disappointed not to have been chosen for it."

"They won't accept her with me around," Dionelle explained, trying to remain patient. "Once dragons accept a whisperer, no one else will do as long as that person is alive and capable. I would have to ask them to release me before they would consider anyone else, and even then it would be a very delicate conversation to have without sparking their wrath."

Reiser only sighed.

"You mustn't be so jealous of them. I have a lot to learn right now, but after I visit Boidossen for my final lessons and Guild assessments at midwinter, I should be prepared for this. Is it really that long to wait to have a happy wife who will be able to keep you happy?"

But it wasn't enough because he still felt like she used her work as an excuse to ignore him and he was unconvinced that she couldn't find something safer. Dionelle was tired of the argument and of his refusal to learn more about what he railed against.

"I've learned enough about farming to keep this place in good order in your absence," she snapped, "but you won't even read a simple book for me."

"You can't expect me to deal with them in your place."

"Of course not! But I expect you to learn enough about what I'm doing to understand the dangers are minimal."

Reiser shook his head, but said nothing, still not liking it.

"You have nothing to say because there's no reason not to let me do this. By spring at the latest I will be fully prepared for the harder aspects—for actually having to negotiate with them and mediate between the dragons and the nobles. Is that really so long to wait for me to settle into the rest of my life?"

"Dionelle, I know I haven't read much, but Ondias is a wealth of knowledge and you know I learn something new from her every time she visits. My concerns about your job are not limited to the dragons. I worry about those terrible nobles—about you being caught between them and the dragons—far more than any danger you might be in talking about art in our yard. You say the difficult part will come when it's time to negotiate, and that's the part that truly worries me. You seem to have the dragons' trust, and I suspect if negotiations go poorly and you say something to upset them, they will direct their wrath at the Dunhams instead of you. But that's not a guarantee. And what if you anger the Dunhams? I think there's far more danger there. The lady pulled her dagger on you once already. This is more than a job just about dragons. It's about diplomacy, politics, and those bloody stupid nobles."

Dionelle was silent for a moment, initially shocked by how much thought and consideration he had actually given the subject. His opinion of the dragons had improved, but he was still resistant to her being a dragon whisperer.

"You act like this is some kind of burden on me, but it's not. I've been spared having to search for a career because one was handed to me, no matter how rudely, and I like what I do. I love that I can already send money home to Mamma and Cusec. You said I could practice my craft at home—you even encouraged it!" she said.

"I want you to practice your craft," he said. "I want you to be happy, I just never expected anything so—exotic. I expected something that would have you more on the edges of the court and less involved with those cursed nobles."

"Yes, the nobles are far more dangerous than the dragons, but that doesn't mean I should give up. I don't know that I can, even if I wanted to. I would first have to find a way not to incur the wrath of the

Dunhams. And then there's the matter of the dragons. Don't you see that, even if someone else was a dragon whisperer, they won't go away? We would see less of them, but not much less because they are fond of me. If I found them a different dragon whisperer and then asked them to leave me alone for good, they'd probably raze this place to the ground at the insult. You need to accept this and you need to prepare yourself and the field workers. There's no reason for you to be afraid."

"Dionelle, they're *dragons*! You can't tell me there's no reason not to be afraid of them."

"No more reason than for you to be afraid of the neighbour's bull. You simply need to arm yourself with the proper knowledge about what you are dealing with. It's no different with the nobles. It just makes my entire task that much more complicated."

He nodded wearily but said nothing, growing tired of the same fight and his inability to make her see the dangers or to convince her to put a little more effort into their relationship. He wanted her to be happy, but didn't want to be completely ignored until the spring. The neglect wore his patience thin, and after every fight, she was usually so angry that she avoided him at all costs, still taking to sleeping across the hall from him.

REISER tried to have patience, but Dionelle was moody about other things than the difficulties of the job she loved so much. She had received word from Sharice that Vyranna had surfaced again. Vyranna had sent a hasty letter informing Sharice she was on her way to Golden Hill, to riches and fame. As Sharice had predicted, Vyranna resumed contact only to flaunt her perceived successes, though Sharice was sceptical about the truth of them.

Sometimes, it just made Dionelle want to reach through the miles separating them and slap her sister. She feared she was beginning to hate her. Then, Dionelle received a message from Vyranna. A multi-page letter arrived one day, a day that had started out pleasantly.

Dionelle was shocked to hear from her sister, even though the letter was unsurprisingly bitter. It was Vyranna to the bone. The parchment envelope was addressed to Dionelle by name, but the greeting at the head of the letter was "To the whore's daughter" and Dionelle was initially confused until she realized that Vyranna's cruelty was no longer bridled by their mother's supervision. So far from Sharice's influence, Vyranna could say exactly what she wanted, including to continue to question

Dionelle's parentage. She simply referred to Sharice as "the whore" and Dionelle as a freak throughout the letter. But Dionelle dutifully read it to the very end, shaking with rage the farther she went.

I know you and the whore never thought you'd hear from me again, and I certainly didn't intend to contact either of you ever again. Good riddance to the lot of you! But my fortunes have changed so dramatically since leaving the whore's prison that I couldn't help myself. I had to share.

I know you think you have such a perfect life, fulfilling your role as a freak and conversing with beasts and monsters. Your perfect husband and your perfect little house. Your assumed perfection makes me sick. It always has. I don't know why they never saw you for what you are: a freak and a bastard. I knew all along. I don't care anymore. May your precious beasts tear you apart and shit you out.

Keep your stupid rancher because I have a wizard now. A rich one with a prominent role in the king's court. That's right, I'm sure the whore told you I was on my way to Golden Hill, well I made it and I couldn't be happier to be here. My wizard treats me as I should be. I have so much freedom and more riches than you could ever imagine in your life as a pathetic bumpkin. Were you slopping any stables today? You're probably up to your knees is cow shit. I spent my day wrapped in silks, sipping fine teas from delicate silver cups on a marble terrace overlooking the city. I can see the king's palace from the other side of the manor. I haven't had to lift a finger since we arrived. There are several peasants in our charge. One of them reminds me of Cusec. I make him wash my feet and change my chamber pot. Scrub it until it shines.

When he needs to be punished, the wizard lets me whip him. It's no substitute for how thrilling it would be to flog dear brother, but it will do. I'm keeping my eye out to see if we can find an especially pale girl to work for us. I'll beat her the worst.

The servants bring trays of aged meats and cheese, fresh loaves, exotic fruits and delicate pastries that would simply stun your inferior sense of culture. I live like a princess now, with golden dishes to dine from and the finest garments in the brightest colours. They bathe me every morning and I don't even have to lift a finger to coif my hair if I don't want to.

Oh, how I could go on and on! But my wizard returns from court soon, and I must be ready for him. His firm hands work deftly on my skin and he worships my body like a goddess while we lay on the finest satin over a feather bed. Sometimes, I think of you and how I'm sure you and that farmer must snivel and whimper in the dark, fumbling to put the right parts together. A few grunts and it's over. I'm right, aren't I? It only draws out my pleasure with the wizard. Every spare moment that he's home is a festival of flesh by firelight. Passion that a freak like you could never even imagine!

So you go ahead and muck your stables and converse with beasts like the freak you are. The whore always used to say we would get what we deserved out of life, and it looks like she was right! And go ahead and cry to her about what I've said. I know you will, you two never could keep anything to yourselves. I look forward to hearing her next reply! She thinks she can bring me down. Let you both just try!

It was signed "Vyranna Victorious". Dionelle wasn't surprised by her sister's vitriol, but she was surprised that she would go out of her way to send her such a scathing letter; that she would reveal her whereabouts just to try to hurt Dionelle and their mother. A thousand rebukes rose to her mind as her fists clenched around the edges of the pages, crumpling them, but she finally set the letter down and shook her head. This was it. This was the end of it.

Dionelle made up her mind that once and for all she no longer had a sister. She would not reply to this filth. She would not justify it with a response and she would leave her sister to fester in her own hatred. Any further letters would be discarded unread because Dionelle was not going to let Vyranna and her rage bring grief to Dionelle's life for another moment.

She picked up the pages in one hand and reached toward the hearth with the other, calling the flames to her hands where they licked at the pages, uncrumpling them as they burned. Between the flames she could see glimpses of her sister's angry, angular writing—hateful slashes of ink on the page—but was unable to actually read any of the words before they were blackened and charred. As a small fire raged in the palms of her hands, her sense of anger, grief, guilt and despair melted away with the writing on the pages.

Reiser walked in as the last flame licked up the last bit of paper, leaving her with hands full of smoldering ashes.

"What's going on?" he asked.

She was silent for a moment, taking a deep, refreshing breath before she dumped the ashes into the hearth and brushed off her hands.

"Vyranna is dead. To me at least."

"Was that a letter from her?"

"Yes. I don't want to speak of it. It doesn't matter. We're never going to see her again and I don't want to think about it. Her self-destructive nature has begun to spiral, and it will bring her to an early grave. In my mind, she's there already."

"My love, I'm sorry," he said, taking her by the shoulders.

"Why? Are you sorry that a woman who caused both of us nothing but hardship is gone?"

"She was your sister."

"Only in name. Sister. It's just a word. She's never been anything but a villain, all her life. I'm not defending her anymore and I'm not letting her cause us anymore grief. My mother has been right all along. Vyranna did this to herself, and I wash my hands of it."

He nodded but was silent. He was concerned by how calm she seemed and wondered what the contents of the letter had been. He doubted he would ever know now, as he certainly wouldn't press the issue. He could never imagine forsaking his sister, but Loniesa had never shown even the smallest fraction of malice toward him as Vyranna had toward Dionelle.

"The anger and grief she causes is not worth the added strain on our marriage," Dionelle said. "Until I've completed my work with Boidossen, we've certainly got enough to worry about."

Unsure of how to support her, Reiser nodded knowing well enough not to bring up any of their other troubles. He had been letting her study in peace and they had enjoyed so many joyful and tender moments scattered throughout the tension; the day had started as one of those pleasant days. Dionelle had slept in the spare room the night before, but had awoken full of mirth, teasing Reiser over breakfast and pinching his side playfully before slipping out of his reach. She had joined him in the field that morning, bringing a playful air with her. During their mid-morning break, she'd started nipping at him again and he alternated between chasing her and chasing the children, who would squeal out laughter every time they managed to evade him. Reiser finally caught Dionelle and slung her over his shoulder and carted her to the barn, despite her indignantly delighted shrieks of protest.

As he laid over her in the hayloft, surrounded by the sweet smells and enveloped in the heat of her body, Dionelle's eyes had been vibrant blue pools of joy, washing the stain of tension from their relationship and making them both forget why they had ever fought. Her eyes still shone as they pulled bits of hay from their hair and she plaited her locks again before heading back into the field.

But that carefree lightness was gone now and he didn't want to upset the balance any further than Vyranna's intrusion had. He thought he understood what Dionelle meant though, realizing that even from hundreds of miles away, Vyranna still managed to hold sway over her emotions.

"Yes," he said at last. "We certainly don't need to worry about her antics right now. I'm sure you're right. Ignoring her very existence is probably the wisest course right now. But I hope you'll tell me if it continues to upset you."

DIONELLE was in the library poring over a book of dragon festivals when she looked up to see Ondias standing on the other side of the table.

"That's a good one," she commented, nodding toward the book. She sat across from Dionelle and continued in a gentle whisper. "Have you read about the Comet Festival yet?"

"Um, I don't think so. I'm in the middle of learning about their Sky Fire Festival. I didn't realize the winter star-shower was so important to them."

"It's the major shower in the year, and I think they believe that if they catch a falling star they will be granted immortality."

"But none of them has ever actually caught one. Have they?"

"I've never heard of an immortal dragon," Ondias replied with a stifled giggle. "I'm sure they'd brag about that sort of thing if it were true."

"So, what's the significance of the comet?" Dionelle asked.

"They gather to celebrate the passing of this particular star, but it only comes once every eighty-two years. Very few of them are fortunate enough to see it more than twice, but those are considered especially esteemed Superiors."

"Do you think my mistress's Superior is one of those few?"

"It's possible," Ondias said. "There aren't many Superiors because they have to reach such an advanced age to be granted the title. I don't know much about the Superiors though—nothing about their personalities or colours or even how many of them there are."

"Perhaps you can get my dragoness talking about it some time. She enjoys talking to you about her world."

"I certainly enjoy learning about it. I would love to see their city in the sky, but few humans are even aware of the mountain range it's located in. They've never allowed one of us to actually enter their valley before."

"Do you think their city is actually in the sky?" Dionelle asked. "Or do you think it's a series of towers, similar to their homes in other mountains?"

"My understanding is that it's a tower, but unlike anything we've glimpsed of their homes closer to human kingdoms. This tower is supposed to reach high above the clouds, hovering in the heights they prefer to fly in—up where it's colder and they can feel more refreshed."

"I wonder if the dragoness will bring us to her home in the Great Mountains."

"It would be unusual, but not unheard of. She is quite fond of you. I got the impression she didn't live so very far from Boidossen's cabin. Half a day's flight, isn't it?"

Dionelle shrugged. "She seems familiar with his location, but hasn't really said where her home is. She and her companions are close together somewhere in the Great Mountains, but it's a very expansive range. They could be just about anywhere and I know it's a fair journey for them to come to Pasdale."

Ondias opened the large tome she'd been carrying, glancing through some of its chapters, trying to discern if it was the right book.

"Studying?" Dionelle asked her.

"I have a major assessment next month," Ondias replied. "I'm expected to be adept at warding spells by then."

"Will you live up to the expectation?" Dionelle asked, surprised by the strain in her friend's voice.

"I think so. I've just got a lot of work ahead of me. I expect to practically live in this library until then. What about you? I thought you preferred to study in the comfort of home."

"It's not quite the comfort it could be," she replied tersely.

95

"Reiser's still being difficult then?"

Dionelle nodded, but kept her gaze on the pages. Ondias bit her lip for a moment and looked awkwardly down at her book again before closing it and tucking it into her bag.

"This one will do for now. Why don't you pack up your book of festivals and we'll go read in the market?" Ondias suggested. "Easier to properly chat that way. I'll treat you to some pixie ice."

Dionelle glanced cautiously to the other scholars studying at the rows of tables and decided it would be better to continue the conversation outside. No matter how hushed their tones, the library was otherwise silent and their voices seemed to carry throughout the entire building. She slid her book into her bag and followed Ondias to the front desk to sign out their finds before heading out into the warm sun of the city streets.

"Is it anything new?" Ondias asked gently.

"Not really," Dionelle replied, sighing in frustration. "He's admitted that it's the job in general and not so much the dragons. He's rightfully put more of his fears with the nobles, but he's still blowing the whole thing completely out of proportion. He feels neglected because I spend so much time studying, but I'm just trying to get it all out of the way as soon as I can. I can't concentrate on my studies at home because I never know when he's going to come in from the fields, see my books, and start the nonsense all over again."

"I wish I could help you to ease his concerns, but he seems to think I'm just foolhardy like you. I mean, we are alike, but neither of us is foolhardy about the dragons."

"I thought you finally had him convinced when you told him about how dangerous other dragon-related careers can be—like the dragon lancers. I thought for a moment that he finally understood that I'm a simple negotiator and in no more danger than anyone else in this city. But now he's on about the nobles. It's like we convince him of one thing and he just goes off and finds something new."

Ondias stopped and bought them each the flavoured ice she had promised and then they sat at one of the tables in the pavilion that stood between the edge of the market and the edge of the sprawling city park.

"I'm sad to agree with him about the nobles," Ondias replied. "I mean, the Pasdale nobles specifically. If you were whispering anywhere with more reasonable leaders, I think it would be okay. But the Dunhams are just—I don't know, they're so many things and none of them are good. Did you know that the advisor they executed on grounds of treason last week was actually executed because he didn't like Lady Karth's gown for the summer festival?"

"How would anyone but you know that?" Dionelle teased. She was tired of hearing more about the nobles and had gotten into the habit of trying to deflect the topic with humour. It seemed like every time she came to the market she heard something new and infuriating—some new tax, some new expense, some unqualified ego-stroker being appointed to a high position, some new execution for usually unproven reasons. They usually held monthly executions, but had special ones as well now, and the gallows were always full. Sometimes they had to execute prisoners in rounds. There were the usual criminals, but always several there for treason as well.

"It was a truly hideous gown—or so I've heard," Ondias went on. "I think it cost nearly as much as that dragon skin cloak she finally tired of. This one was made of gold. Honest to the moons, it was gold from head to toe. She got a wizard to charm the gold leaf so that it wouldn't tear and then had the dress made out of it. Layers and layers of gold leaf and I guess she looked like a big scaly golden fish."

Both women giggled at that, and Dionelle was pleased to think that she would have to relay this one back to Reiser. She seldom thought of him while she was away from home and it relieved her to still think of him pleasantly. It reinforced her belief that things would be better by the spring.

"Well, if you want to study with me, I welcome the company," Ondias offered. "I would welcome the chance to have another sorceress to practice with. You might even find something to teach me about dragons too."

Dionelle smiled furtively. "I doubt anyone could find anything to teach you about dragons. Except, perhaps, the dragons themselves."

Ondias only laughed.

"Would you prefer to study at the library or here in the market?" Dionelle asked. "I can meet you every day if you want. Reiser heads for the fields shortly after dawn and would be unlikely to really miss my presence until dinnertime. He's quite busy with the harvest at the moment. He may end up needing my help at some point, but otherwise I would be free to meet you."

"I think we should meet here until the weather turns. Every morning then?"

"Until I have to leave for my apprenticeship," Dionelle promised.

They spread out their books and read silently together, casually nibbling on their ice treats and basking in the late-season warmth, knowing that all too soon the bitter winter would sweep over the mountains and make them long for the summer's heat.

CHAPTER 7

REISER stood on the porch and watched Dionelle fix the last of her things to the mare. He pulled his robes tighter to him, trying to ward off the bitter cold, and waited until she was ready to go, longing for the warmth of the fire again. This time, he was relieved she was leaving and he could see that she was even more relieved than when she had gone to her summer lessons. He was looking forward to a month alone with no worries of having to entertain the dragons or having the tension between them continue to smother him.

She had only grown angrier as the autumn had worn on and barely spoke to him at all. Their days had become a routine of civility and their marriage seemed like a foolish formality. He wasn't sure where it had gone wrong, because he had tried to do as she asked. He hadn't said anything about her job, but let her talk about it when she wanted to. There was more going on, but he'd lost her to the earlier tension and didn't know how to reach her through the wall of anger she had built. She hadn't learned to confide in him and now that there was a problem beyond their relationship she didn't know how to talk to him about it. She seemed lonely and often slept across the hall by herself—and had even gone so far as to move many of her things there—though she had spent last night with him.

He had enjoyed having her with him and feeling the exquisite warmth of her skin on his, and it gave him hope that she was right and their life would gain meaning, peace and stability once she returned. It only made him that much more happy to see her leave. After months of anxiety, he looked forward to peace.

He had begun to learn more about the dragons again, talking in more depth with Dionelle and Ondias, as well as occasionally reading the book of dragon lore she had given him, but his wife was still deeply troubled despite his attempts to appease her over the dragon issue. She was under pressure with her Guild entrance assessments coming up, but something was also wrong in the Joasera family. He wasn't sure of the nature of the problem because Dionelle wouldn't talk about it or show him the letters from her mother and Cusec. She still burned Vyranna's letters unread. He knew that Vyranna was involved with a wizard, and not a good one, but that was it.

"My love, please don't brood in my absence," she pleaded, startling him out of his thoughts. He had barely noticed that she was ready to leave and had come over to him.

"Do you really still love me?" he asked openly.

She was hurt and surprised by the question, but reached up to touch his face with her hand white as the snow gathering around them. Her skin lacked all the bitter cold of the snow, and she was always warm with an internal fire that baked off of her like a fever. She pulled his face down to hers and kissed him with a fierceness he'd never known from her before, chasing away the chill of winter.

"Do you think I'd go through all of this if I didn't?" she finally replied. "When I get back, I won't have so many troubles weighing me down."

"Will you share them with me?"

"I will make a better effort at it, yes. These past months haven't been your fault, and I should have said that sooner. I don't know how to talk about what's wrong—I haven't spoken to Ondias either, if that makes you feel better. I don't really know what to say about it—how to begin. But I will miss you terribly."

Reiser was surprised and relieved and heartbroken all at once. He didn't know what to say, but took her hand and kissed the back of it. He was reluctant to let go of her now, wanting to hear more and then to hold her in silence.

She gave him the shy smile he had missed so much and then turned from him, mounting up and leading the mare down the lane. She gave one final wave before disappearing into the blowing snow. Now he wished that she wasn't leaving. He hadn't known such passion and intensity had existed in her and he realized he had missed out on it over the past months. Even once he was back in the warm house he could still feel the heat of her hand on his cheek and her lips on his. It called up memories of the heat of her body against his the night before and he missed her already.

The days had been so full of uncertainty and resentment that it actually felt good to miss her absence—it meant that he still cared for her deeply and that their relationship was still salvageable—and now he truly looked forward to her return, understanding what she meant when she insisted the spring would be better. He sat at the hearth, contemplating the fire-coloured book of dragon lore, but finally picked up one of the other books she had left behind, thumbing through it. It was a spellbook and he could make little sense of it, so he finally set it aside and picked up the orange book again. It had been weeks since he had even thought of it, mostly relying on Ondias for information, so he would start again at the beginning and have it finished by the time she returned.

Reading it would either set his mind at ease that she really was safe as a dragon whisperer, or it would give him what he needed to talk her into a safer area of study. It would settle the matter, either way, and he had the new puzzle she had left him with—the problem with her sister and family. He wanted to sit and read the dragon lore that instant, but there were stables to muck and livestock to feed and dinner to be made, so it would have to wait until the evening.

REISER had progressed a good way through the book, nearing the end, and had even tracked down Ondias in the city to talk to her. The book could only teach him so much, and with so many contradictions in their practices, Reiser found he needed someone to help clarify some of the finer points of dragon culture. She came to visit him a couple of times a week and stayed for dinner to chat, so when the dragoness knocked on his door during an unusually bitter cold snap, he was shocked to see her but prepared to talk. He opened the door, expecting a human, but instead the dragoness was lying in his dooryard with her chin resting on his steps. Her face filled the entire view from the doorway, with her great horns rising up out of view.

"Mistress!" he exclaimed, trying to keep his surprise to a minimum because he knew dragons cared very little for the highs and lows of human emotion. "This is pleasantly unexpected, and I appreciate you not disturbing the neighbours."

"It pleases me that they are less disturbed by my presence. It makes stealth worthwhile."

"They are learning, and I truly appreciate your patience with us," he replied carefully. "I don't believe I am educated or handsome enough to hold counsel with you, so what brings you to my home while Dionelle is away?"

Dionelle had told the dragons how to find Boidossen's cabin in the foothills, and the dragoness had admitted to being familiar with the location. They could continue to converse with her while she apprenticed, if that was what they desired, so Reiser was shocked to see them when they knew she wasn't due back for almost a week.

"No one is answering my taps or my cries at the cabin. The shutters are drawn and there are no lights within. I do not know where your wife and the wizard have gone, but they are not there. Lady Karth was unable to enlighten me about Dionelle's whereabouts."

"Then it was natural you would come here to look for her, but I am afraid I have not seen her since she left at midwinter."

The dragoness narrowed her eyes at him, studying him closely.

"Mistress, I have learned your value of truth and I swear to you that I have not seen my wife for weeks. Were she here, I know it would bring her joy to see you and I would not deny her that."

"You have been giving her difficulties about this," the dragoness pointed out. "You were willing to hide her in the past."

"I was mistaken. I believed she was in danger, and perhaps she was but it is clear to me now that the nobles are more danger to her than you ever could be."

"You have been learning then."

"I have tried."

"I must see your wife."

"Mistress, I apologize, but I don't know where she is. She is not here, and if she is not at the wizard's cabin, then the only place I can think of is her mother's house. There have been some difficulties with her sister—perhaps she has mentioned that—and if something happened, she may have rushed there without getting a message to me first."

"How do I find her mother?"

Reiser paused, not sure how Sharice would respond to a dragon suddenly showing up at her door, but figured that living with Dionelle for twenty years would have them prepared enough. He told the dragoness how to find Sharice.

"But she will be startled and stealth may again be to your benefit if you go there. Dionelle has a young brother and I don't know how accustomed he is to speaking with your kind. His manners will likely be lacking. Please remember that they are Dionelle's family and that she would risk death in not speaking to you if you were to harm them in any way."

"Do you know how much sway your wife holds over me?" the dragoness replied.

"As much as she holds over me, I would reckon."

"She is a mystery, and a beautiful one. I'm not sure which aspect intrigues me more."

"Then remember that when you visit Sharice, and be sure to hold your temper if she forgets her manners. She hasn't spoken with dragons in years and is likely to have forgotten."

"Yes, I will keep that in mind."

"If Dionelle is not with her mother, she may have gone with Boidossen to the Wizards Guild. She had to complete her entrance assessments, and I don't know what that entails. If you think it's likely they would be there, it is another good place to try."

"Ah yes, I had not thought of her Guild acceptance. I will try both places. Thank you."

"Mistress, before you go, may I ask a favour of you."

"I don't usually allow it."

"I know, but will you make an exception—not for me but for my wife?"

"Very well, what is it?"

"Will you bring a message back to me when you find her? You are far swifter than any messenger she could find. All I need to know is where she is and that she is safe."

The dragoness narrowed her eyes at him, but nodded. "That is a small favour but not beyond my capabilities."

"My thanks," he replied with a bow. "Safe flights."

REISER stood in the cabin door, terrified and wondering if he should go any farther into the house to look for Dionelle or just flee. The unbearable stench when he opened the door, made overpowering by the unusually warm day, had been warning enough, but he was quick to spot the wizard—or what he could only guess had once been the wizard—in an unrecognizable heap in the middle of the floor. It was the robes and the still-intact unruly grey hair that made the body identifiable, and it had certainly not been a good death.

When the dragoness had returned in the middle of the night to tell him that Sharice hadn't seen or heard from Dionelle since before midwinter, and the Guild hadn't heard from either of them at all, Reiser had grown concerned. When Dionelle hadn't returned from the foothills when she was supposed to, he had grown even more anxious. He waited three days, in case the unruly weather—unseasonal amounts of rain—had held her up, and then he went in search of her.

He stood uncertainly at the door, his scarves thrust tightly against his face to guard against the foul smell of death, wondering what to do. He decided he had to know, one way or the other, what had become of his wife, so he gingerly stepped around the mess in front of the hearth that had once been a powerful wizard. He crept through the small cabin, careful not to touch anything and holding his breath as much as possible and breathing shallowly otherwise, not wanting to make a sound. He nudged open the doors to the two small bedrooms at the back of the cabin, steeling himself against what he was likely to find, but there was nothing. All of Dionelle's possessions were in the smaller room, still in the bag she had brought them there in. Her fire cloak was hanging at the front door and Reiser snatched it on his way out, shutting the door tightly behind him.

Using his walking staff, he dug through the thick, slushy snow surrounding the cabin, in case she had met her doom outside in an attempt to flee. He could find nothing, because the drifts, though melting in the unusual warmth, were far too high for him to tackle on his own. There was a small stable in the back, and all he found there was his mare and the wizard's horse, unharmed, but half-starved and ill from neglect. He opened the doors for them so they could at least forage, and then he turned back to his own horse. Terrified and helpless, he had no choice but to mount up and make the three-day journey back to Pasdale to report his findings to Lady Karth.

Boidossen's horse wandered out into the wilderness, but the mare followed Reiser all the way back to the city. After the warmth of the day at the cabin, the weather took a bitterly cold swing and it was three nightmarish days back through craggy, icy terrain and an oncoming storm that he had to race back to safety, on top of his fears for Dionelle. He made it back to Pasdale just as the winter storm reached the peak of its fury, but he didn't linger at his house once he made it back. He stabled the exhausted mare and made sure one of the workers would fetch an animal doctor to properly care for her, before he ventured back out into the blizzard, heading into the city.

It was growing late and he was tired and hungry, but he went straight to the palace to talk to the Lord and Lady Dunham about Dionelle's disappearance. He was merely a rancher though, and he was having difficulties getting past the guards of the palace. He kept insisting it had to do with the kingdom's dragon whisperer, and someone finally let him in.

"This had better be worthwhile, rancher," Lady Karth snapped as she strode into the room he'd been left to wait in.

"Dionelle is missing," he blurted, in no mood to waste time with formalities.

"Do not toy with me, you stupid man. How could she be missing?"

"Boidossen is dead. When Dionelle didn't return from the foothills on time I went out there to see what was going on and found the old wizard torn apart. There was no sign of my wife, though she could be buried in the snow somewhere. She's not at her mother's or the Wizards Guild, the dragoness already went looking for her."

"You let the dragons know she's missing?" Lady Karth exploded.

"I haven't told them anything, but the dragoness is the one who brought the matter to my attention. They went to the cabin looking for Dionelle and when they got no answers they came to me. I sent them to Dionelle's mother and the Guild, figuring she must have gone to one or the other due to some crisis or other. Her sister has fallen in league with the wrong kind of wizard, and it seemed a likely reason for Dionelle to bypass coming home and with no warning. And she was completing her final Guild assessments, which I know little about and thought maybe she would be there. But she's nowhere, m'lady, and I have nowhere else to turn."

"If the wizard is dead, it is likely that she is too," the lady snapped. "We need to be certain or it will be war with the dragons. She has been far too good at keeping them appeased to replace her easily, and not at all unless we can prove to them that she is dead."

"She could still be alive."

"Do not be a fool! She is dead in the snow somewhere. Even if she survived whatever attacked the wizard, we would have had some sign of her by now if she was still alive. You had best accept that now."

Reiser was far too angry over the noblewoman's apathy and cruelty to let the possibility of Dionelle's death sink in. Lady Karth was simply concerned about having lost another dragon whisperer, but Reiser hadn't seen anything to indicate that Dionelle had been killed. If she had been dead outside the cabin, he was certain the dragoness would have noticed something.

"We need answers immediately—regardless of what they are," Lady Karth said tersely. "I will dispatch my top wizard with a military escort at first light, but you will speak with my wizard first. Wait here."

Reiser just wanted to get up and leave, to find the dragons and see if they could help, but if the wizard was going to be in charge of getting to the truth of whatever had happened at Boidossen's cabin, then Reiser would talk to him in the hopes he would be more approachable than the deplorable lady.

The royal wizard was a fairly young man, in his thirties and hardly what Reiser had expected after dealing so frequently with Boidossen and his ancient colleagues. His raven hair was shortly cropped and he was clean shaven, wearing a simple noble's suit instead of the wizarding robes Reiser had grown accustomed to.

"I am Zev," he introduced. "The lady wasn't good enough to leave me with your name."

"I don't believe she actually knows my name. I'm Reiser Ovailen."

"Reiser, I'm going to do my best to have other wizards with me when I go, and perhaps even have the dragoness who is so fond of your wife meet us at the cabin."

"What would that achieve?"

"Well, first I need to learn more from you. Lady Karth said only that Boidossen was torn apart, but I need more than that to go on. Tell me everything you can about that cabin and why you seem so certain that your wife isn't dead."

Reiser explained his convictions based on what the dragoness had seen and not seen when she had gone to the cabin and found it silent.

"Wait, the door and shutters had all been drawn?"

"Everything had been closed tightly, including the front door."

"That immediately rules out an animal. Tell me more—about the inside of the cabin and what you saw when you found the wizard. It may be difficult, but every detail you can give me will help me narrow this down so I can be better prepared when I get out there."

Reiser described the scene in as much detail as he could remember, but he had taken little more than a cursory glance at the wizard, acknowledging only that it was in fact his desiccated corpse, and then had done his best not to look at the body. He had been concerned only in finding Dionelle.

"The cabin was in fairly good order?" Zev asked.

"There was a lot of blood. Dried blood," Reiser replied, swallowing hard.

"Yes, it sounds like there would have been if the old man was in such bad shape. But the rest of the house was in good order? Were there many books on the floor? Any furniture tipped over?"

"No," Reiser said, surprised by the recollection. "There was a shattered bowl or something on the floor near the body, but that was it."

"No struggle..." the wizard mused aloud. "Something took the old man by surprise and then left the house completely closed up and locked properly."

Reiser said nothing.

"And all of your wife's things were still in the cabin?"

"Yes."

"So she didn't leave on her own. If she had gone for help, she would have brought something."

"Her winter robes were in her room, and her fire cloak was still hanging by the door. I didn't look for her boots."

"Based on what you have said, I would expect to find her boots still there. It sounds to me like she is either dead in the snow as the lady suspects, or she has been taken."

Reiser's chest tightened and he felt his throat grow hot as he struggled to breathe.

"Death would be more comforting to you at this point, wouldn't it? Answers are better than none."

"Who would take her? And why?"

"I will not be able to answer that until after I have seen that cabin. We must do a thorough search of the surrounding woods as well. There is the chance that it was an animal and that Dionelle is the one who closed the door as she fled, so we will need to search the snow to see if she escaped the house but not her death. But you know as well as I do that the dragoness would have noticed a body in the snow."

"Dionelle's skin is as white as the snow," Reiser said.

"But her clothes and blood are not," the wizard said gently.

Reiser shook his head, understanding but not wanting to.

"I'm afraid I can't give you better answers," Zev lamented, "but I will know more in a week's time. Once we discover what killed the wizard we will have a better idea of who took your wife and to what end. It is possible that some enemy of the Dunhams has taken their dragon whisperer in hopes of provoking the dragons into destroying the kingdom, or to keep her as ransom."

"You think she's caught in the middle of some political scheme?"

"It's likely. The Dunhams are as unpopular among other kingdoms as they are in their own."

"She may as well be dead!"

"Can you speak to the dragons on her behalf?"

"I have once."

"If we can find out who has her, you may be able to convince them to help save her. Do you know much about dragons?"

"More then I ever would have imagined. They're fond of her, have locked onto her, and will do whatever is necessary to keep interacting with her."

"It is unwise to come between dragons and someone or something they have become fixated on," Zev agreed. "All we have to do is find out where she is and leave the rest up to them."

Reiser finally had some hope to latch onto. "She is immune to fire and they could level an entire city without harming her."

Zev nodded, but was still cautious. "Don't allow yourself too much hope until I can get some answers. Tell me where you live, and I will come to you directly."

Reiser let the wizard know how to find him and quickly left the palace before he had to face either of the nobles again. He couldn't bear anymore of their pessimism, selfishness, or apathy. They didn't care what had happened to Dionelle, only that they find out the truth so they could move on in dealing with the dragons. They would prefer to find Dionelle alive to save them finding a new dragon whisperer, but the extent to which they cared involved only how the situation affected them personally.

Zev's concern had been refreshing after the cruel apathy of Lady Karth, and Reiser was relieved he wouldn't have to deal with the noblewoman again on the matter. Zev would make a suitable messenger.

Reiser found Ondias at the house she roomed in and let her know what had happened. He wanted her advice on how to deal with the dragons. They wouldn't stand to be lied to, but the lady had made it perfectly clear that she didn't want them to know Dionelle was missing.

"That woman is a moron!" Ondias spat. "You mustn't lie to them if they ask you where Dionelle is, especially not if you hope to enlist their help in finding her again. The dragons are far more powerful allies than the kings of this world can ever dream of and you need them on your side."

REISER hadn't had to break the news to the dragons yet and hoped he never had to, but things were not looking promising. Zev had used the fire of a sorceress with similar talents to Dionelle's to melt the surrounding snow. A messenger had sent that much news back to Reiser, but it had been over a week since his meeting with the royal wizard and he had heard nothing new. He had long since finished the book of dragon lore Dionelle had given him and had moved on to other books Ondias had loaned him.

He had first begun to learn about dragons in the hope he could use the knowledge to persuade Dionelle to switch to a safer job, but now that he was learning so much about them he had begun to truly appreciate the strange creatures. He understood that Dionelle was truly in far more danger from the nobles than she had ever been from the dragons, and though the dragons had terribly inflated egos, they still had infinitely more integrity than the nobles and most humans did. A dragon whisperer's work was vital to the peace of a kingdom and he was proud of Dionelle's work now. He hoped to find her alive so that she could continue to do it.

Reiser had been flipping through one of Ondias's books one evening when he received a knock at his door. There was a blonde woman with brilliant green eyes standing on his porch wrapped in brightly coloured wizarding robes that swirled wildly in the unusually strong winds.

"May I help you?" he asked politely.

"My name is Nandara and I bring you news from Zev," the sorceress replied.

"Have they found Dionelle?" he asked earnestly, inviting her to sit by the fire.

She shook her head. "It is good news and bad news. Good that we did not find her so it is likely she is still alive. The bad news is that it looks unlikely that we will ever find her."

"What! How can you be so certain? Where is Zev and why did he send you?"

"Zev is still working with the others to find out why Boidossen was targeted and murdered, and who was behind it. He called on me to help when he realized what they were dealing with, but also so I could help melt the snow to search for your wife. Boidossen was killed by an elemental demon and I am a mistress of the elements. Your wife deals primarily in fire, but I command earth, air and water as well."

"A demon!" Reiser gasped. "I didn't think they could do such damage. Aren't they limited to possession?"

"When they act of their own accord, they are motivated to cause mischief and little more. Someone was commanding the demon and so it took as much of its true form as it can in our realm. Normally, only their essence can cross into this world and they are limited to possessions. They can possess anything from people to stones, though this one possessed the very fire in Boidossen's hearth. That is how it caught him by surprise the way it did. We found evidence of some scorching around his numerous wounds."

"A fire demon," he muttered, still terrified. "Is that why Dionelle is still alive? Because she is immune to fire?"

"It's possible."

"Where is she then? She can't have just disappeared!"

"She is still missing and at this point it is impossible to say where she is. The demon could have possessed her and made her walk just about anywhere, to whomever sent the demon in the first place."

"The demon didn't act alone?"

"No, someone sent it. This is too targeted and far too violent for simple demon mischief. I have never seen anything like this and neither has my master, who is quite old even as far as wizards go."

"Could the demon have possessed her and made her walk deep into the forest to freeze to death?"

Nandara sighed wearily. "That is a possibility and we are continuing to search the surrounding forest. We know a wizard in the area who can communicate with wild animals and he's going to put them on the lookout for her."

"You're not really any closer to finding answers then, are you?"

"No, not really. We know how Boidossen was killed, and that's it. Once we learn more about his death and who was responsible, we will be able to find out more about what happened to your wife and whether she was a target as well."

Reiser shook his head, unsure of how to go on, to keep going through his days without knowing what had happened to Dionelle. The story Nandara had for him was unbelievable and he couldn't believe anyone would want to hurt Dionelle or the wizard.

"Someone will keep in contact with you as we learn more," Nandara promised, "but it will take time. There are few wizards powerful enough to command elemental demons so we will certainly find out which one was behind the attack, but it will take some time.

"If you think of anything, please let us know. Anything Dionelle said to you about anyone who seemed angry with her or the wizard, or anyone else with a power for fire like she had. Just anything."

Reiser nodded dumbly, knowing there was nothing he could ever add. Dionelle had barely spoken to him for months, so if anything had happened since the summer, he had no way of knowing about it.

Before she left, Nandara gave him one small piece of good news.

"In our investigation, we discovered something of interest to you amongst the old man's papers. It would seem that your wife passed all of her entrance assessments, as we found the formal documentation for her entrance to the Wizards Guild filled out by Boidossen. Her acceptance is being quickly processed and you will soon have the entire Wizards Guild putting the same effort into finding her as they are in seeking answers to Boidossen's death. I know that seems like small consolation right now, but it will mean you will soon have someone other than the fickle Dunhams formally helping to find your wife."

CHAPTER 8

REISER stood impatiently at Ondias's door, waiting for her to answer. He had spent the last week, since Nandara's visit, pacing his house, mucking his stables, and doing his best to go on with his life, but he had to know what had happened to Dionelle before he could decide what the rest of his life would be. Ondias had been her confidante and he would see if he could get any useful information from her.

"Reiser! What's going on?"

"I need to talk to you about Dionelle. May I come in?"

"I'm afraid it's a girls' residence and the mistress doesn't permit men—she doesn't want anyone getting the idea that this is just some kind of brothel."

Reiser smiled wanly. "Very well, will you come back with me then? I need your help."

"Is it about Dionelle? I hear things about her, but nothing solid."

"What have you heard?"

"Silly things, mostly. Is she dead?"

"No one knows."

Ondias cringed and let out a sigh. "Give me a moment to collect some things and I will come with you. Would you like me to stay long?"

"As long as you like. I feel like I'm going mad and maybe you can help me stay grounded."

"All right, just give me a moment."

Bundled against the cold and carrying a fair-sized bag, Ondias walked out of the city and across the fields with Reiser, back to his farmhouse. As they walked, Reiser explained to her what Nandara had revealed. The more he thought about it, the more he was sure it had something to do with Dionelle. Nandara had even suggested that the attack was targeted, and why, after all his life, would someone choose such a late age to target Boidossen, when Dionelle had just appeared in the wizarding world with her fire immunity and dragon whispering.

"I'm sure this kingdom has enemies with connections to wizards powerful enough to command elemental demons like that," Ondias agreed.

"Dionelle hasn't said anything to you? She always insisted that the dragons weren't a danger, but that humans might be. Did she mean something by that? Someone other than that awful Lady Karth?"

"Never. Her only complaint about the job was the nobles. She never named anyone specific other than the Dunhams though. There must be something. She's the one missing now, so it had to have been a targeted attack, or she'd just be dead alongside Boidossen."

"The demons couldn't harm her with fire, but if they chose to possess a stone, they certainly could have beaten her with it. Or possessed her and made her fall on a sword. The more I think about it, the harder it is for me to believe that she's dead. We would have found her—she would have been in that house if she were dead. Or do I just want to believe that?"

"It's perfectly reasonable. The sorceress made it quite clear that they're investigating Boidossen's death exclusively and hope to find out about Dionelle through that. But I think we need to sift through her life and see what we can come up with separately. If we find anything, we can call Nandara back and see if they have anything new. We can compare our discoveries."

"We need to find something. She wasn't talking to me, you know that. She only trusted the neighbours with dinner recipes, and dragons have little care about the problems of humans, so you're the only one she would reveal anything to."

"What about her mother? She writes to her family all the time. They're in constant contact."

"Did she say anything to you? She would tell me very little, except that her sister was so troubled."

"Does she keep her letters?"

"I don't know. She burns the ones from her sister."

"Well, we're going to find out what she does with the rest."

They reached the house and Ondias marched straight up the stairs to their bedroom.

"Please, Ondias, what are you doing?"

"You've probably thought of doing this already, but if you feel too uncomfortable digging through her things to find information, I assure you, I have no problem doing it myself," she explained with a mischievous grin. "She may even have a journal, if not the letters from her mother. If we're lucky, we'll find both."

"She wasn't staying in here regularly," Reiser admitted sadly.

Ondias gave him a startled look.

"She never indicated anything was wrong. She always seemed happy in your marriage, though your refusal to learn about the dragons did irritate her."

"More than she let you know," he replied. "She used the spare room as a sanctuary to study at home—somewhere she could shut everything out and concentrate. But it wasn't just that. We need to find out what the rest was."

"All right, so she was usually sleeping across the hall?" Ondias went across the hall and began dumping Dionelle's things out onto the bed. She turned out all the drawers and pulled everything out of the wardrobe. There wasn't much left in the room, as Reiser had originally moved everything into his room for her, leaving only a few things for guests. Dionelle had become a guest in her own home.

Once everything had been emptied onto the bed, Ondias began inspecting the bare wardrobe.

"All right, search everything for hidden doors or compartments. Then we'll search all the pockets and packages that came out of the drawers as we put it all away again."

As Reiser had suspected, Dionelle hadn't bothered creating any secret compartments to hide things from him, and they quickly began digging through pockets of garments that had come out of the wardrobe. The boxes seemed like the best place to go next and so they did. There were plenty of mementos, including several letters from Reiser while they were still courting.

"She keeps everything, this is good. There will be letters from her mother, recent ones, and if anything has happened at home to lead to this, we'll find it."

Reiser found her jewellery box, though there was very little in it—mostly homemade beaded jewellery she had likely had since she was a girl. The only thing of real value was the pendant Boidossen had given Dionelle for her wedding, the blue stone with the silver light trapped in it.

"That's so beautiful! Has it been enchanted?" Ondias asked when she saw him with it.

"Yes. We're soulmates, and love's light burst around us in the temple during our wedding. This rock, a love rock, caught the light."

"Oh," she said awkwardly. It saddened her to see that something that had started out so true had gone so wrong. "It's beautiful," she finally said. "All the more reason to find her."

They both went back to rifling through Dionelle's things, but Reiser put the pendant around his neck, tucking it under his clothes and out of sight before returning the jewellery box to the wardrobe.

They found her more recent letters from her mother and brother not long afterward, and Reiser wanted to read them, but Ondias insisted on going through everything to see if she kept a journal first. If there was a journal, everything would make more sense to read it with the letters, in chronological order.

"You're a clever woman," Reiser commented with a smile.

The journal proved to be a harder find, and they had gone through everything and cleaned up entirely when Ondias finally lifted the mattress of the bed to find a small notebook stuffed away underneath.

"I can't bear to know how much she hated me," Reiser said, handing the book to Ondias. "I won't read it. You take this and I will read the letters."

She wanted to try to reassure him that Dionelle had never hated him, but didn't want to lie either. She hadn't realized that Dionelle had remained so distant from Reiser until learning she often confined herself to the spare room, and now she didn't know where her friend's heart truly lay. So she took the journal without a word.

They ventured down to the hearth and started sorting through Dionelle's life, comparing the letters to journal entries. Reiser didn't have to read the journal to know that Dionelle had suffered since moving to Pasdale because her mother's responses to her letters spoke volumes. But he was at least assured that it wasn't all bad and was relieved that she was full of hope. Sharice's letters were often reassuring, trying to convince Dionelle that it would get better once everything settled. Dionelle had hung her hopes on her winter apprenticing as being the turning point, and if she hadn't gone missing she would have been right.

What Dionelle thought of married life quickly fell to the wayside in her conversations with Sharice though. The majority of Dionelle's unhappiness was caused by her sister and, to a lesser extent, her inability to talk to Reiser about any of it. Reiser cursed himself for not doing more to set her at ease and trust him.

Vyranna was little more than a common whore living in Golden Hill with a wizard named Vozawr. The conversations seemed steeped in secrecy though, and there was something the two women kept referring to without naming, something Vyranna knew about Dionelle—something potentially damaging. It had also become apparent that Vyranna was using her body to control the wizard and letting him have his way with her. In exchange, she had her way with the focus of his power.

"We need to tell Nandara and Zev about this," Ondias said. "I know Dionelle tries to think better of her sister, but I don't believe there's an ounce of compassion in that woman and she certainly seems to believe she had some sort of claim on you."

"Yes, she was insanely jealous though it didn't truly come out until the day after we were married. She's a complete fool. And a vindictive fool."

Ondias shook her head and kept reading, though there was little in the journal to surprise her as she had known Vyranna was a problem and that things had been less than perfect in Reiser and Dionelle's marriage. The truth about what kind of trouble Vyranna had made for herself was disturbing though, and they would have to find out what Sharice and Dionelle had been leaving unsaid.

"We should meet with Zev and Nandara tomorrow," Reiser suggested. "There isn't much new information here, but I'm sure they will want to look into Vyranna's wizard to see what kind of power he has, and narrowing their search to begin with him will save them a great deal of time if he is the culprit—and it seems likely that he is. Vyranna manipulating a powerful wizard is a very dangerous thing, and I have no doubts that he is powerful or she wouldn't have latched onto him like this or for this long. It seems like he's the one she left home with and that's a long time for Vyranna to put up with anyone."

"If Dionelle was the true target in Boidossen's death, her awful sister is a more likely suspect than some enemy of the Dunhams or the king. Dragon whisperers are seldom the focus of such attacks, and the ones that are are usually far more politically connected than Dionelle is. She's the wife of a simple farmer, not the charming daughter of the court's elite."

"It's late and I think we've found all the answers we will for tonight," Reiser said. "Help me put these away and we'll go to Nandara and Zev in the morning."

"I'm sorry, I really am. I know you think she hates you, but if she did, I would have known about it. She would have told me if it was as bad as you think. I know it. The journal is full of frustration, but not hatred or despair."

"We barely spoke," he protested. "She would barely even sleep in the same room as me."

"She was frustrated, that's all. She was a bit frustrated with you, but mostly she was frustrated that she couldn't speed things up and get her life to a comfortable place where you could both be happy. You were happy once, weren't you?"

"Yes, at first. Our wedding day was strange but so full of joy. We held onto it for a while, before the Dunhams and the dragons got in the way."

Ondias was curious now and Reiser told her of the day they had been married.

"It was arranged by our parents," he started, "and I hadn't seen her in years. I'm sure you can imagine that I was nervous..."

WITH a stomach full of butterflies, Reiser eased the wagon to a halt in front of the Joaseras' ramshackle, two-storey home. The small centre of the town was atop a gentle knoll and the Joasera household was out farther in the rolling prairie at the edge of a field at the end of their lane. It was a warm, pleasant day with the fresh, sweet scent of spring in the air, but Reiser couldn't remember being so nervous before in his life.

He was early and hoped they wouldn't mind, but he had been unable to sleep the night before and had simply started his journey early, leaving well before dawn. He slowly climbed down from the wagon, careful not to wrinkle the expensive new cloak he'd bought just for this occasion. He walked nervously through the front gate and up the stone walkway to greet his bride. It had been nearly ten years, at her father's funeral, when he had last seen her, and his last image of her was of a scrawny boy-figured girl with scraggly white hair carelessly thrown back into a loose braid. He couldn't quite say he had fallen in love with her, but through her letters over the years, he had grown quite fond of her. He had been especially touched by the last two letters she had sent to him.

His mother had died abruptly of a brain sickness in the middle of the winter. As a result, he had lost his father to a sickness of the heart and soul that spring, not a month ago. After each of his parents' deaths, she had sent a letter showing deep empathy, expressing her concerns, and giving her regrets that no one from her family could afford the trip to Pasdale to be with him.

With both his parents gone, Reiser was alone in their farmhouse. Without Draidel, the Joasera family had come into tough times and the small amount of money he had left his family had quickly dried up. The past five years had been particularly trying for the Joaseras. Their extended family members did their best to help, but it wasn't always enough. So, with the recent deaths of Lou and Sivyla Ovailen added to the long ago loss of Draidel Joasera, Dionelle and Reiser finalized the decision made by their parents twenty years earlier.

Reiser knocked at the door and waited nervously, straightening his burgundy velvet cloak. After only a moment, it was Vyranna who opened the door for him.

"You're early," she said awkwardly. "Wait here and I'll get Mamma."

She left the door open and disappeared down the hall and into the kitchen. He heard her calling for Sharice out back and he stepped into the mud room to wait. He heard soft footsteps on the stairs, and looked in that direction expecting to see Cusec, the youngest Joasera and only boy. Reiser was surprised by who he saw instead—it certainly wasn't the scrawny girl he remembered.

They both froze in equal shock.

Her straight white hair was still long, but the strands around her face had been pulled back and braided into a crown around her head. She was much taller and, though she was still quite thin, she now possessed the curves that defined her gender. Frozen on the stairs, she was draped in a white bridal gown and staring at him with her intense, fiery gaze. She looked almost ghostly in the mysteriously beautiful way that was unique to her. Her burning eyes and the dark blue pendant she wore were the only indication that she wasn't an apparition. The pendant had been an early wedding gift from Boidossen, the wizard in the forest at the foothills of the Great Mountains, whom Dionelle apprenticed under. Her fiery gaze and the talents that accompanied them were still a mystery.

"You're early," she said with a smile, pleased.

She glided down the stairs toward him and he took her long, delicate hands in his. She looked up at him expectantly with her strange and captivating amber-blue eyes and, if he hadn't been in love with her before, he surely was now. An orange light flickered quickly in her eyes and for a moment they truly looked like they were on fire. Still unable to say anything, Reiser kissed her forehead. She smelled faintly of lilac and it made his head spin.

"Well, there he is!" Sharice said from the door to the kitchen. Reiser and Dionelle turned toward the sound of her voice and saw her standing with Vyranna, beaming.

Reiser was quick to notice the resentment in Vyranna's expression and was confused. Dionelle's letters had mentioned her sister's jealousy, but he hadn't believed how deep the feelings ran until now.

After Draidel's death, Reiser and the Joasera girls had been brought up to speed on the decision made by their parents before Dionelle had even been born. They left it up to the three of them to work out, if they thought there was anything to work out at all, and a fight between the two girls was what they had all expected, but that wasn't what had happened at all.

Dionelle's affection for Reiser was only strengthened by the discovery of their betrothal, and he was quickly forsaken by Vyranna. Saucy and bold as she was, she claimed she had no interest in ever being tamed by a man, especially not Reiser. She even went so far as to scorn her sister for being smitten with him, as she felt men were foolish and useless. She had sworn that she'd never need anyone but herself. She had obviously had a change of heart since then, but it was her decision and hers alone, and Reiser couldn't understand why she had become so bitter about it.

"And there's my angel," Sharice said, as Dionelle went to her mother and hugged her. "Looking beautiful as ever."

Dionelle realized that her mother was weeping. "Ma, what is it?"

Sharice shook her head and smiled at her daughters. "You kids have been so good."

Vyranna draped her arms over her mother's and sister's shoulders. "Are we ready?" she questioned, trying to be happy for Dionelle and almost succeeding.

"We're just waiting on Cusec," Dionelle replied.

"I'll go get him," Vyranna offered and hurried upstairs to fetch their brother.

Vyranna finally returned with Cusec, who was hastily trying to straighten up his clothing. He had been a toddler at his father's funeral—the last time Reiser had seen him—and the boy didn't remember him at all, shying behind his mother. He was upset over the marriage, fearing he would lose his beloved sister for good.

"We're all set now," Vyranna chirped with false enthusiasm.

"It's still early," Sharice said. "Reiser, would you like something to eat or drink? You've had a long trip."

"Water will be just fine, thank you."

While Sharice went to the kitchen to get him some water, the other four moved into the parlour.

"I'm going to get everything ready," Vyranna offered. "That way we'll be all ready to go when it's time."

After an uncertain glance at the newcomer, Cusec followed his eldest sister out of the room.

"I'm glad to see I've made such a wonderful impression on your family," Reiser commented dryly as he watched after Cusec and Vyranna.

"Cusec's just shy and Vyranna is just herself," Dionelle replied with a sly smile.

Reiser dropped into one of the large, soft chairs in front of the hearth. Dionelle brushed off the bricks to keep from getting her dress dirty and then sat in front of the dying fire.

"Was the trip long?" she questioned. "I can't remember ever travelling to Pasdale or back again. I would always sleep."

"It's not so long," he replied. "And it passes quicker with company."

"Then I'll try to stay awake tomorrow," she said, poking at the embers with an iron rod.

Sharice came into the room with a tray of cups and a pitcher of water.

"Where are the other two?" she asked.

"They went to get everything ready," Dionelle said.

Sharice set the tray on the low table and turned apologetically to Reiser and Dionelle. "I'm sorry that I can't stay and chat, but there's still so much to be done for this afternoon."

"Of course," Reiser said sympathetically. "We'll be fine until it's time to go."

He watched Sharice until she was out of the room and then turned his attention to Dionelle, who had a look of pure determination as she concentrated on the embers in the hearth, which now seemed to be glowing with new life. Then the back door clattered loudly, startling her, and flames exploded from the embers. It was a brief flare, but Dionelle jumped back—more to protect her clothes than herself—dropping the iron into the embers.

Before Reiser could register what was going on, she rolled up the sleeve of her pure white dress and buried her hand up to the wrist in the hot embers, trying to retrieve the poker.

"Dionelle!" he cried out in alarm, jumping to his feet.

"What?" She stood quickly, the poker in hand, looking about, afraid that the fire may have escaped from its place among the stones. Then she remembered that Reiser had only heard about her talent and had never witnessed it firsthand. She looked down at the hot poker and then back to him.

"It's all right," she assured him. "Watch—"

He looked on, unsettled, as she reached her other hand into the hearth and grabbed a handful of the bright orange embers. She held them out in her upturned palm as if they were stones from the ground rather than glowing coals. She concentrated on them as she had earlier and flames began to lick up from the coals until she had a small blaze in the palm of her hand.

"See?"

Then she nonchalantly tossed them back into the hearth and set the iron poker back down beside the fire.

"I suppose I should have warned you. I'm sorry," she apologized as she searched around for something to clean the soot off her hands before she blackened her clean new dress.

"It's all right. You just startled me is all. I'll be more prepared next time."

"I'm just so used to it that I don't even notice anymore. It's natural for me, with fire anyway. Everything else I have to think about, but fire has never been able to harm me and I've always had control over it," she explained. "Have you heard the story about how Mamma and Da found out about my immunity to fire?"

Reiser shook his head apprehensively, questioning for the first time just what he'd gotten himself into.

"Everyone knew I was odd from the moment I was born, and found out I had magic when I was a few months old because I levitated a toy I wanted. The fire though—that was different. It was the middle of my second winter and Ma and Da had left me with Vyranna. She stole my toys and left me by myself. As an inquisitive baby with no toys, I must have become preoccupied with the fire. When my parents came back, I had crawled right inside the hearth with the fire blazing. I can't imagine their initial terror at the discovery. Da burned his arm quite badly trying to get me out of there. Then they realized my clothes had already long burned away and that I was laughing and unharmed. They coaxed me back out, dressed me, and rushed me to the resident wizard. He hadn't seen many cases of fire immunity and had never heard of it in an infant before. After that, he performed several rounds of tests to find out the extent of my powers."

Reiser was awestruck. "Have they come any closer to the cause of it?"

Dionelle's expression darkened and became thoughtful as she took a moment before answering him, checking to make sure the rest of her family was out of earshot.

"Boidossen recently journeyed to the bicentennial Wizards Guild assembly and I believe he discovered something. He keeps it to himself though, so I have only my suspicions. I've said nothing about it to anyone else—not yet."

"Best to get one thing out of the way at a time," he replied.

"Yes, exactly. Besides, Vyranna likes to use my differences to degrade me. She calls me a freak."

"I had always hoped she would grow out of her cruelty," he replied, shaking his head.

"Instead she's honed it like a well-tooled blade, but I usually just ignore her. Now, before either of us has a chance to change our minds, let's get everyone to the temple!"

They went into the back yard to help Sharice finish setting up benches and decorations of vines and flowers. All the food preparations were complete except for the cooking that would be done after the marriage ritual was over. After loading the family Spirit Book into the wagon, along with a few ornamental pieces, Vyranna and Cusec joined everyone else in the back yard to help finish preparations. Sharice convinced Dionelle and Reiser to sit idly under one of the vined arches to keep from dirtying their wedding garb.

Once they were done in the back, Sharice went up to change into her formal gown and robes made of rich blue silk, while the others fastened the horses to the wagon. Then the Joasera family left in their wagon and Reiser followed behind in his, as it was in bad taste for the bride and groom to arrive at the temple together. When they arrived at the temple, they found it buzzing with activity.

The Joaseras were popular in their village and many people had turned out for the occasion. Reiser's sister, Loniesa, had recently borne a child and was in no condition to make the journey, but a handful of Reiser's extended family and one friend from Pasdale were in attendance. Boidossen had also come in his finest wizarding robes of iridescent silver, and his normally dishevelled, ankle-length grey hair and beard had been ornately plaited for the occasion.

The crowd outside the temple cheered when the couple arrived and Reiser met Dionelle at her family's wagon. He took a deep, steadying breath.

"Are you ready for this?" he asked her.

"All my life!" she said with a winning smile. He took her hand and they walked together through the throng of people and up the temple steps. As was custom, they entered together and the crowd eagerly followed.

The day outside had been bright and warm, but the temple was lit primarily by torchlight and the air was cool, though not uncomfortably so. The brightest part of the building was the dome at the centre which had skylights to let in the sun and bless the ritual circle with its sacred light. The great temples in the cities often boasted domes made entirely of glass, but the skylight panels were all that Dionelle's nameless little town could afford. They still let in plenty of light and the white marble floors, etched with silver, were dazzling in the shafts of midday sun.

It was this very temple where they had last seen each other for Draidel's funeral. His body had been brought to the ritual circle so his spirit could be blessed before being carried out to the back of the temple for his pyre. That day had been just as emotionally charged as today was, but had held a sombre tone while the temple now buzzed with excitement and had been cheerfully decorated with flowers and bright tapestries.

The monk greeted them as they entered the central dome room where all the rituals took place. He smiled warmly and guided them into the circle, while their family and friends followed close behind and began to gather around the edges, sitting on the tiered marble-slab seating as they waited for the ritual to begin.

Reiser and Dionelle were nervous now as they watched those dearest to them file into the room, occasionally stealing glances at each other. Dionelle lacked much of her sister's boldness and was often soft-spoken and shy, so her pale cheeks were flushed with colour and turned almost rose-red each time she actually met his gaze. She had begun to tremble nervously and he gave her hand a reassuring squeeze.

The monk finally moved to a bar of light just outside the circle, signalling the beginning of the ritual, and the murmuring crowd fell silent. Reiser and Dionelle, still hand in hand, turned to face him and he began to chant the Prayer of Good Fortune—the rest of the crowd joined in. Next, they chanted a warding spell to protect the new couple from harm and jealousy and Reiser tried not to look at Vyranna during that one. The chanting finally quieted and the monk read from the Rites of Love, giving brief counsel to the nervous bride and groom, who were practically strangers to each other.

"Today, you begin a new life together—a blossom sprouting from the solid root foundation of your families. You will face difficulties in the coming days and months as you learn to grow with one another, but no matter your difficulties, remember the foundation you share in your family and the dedication they showed in bringing you together. Show that same dedication to each other. Never speak a cruel or angry word when plain silence will suffice."

Reiser tried to concentrate on the monk's words, but had glanced in Vyranna's direction, only to see her openly scowling and now he couldn't focus on anything but a growing sense of dread. The monk continued to extol the virtues of close-knit family and it only heightened Reiser's awareness of Vyranna's hostility. He knew that after tomorrow, he would see very little of Dionelle's family, but he did not want to start their first day married with a rift.

"...and now Reiser and Dionelle," the monk said and Reiser snapped back to attention at the sound of his name, "you are here among our good townsfolk, your friends and family, to solemnize the arrangement of marriage that your parents put forth in your childhood. Do you vow to remain true to the sacred tradition of marriage?"

He waited expectantly for their response.

Reiser was more nervous than ever now, but Dionelle squeezed his hand and he glanced over to see her smiling up at him.

"Yes," he replied.

"Of course," she said.

They exhaled deeply and turned to face the monk again. Reiser's mind had gone completely numb and even though he refused to look in Vyranna's direction, he could feel the anger emanating from her, like sand being blasted at him in a hot summer gale. He squeezed Dionelle's hand again, trying to draw love and security from her, but she was still a virtual stranger to him and he began to tremble, internally panicking, and missing his parents more profoundly than he ever had before. It was far too late to change his mind though—they had already given their vow. The rest of the ritual was purely for show and the monk was currently blessing them with fertility.

"And now I invite you to seal your vow," the monk ended, spreading his arms as if he meant to embrace them.

Now Reiser and Dionelle were expected to kiss—not some quick peck on the forehead, but a proper lover's kiss—and the sun seemed far too bright; the air too cold and close. Reiser wanted nothing more than to be outside in the fresh air, and in his wagon heading home where everything was familiar and safe. But then Dionelle took his hand in both of hers and he turned to face her, seeing she was calm and resolute now. She was smiling and her eyes were stunning blue flames without a hint of amber. She reached up and touched the side of his face, holding him in her gaze, and he felt the calmness in her expression melting into him.

Her touch was steadying and her gaze mesmerizing, and he was having a hard time remembering what all the fuss had been about, suddenly feeling grounded again. He still felt clumsy and awkward as he gently brushed his knuckles over her cheek before sliding his hands behind her to pull her close to him. But he easily found her lips—soft and warm—his whole body tingling, starting at his spine, as she cupped her hand at the back of his neck. At first, the rush of air seemed completely natural to him, but the surprised gasps of those in attendance had him pulling back from Dionelle in awe. They were surrounded by swirling silver light.

It seemed to be coming from the silver etched into the marble, but was so bright that he could barely see anything at all. If not for the feeling of complete serenity, he would have feared that the warding spell had failed and this was some sort of demon trickery—perhaps an elemental of fire or air. His new bride's white skin was glowing in the light and she looked radiant, smiling in delight. The light was warm and neither of them felt threatened—bathed in a warm, loving glow. Dionelle reached out and let the light wash between her splayed fingers, but when she turned and dropped her other hand away from Reiser, the light finally evanesced and in its wake, the afternoon sun seemed to pale in comparison.

The ritual was officially over, but no one moved, stunned by the appearance of the mystery light, and the new couple turned questioningly to the monk, who seemed equally stunned.

"It was love's light," Boidossen finally explained, from his seat on the front tier beside Sharice.

"I've never seen it before in my life!" the monk exclaimed. "I had come to believe it was a myth."

"Few couples are ever blessed enough to be a true match," the wizard replied.

Reiser was still so at peace from the comforting warmth of the light that he wasn't at all concerned by the dark look on Vyranna's face. He only felt sorry for her as he turned his attention back to Dionelle. He noticed that a silver light was swirling in the dark blue of Dionelle's pendant, and he brushed it with his fingertips, amazed that it had happened at all. A chorus of chatter had risen all around them as everyone began excitedly talking about what they had just witnessed, but the newlyweds heard only the wizard's voice above the din. He was standing at the edge of the circle.

"It's a love stone," Boidossen explained, regarding Dionelle's pendant. "It's the only thing that can capture love's light once it's been released from the energy of two souls finally united to one."

"Is that what that was?" Reiser asked, feeling like he was slowly waking from a strange dream.

"What does that mean?" Dionelle demanded. "Was this destiny?"

"Yes, my dear," the wizard replied. "You are a very lucky woman."

She apprehensively glanced down at the pendant. "I think only time will reveal the true extent of my luck."

The wizard patted her hand and smiled. "I know you're nervous now, but it will look more promising once you're home and have had some time to grow accustomed to each other in solitude."

As the noise in the temple quieted again, the monk guided them out of the circle and to the altar under one of the skylights where they would get their marriage tattoos. Dionelle had been nervous about the tattoo, her eyes often drawn to her mother's in the weeks leading up to this day. She and Reiser would get a simple line across the top of their right wrists to indicate their union. Sharice's marriage tattoo now had a simple diagonal line through the middle of it to indicate her widowhood. A double diagonal line through the tattoo would indicate divorce. Each subsequent marriage meant more lines across the wrist and each divorce or death resulted in more diagonal lines, but Dionelle had never seen anyone married even three times because of the stigma attached to people who were unlucky enough to have been through two spouses already.

The monk led Dionelle to sit across from him first and she grew truly nervous for the first time that day—worried not only about the permanence but about the pain of the inking needle. Sharice had assured her it wouldn't hurt, but she'd said the same thing about a woman's first sexual encounter, so Dionelle no longer believed her mother on issues regarding pain.

The monk massaged a pleasant-smelling antiseptic salve onto the area and instructed her to remain as still as she could.

"It will be over before you know it," he said gently.

She flinched at first, the needle leaving a hot, painful line in its wake, but it soon dulled and began to feel more like an irritating bug bite. He cleaned her wrist again after he was finished, and lathered on a sealing salve that left the new mark tingling pleasantly. She stood behind Reiser with her hand gently on his shoulder while he sat through his turn getting tattooed. They finally stood again, sombre now, as the monk introduced them to the gathered crowd. The permanence of their tattoos truly brought the permanence of their union into sharp focus and they exchanged a nervous glance, but said nothing as they joined their friends and family, who had begun to cheer.

Trying to forget their uncertainties, they left the temple hand-in-hand again, and climbed into Reiser's wagon to lead the procession back to the Joaseras' for the wedding feast. Vyranna and her angry jealousy faded into the background as Reiser sat to dinner with his new bride, and local minstrels brought their talents to the feast to wish the new couple happiness through songs of love, prosperity and good health. A few cups of wine helped Dionelle find her dancing feet and they celebrated with all their well-wishers late into the night. Even the moons were long asleep and the sky lit by only starlight when the festivities began to wind down and reality began to creep back in.

Dionelle noticed for the first time that she hadn't heard a word from her sister—kind or otherwise—since they had arrived at the temple. It was customary for the bride and groom to return to their homestead after the wedding feast, but the journey was too far and they would be staying with Dionelle's family that night. Sharice had offered the couple her room, but Dionelle wouldn't force her mother out of her bed. She insisted on sleeping in her room, which she shared with both of her siblings, so Reiser opted to sleep on the sofa in the parlour.

Reiser had bundled his soft cloak into a makeshift pillow, but it was lumpy and uncomfortable, and the sparse blanket Sharice had given him did little to ward against the cool spring night. The fire had burned low and he was too exhausted to get up and get a proper blaze going again. The day had been surreal and he was concerned about what the morning would bring, when he would have to pack his strange bride into his wagon and return to a life that would never be the same again.

He had been so consumed by his thoughts of the profound change his life had taken, that he didn't hear Dionelle come down the stairs and didn't notice her presence until the fire in the hearth swelled on its own. He looked up and saw her in the doorway, tears streaming down her raw, red cheeks.

"What's happened?" he asked, sitting up quickly.

She came to him uncertainly and sat beside him, wringing her hands shyly.

"It's Vyranna," she finally whispered. "She says the most hateful things sometimes, and is only fuelling Cusec's uncertainties, so she succeeds in turning him against me as well."

"Tomorrow you will be beyond her cruelty."

"Can't you take her away instead? I don't want to leave my family."

"It's not permanent. We can still visit them and they can visit us. Every couple in the world has found a way through this and we will too. At least we have the advantage of being well-matched."

She smiled wanly at him, but looked away.

"Will you stay with me tonight?" he asked her. "It's cold down here and I prefer your company to the solitude of my thoughts."

"I suppose I should," she replied, but she was clearly hesitant. "I *am* your wife now."

"My love, you don't have to do anything you don't want to."

"Do you really love me?" she asked, looking at him again, her eyes a perfect mirror for the firelight.

"I think so."

"We barely know each other," she protested.

"But time is on our side and we've got all the days ahead of us to learn and grow together. It will be strange at first—it is strange—but we will get through just the same as everyone else ever has."

"I thought I was ready for this," she replied. "But I don't think I gave it any real thought at all. Not even all these years of my sister's smart remarks, or the past days full of packing or preparation—none of those things made it seem real. Marriage was just a word—just something to do, like going to school or playing in the field or lighting a fire. You lost your folks, and Da has been dead for so long it's like he was barely here at all, and it was just natural that we get married—we were betrothed after all, and that's what betrothed people do. It's going to be such a change and it already seems like a huge change though really all we've done is spoken a few words and had a party."

"It's going to be difficult," he admitted, "but I think it will be easier once we get home and have some time away from Vyranna's anger."

"Now that it's come to it, I can't bear to leave them. They've been my whole life, and I don't know what I'd do without them—even without Vyranna's unreasonable temper."

"It's a big change for us both." Reiser reached out and stroked her cheek, but she shied away from his touch.

"I'm not ready for any of this," she whispered, fresh tears streaming down her cheeks. "Even beyond leaving my family, there's so much more to being married and I hadn't given most of it a thought until Mamma sat down with me earlier in the day to talk about taking to my marriage bed. It was actually a relief for me to sleep in my own room—except my sister won't even let me have that comfort."

Reiser was at a loss and said nothing, only sitting silently beside her and staring into the firelight that rose and fell in time with each breath she took. He longed for her and wished that she didn't keep shying away from his touch because, ever since he first saw her on the stairs, she'd stirred his desires, and he wanted nothing more than to push back her night robes to reach her soft, pale skin and feel her true warmth. Betrothed or not, he'd had lovers before—in the hayloft of barn dances after too much ale, and he imagined Dionelle had likely done the same—

it wasn't that unusual. Being so near to her now—his vulnerable bride still smelling faintly of lilac—only resurrected the desires of past trysts.

"I will stay down here," she said at last. "Anything is better than Vyranna's harsh words and Cusec's fears."

"It will all look better once you've had some sleep. Everything is a crisis when you're exhausted."

He spread out the blanket he'd been wrapped in and shuffled over on the sofa to make more room for her to lay beside him. It was narrow, but she nervously curled against him and he draped an arm over her to keep her securely at his side, not wanting her to take a fall in the night. She pressed her cheek against his shoulder, but remained tense long after the comfort of her warmth had helped him fall asleep.

CHAPTER 9

REISER stood, pacing in front of his hearth, while Nandara explained the latest findings to him. It had been five agonizing weeks since he had given her and Zev the news about Dionelle's sister and they had only just now managed to gather any kind of conclusions, though they still didn't have the answers to satisfy Reiser.

"So, all you're saying is our suspicions were correct but we're still no closer to finding my wife?"

"Extensive interrogations haven't been able to reveal Dionelle's whereabouts. Vyranna, before going almost completely mad, assured us she would never bring her sister anywhere in her sight again, so it's unlikely Dionelle is hidden somewhere in Golden Hill."

"But they wouldn't tell you where they've hidden her?"

"No, they haven't. She's likely alive though, wherever she is. Vozawr would say nothing at all, but Vyranna was happy to gloat about what they had done and I believe if her sister was dead she would brag about it and possibly try to contact you. She's horribly obsessed with you."

"None of this is news or helpful."

"Reiser, you've got to calm down and be patient," Ondias said from her place beside the sorceress. "When the clues to her whereabouts are scattered all over the lands like this, it's going to take some time to get the answers we need to find Dionelle."

"The Guild is going to call a special meeting to discuss Vozawr's grave crime, but it won't be for another fortnight," Nandara explained. "Gathering that many wizards and sorceresses in one place takes time. They will force him to talk, whether he wants to or not, and then we will have our answers."

"In the meantime, I'm going to go find out what Sharice knows," Reiser insisted. "There's something else going on that may help lead our search in the right direction."

REISER had just finished his breakfast and was tidying up while he waited for Ondias to arrive. She was going to help keep his home in order while he went to see what he could find out from Sharice. He had just put the breakfast dishes away when the peaceful morning was split by the fiercest dragoncries he'd heard since Dionelle had moved to Pasdale. Terrified, he grabbed her cloak and ran out into the lane, slipping in the slushy muck of an unusually early thaw, as the dragoness and five others landed in his yard, snarling and writhing, and clearly furious.

"Mistress, please!" he begged, pulling the cloak up around his head, in case he needed it to guard against their fire. "I cannot talk to you over all this noise."

"Why does your wife ignore our summons?" the dragoness demanded, crouching down dangerously close to him and snarling.

"She has no way of knowing about them. Why haven't you been seeking her counsel here?"

"We need her to negotiate with that awful noblewoman. Why is she not capable of knowing of our summons?"

"She's missing, Mistress."

"Lady Karth Dunham warned me you would try to say that!"

"Between me and the lady, who do you think knows better than to lie to you?" Reiser countered.

"Yes, that is true. After all, she is the one who needs a dragon whisperer. I can speak with you openly. Why would the lady be foolish enough to lie? She led us to believe that she was simply keeping Dionelle from us out of some kind of political leverage. That woman is so foolish! Today, she said that Dionelle refused to come to the summons and that she no longer wished to speak with us! Lady Karth indicated Dionelle would be executed over the refusal."

"That story would have worked well for her, because then she could stop stalling and find a new dragon whisperer. Dionelle is missing and very likely still alive, meaning you will not speak to another until Dionelle has been found, but I am afraid there is very little hope of finding her any time soon. The Dunhams are clearly not inclined to spend the money or put in the effort that would speed up the search. They prefer deceit."

"When did Dionelle vanish?"

"You said there was no answer at the wizard's cabin. He was in there dead and she was already missing. Her awful sister found a wizard with the power to control fire demons and he sent them to that cabin to kill the wizard and do away with Dionelle. She is alive, but we don't know where. The Wizards Guild expects to get proper answers out of Vozawr in a fortnight."

"Vozawr!" the dragoness roared. "Never have I encountered a fouler wizard than he, and I wish he had not been immune to my flame or quicker than my bite!"

"He is well-matched with Dionelle's treacherous sister then. I am on my way to Sharice to see if I can find some more information about Dionelle—some secret the two women have been keeping from me. I hope it will help me find out where she is. I know Lady Karth is unbearable, but please, try to put up with her a little longer. Your patience is appreciated and I hope you won't be pushed into any rash decisions by that woman's deceit."

"I shall keep your advice in mind, and while I am content to wait until Dionelle can be found, there are many of my kind not willing to believe this tale you are weaving. They will think it is nothing more than a tale."

"It must anger you that they think you are foolish enough to let a human trick you."

"They have more influence than I do, and it will be difficult for me to keep them appeased for long."

"I must go then, so I can find the answers we need. Good day, Mistress."

"REISER!" Sharice gasped, shocked to answer the knock at her door and find him there. He had sent her a letter to tell her that it was likely Vyranna had had something to do with Dionelle's disappearance, but he hadn't had time to give her the courtesy of a warning before he arrived at her house.

"What's happened? What's going on?" she asked, panicked. Sharice could accept that her daughter was missing—she already had to accept it for a while with Vyranna, even though she was still lost—but she wouldn't handle hearing that Dionelle was dead.

"I need some answers from you," he said, as she opened the door wide to let him in. She had a pile of mending at her chair beside the hearth, but otherwise the house was as tidy as always. Cuser was growing into a helpful young man, though he was nowhere to be seen.

"Answers? I don't understand. I thought you got everything you needed from my letters to Dionelle."

"In your letters and in her journal, her 'past' and her 'nature' kept coming up in a negative light, though both of you were terribly careful not to elaborate in the slightest. What's going on?"

"I suppose in light of what you've discovered about Vozawr, it's likely relevant," Sharice replied with a weary sigh. "We've suspected for a long time that Dionelle's appearance and power is completely unnatural and as she got older, she began to press the issue with Boidossen, mostly because she could no longer tolerate Vyranna's accusations that she was a bastard. Almost two years ago now, he came here with another of his colleagues to ask me questions about my pregnancy and Dionelle's conception—searching for anything odd that might indicate the cause of her nature."

"There was something then? You discovered what made her the way she is?"

"Yes. My pregnancy was normal, but her conception was anything but. Draidel had been very ill for several months surrounding it, but it was only recently we learned the truth of his illness. He hadn't been ill so much as it was like he had gone mad. He was violent, though never towards anyone particularly, and often incomprehensible, grunting and muttering to himself. He had become unnaturally preoccupied with fire and burnt himself quite badly a few times—on purpose—just to feel the heat. I know exactly when Dionelle was conceived because it was the only time he took interest in me in the entire time he was unwell. I'd had a dreadful fever and he had been attracted to the heat of my body."

"And this meant something to the wizards?"

"Yes, it was a demon. It's rare for them to possess humans at all without being invited for the sake of spellwork, and even more rare for it to last so long without resulting in death—though it certainly took many years from his life."

"A fire demon," Reiser said, the words falling from his numb lips. He had begun to tremble.

"Yes. His behaviour was typical of demon possession, and the obsession with heat and fire meant it was a fire demon. While it's unusual, it's not unheard of. Conception during a demon possession is unprecedented though. Dionelle is unique."

"The demon had something to with her appearance then?"

Sharice nodded gravely. "Your wife—my daughter—is part fire demon."

CHAPTER 10

ONDIAS was baking cookies for the peasant children who were helping her look after the livestock when she heard the rattle of a wagon in the lane. Hoping it was Reiser finally back from his mother-in-law's, she ran to the door to greet him, hoping he had answers. She was rudely surprised by who she found instead.

"I hoped I might find you here," Lady Karth snarled. "I understand you schooled Dionelle in dragon culture."

"She already knew a lot when I met her," Ondias stammered, uncertain of where the conversation was heading, but knowing it had to be something unpleasant.

"Tell me, girl, how much do you know about dragons?"

"Plenty," she replied curtly.

"The neighbours indicated that they have seen you talking to them with my dragon whisperer."

"They've let me sit in a time or two when I was visiting and they came for counsel."

"Good enough." Lady Karth nodded to two of the guards travelling with her, and they immediately seized Ondias.

"Stop! What's going on? Leave me be!"

"I cannot wait any longer, war is at hand."

"You cannot be serious!" Ondias protested. "They know Dionelle is still alive! They absolutely will not accept me in her place. You're just going to get me killed!"

"That is little concern of mine."

"They'll tear you apart as soon as they're done with me!" Ondias spat.

ONDIAS stood, trembling, in the great stone hall where Lord and Lady Dunham hosted the dragons. She had thought Dionelle had exaggerated its ugliness and was horrified to see the truth. She wished she had had at least enough warning to grab Dionelle's fire cloak before being carted away to this madness. The cloak wouldn't protect her from much of the heat, but at least it would spare her a direct scorching. She had no idea how she would come out of this alive, but she tried to remain as calm as possible, carefully plaiting her hair and trying to catch it in the inadequate light coming in through the high doorway the dragons used.

She only recognized two of the dragons in the room with her, but was relieved that one of them was the black dragoness and the other was the brilliant blue one who had played dragonsong for Dionelle. The dragoness, as usual, was in charge of the meeting, and that would bode well for Ondias, as the dragoness understood the full extent of the situation. She was still unlikely to accept Ondias in Dionelle's stead, and Ondias had decided it was best not to even try. She was dead either way, but death by hanging seemed preferable to death by dragon.

"What is this?" the dragoness finally asked.

"Mistress, this is not my doing," Ondias insisted. "I am not a dragon whisperer and I will not attempt to speak business here—that is the sole responsibility of Dionelle, who is still missing."

"Talk to them or you face the gallows!" Lady Karth hissed from the other room, slamming her hand against the glass in threat.

Ondias remained defiantly silent. The dragoness unleashed her fury on the glass and when her fire couldn't harm it, she threw her body against it, shattering it under her sheer weight. The nobles behind it scattered as she breathed more fury at them through the opening she had created. Then she took flight and disappeared out the wide doorway with the rest of her flight following. Ondias had been knocked aside, but was relieved to be neither gored, nor crushed, nor scorched.

"That was very foolish of you," Lady Karth growled, grabbing Ondias by the arm and dragging her away. "I will gut you myself if I must!"

"I take death by gallows over death by dragon any day. At least there will be something left to send home to Mamma for my pyre."

REISER stabled the horses and returned his wagon to its shed but there was still no sign of anyone to greet him—not even the two boys he had left to help Ondias look after the homestead and livestock. He was troubled by it, expecting Ondias to run out to greet him to see what he'd found out. He had hoped she would run out to greet him because he was bursting to tell someone what he had learned about Dionelle. He couldn't see how all the pieces fit together yet, but he knew they would before long. The first traces of spring were in the air and he yearned to have his wife back before their anniversary. It was a small hope but he clung to it.

The house seemed silent and even a little dark, though he could see smoke rising from the chimney. Someone was home, so perhaps Ondias had fallen asleep. He pushed open the front door and was shocked to see Nandara sitting in front of his hearth, coaxing fire from coals in much the same fashion Dionelle always had.

"Reiser!" she cried, standing to meet him. She had been so focussed on her spells that she hadn't heard him arrive until he clattered through the front door.

"What's going on?" he finally managed to say, concerned over the troubled expression Nandara wore.

"We don't have much time! They will execute her in hours and we must stop them—this is Lady Karth's cruelty at its worst."

"Who are they executing?" he asked, horrified, thinking they had found Dionelle.

"Ondias! Lady Karth tried to force her into dragon whispering but the girl was clever enough to keep her mouth shut. She's at the gallows now and the execution is at sunset."

"They're going to execute her for refusing to do Dionelle's job?" he asked, astounded. He sat helplessly on the sofa and Nandara resumed her place by the fire.

"That ignorant noblewoman thinks just anyone can talk to dragons if they know what they're doing, but anyone who knows what they're doing knows that the dragons are fixated on your wife. Lady Karth seems to think she can bend the dragons to her will and force them to talk to whomever she deems fit. Ondias incited their fury with the lady though, and they nearly did what we all have been hoping for, and roast her alive."

"That likely didn't bode well for Ondias," Reiser said, shaking his head.

"Not at all. They normally hold mass executions at the end of every month, but have made a special exception for Ondias and are executing her on grounds of treason, claiming she is in league with the dragons."

"Really, she is. We all are," Reiser muttered. "But what can we do? We can't storm the castle, just the two of us. Saving Ondias would require a full civilian uprising by sunset."

"Ondias is a sweet girl and popular among scholars of the court and the wizards, and there is already a great deal of outrage over this and everything else. If Lady Karth's treachery continues to escalate in this manner and her husband continues to do nothing, then a full uprising is exactly what they're going to earn, but that's not going to save Ondias. We need the dragons," Nandara replied, turning back to the fire she had been brooding over when he arrived.

Nandara flung her arms toward the hot coals and screaming flames leapt up, firing straight up the chimney like a cannon.

"What was that?"

"I just summoned the dragons. It's how Lady Karth gets me to do it at her palace and they should be here within the hour."

"Dragons! But they're furious about Dionelle being gone."

"Yes, but the dragoness will listen to you because you are the only link she has left to Dionelle. We will let her know that we are getting closer to finding her. You let her know that you have new information, because the look on your face suggests that you do, and we will use that to get her to help us. Your information will be our bargaining chip."

"We're going to send the dragons to save Ondias?" he replied in awe. "They would do that?"

"They will do nearly anything for Dionelle and to anger Lady Karth. After the lies and deceit, they will be particularly angry at the nobles over the insult of forcing an unwelcome dragon whisperer upon them. Rescuing Ondias will satisfy their desires, and the dragoness does like Ondias, just not as much as Dionelle. Dragons can be our allies when we are careful with our words and act with honour."

"Yes, I never would have believed it possible to side with dragons over humans, but the dragons have never even hinted at being capable of the sort of treachery Lady Karth continues to deal to us. Won't this continued escalation incite a war?"

"The dragons will be appeased for the time being if they can successfully rescue Ondias and turn their attention to finding Dionelle. If the Dunhams have any sense at all, they will not immediately strike back at the dragons for preventing the execution."

"But escalation is inevitable? Is there any way to avoid war?"

"I'm sure this can still be salvaged, but proper negotiations need to begin soon. We need Dionelle."

"I hope my information is enough to keep the dragons satisfied."

"You discovered something very important then?"

"Vyranna knew the truth about Dionelle and used that to gain support with Vozawr. The two of them are certainly behind the attack. I will explain everything once we have freed Ondias and have Zev back here as well."

"Very well, I will send a message to him."

"We're going to have to find somewhere to hide Ondias until this is over," Reiser pointed out. "Possibly forever depending on Lady Karth's wrath."

"We've got to unseat the Dunhams," Nandara insisted. "An uprising is certainly brewing and has been for many years, though quietly. Problems with the dragons have been escalating and we have begun to petition the king to have his nephew removed from his post here. He is a poor representative of the king and we have done all we can to prove that. The unreasonable taxes and luxuriant spending aren't enough alone, nor is the rampant nepotism, but the unwarranted executions have been a concern. These new actions will likely help our cause, but the king is fond of his nephew."

"More fond of him than peace with the dragons?"

"I hope not. When word reaches him that the dragons are rebelling against the Dunhams' rule to such a degree, then I believe he will have little choice but to find another relative to supplant his nephew. Remember that when you negotiate with the dragoness."

"I will certainly keep it in mind, but we still need to find a temporary hiding place for Ondias. She cannot stay here."

"Her family lives on the western outskirts of Pasdale and would be too easy to find. Have you got something in mind?" Nandara asked.

"We should send her to Dionelle's mother. Sharice will look after her now that I've made her aware of just how bad the situation here has become. When she learns of this latest plot, she will be ready to help. It's a day's journey from here, but it's still far enough that it will take the nobles some time to locate the Joasera household. The Dunhams never bothered to learn much about Dionelle beyond her capabilities and the fact that she's my wife. They may not even know her full name."

Nandara nodded. "That will do for the short term, but it won't take more than a fortnight for the Dunhams to learn Ondias's whereabouts. Sharice is going to have to find a new place for the girl."

"Can the Wizards Guild do anything to protect her?"

"It's possible. They are pressing for the removal of the Dunhams, and this will help the cause. Ondias will be a political refugee, but it will take some time to go through the proper channels within the Guild to obtain that status for her."

"Can you do it in less than a fortnight?"

"I will do my best. For now, we have to worry about the dragons and getting Ondias out of that castle or else none of our other plans will matter."

"We won't have long after the dragons get her out," Reiser said. "The Dunhams will know we had something to do with it."

"They will know *you* had something to do with it," Nandara corrected. "You mustn't let them know of my involvement. Tell her the dragons came to you and that you acted alone."

"Then I will be the one on the gallows for treason!"

"The dragons will protect you because you know how to find Dionelle."

"But I don't!"

"I think you have the information we need."

Reiser sprang to his feet as the first of the distant dragoncries reached them. He grabbed Dionelle's fire cloak and went out the front door. He saw the great black form of the dragoness first as she soared over the northern horizon and swooped across the plains toward him. He was nervous and uncertain of how to begin. She had only two others with her—the grey one Dionelle had scolded for trying to eat the neighbour's cows, and another large, white and blue female. She had royal blue horns, claws and wings with a silvery blue underbelly that shimmered as she landed near him.

"What is the meaning of this summoning?" the white dragoness demanded.

"Pardon me, Mistress, but we have never met before," Reiser stammered with a bow. "I am Dionelle's husband and I have new information of her whereabouts, but it must wait because her best friend is in grave danger."

"At the gallows; yes, we know," the white dragoness replied. "That is no concern of mine."

"Isn't it? You have no cares for Dionelle's best friend? I don't know that she would be terribly pleased to discover you let that horrible noblewoman murder Ondias. She may not be willing to do this job any longer."

"You expect to find her then?"

"I just returned from visiting her mother, and have discovered some extremely valuable new information. I am not clever enough to see how it is relevant, but I am clever enough to know that it is."

"And you won't give us that information unless we help Ondias," the black dragoness said.

"That's right, Mistress. Lady Karth has gone too far. She does not care about the sensitivities of your kind, as you undoubtedly have noticed, and she doesn't appear to care about the sensitivities of her own kind. The Wizards Guild is pressing the king to have the Dunhams removed from power and if you act now to save Ondias from execution, it will send a strong message to the king. Do you remember the circumstances under which you first met my wife? How they left her shivering and naked because they didn't care? You can stop that kind of behaviour with something as simple as snatching a young woman from the gallows."

The black dragoness glanced over at the white one, who was clearly her superior, and gave a slight bow.

"Mistress," the black dragoness began, "I believe this is a small act on our part if it means having nobler nobles to deal with."

"The Dunhams are some of the worst our kind has ever dealt with and it would please me to have them replaced. Having Dionelle to converse with has certainly eased the burden of dealing with the Dunhams," the white dragoness conceded.

"The Dunhams have no interest in finding Dionelle," Reiser said. "They have given up and continue on as though she is dead, despite strong evidence to suggest the contrary. There is hope we can still find Dionelle, but I need Ondias and I need some time."

"Very well," the white dragoness said. "Shall we bring the girl back here?"

"Yes, but please linger because we may need you to bring her elsewhere. Until we can convince the king that the Dunhams are unworthy representatives, we need to keep Ondias hidden."

"We will aid you," the white dragoness promised. "I will go to the king myself and press this cause with him."

"Mistress, that would be extremely helpful."

"I want answers from you about your wife before I leave for the king," she demanded.

"As soon as Ondias is free of the Dunhams, I will give you your answers," Reiser promised.

The white dragoness nodded to the others, and they immediately took flight, heading straight for the palace in Pasdale, shrieking their awful cry the entire way there. Once they left, Nandara joined him in the fields to watch their swift descent into the city.

"Those are battle cries," Nandara said. "The Dunhams are going to believe the dragons have declared war."

"In a way, they have."

"Zev is on his way, though I'm not certain if he will arrive before the dragons return."

"We won't have much time to speak before they will need to get Ondias away from Pasdale. If he isn't here, we will have to fill him in later."

They could still hear the dragoncries and turned back toward the city, waiting and hoping the dragons didn't cause too much carnage and that they were in time.

ONDIAS was tied to a stake at the foot of the gallows, on display, and would have been pelted with rotten produce if it was a true execution. There weren't many people gathered, despite the notices that a traitor was to be hanged at sundown. Those who had gathered were subdued, mostly there out of boredom.

When the Dunhams arrived shortly before sundown, Ondias broke her silence and began shouting at them.

"Awfully small crowd, don't you think? I guess no one wants to see the murder of an innocent woman."

"Shut your mouth, girl!" Lord Dunham snapped.

"You're going to make me a martyr. That's all this is going to achieve! Reiser is going to find Dionelle and when she finds out what you've done to me, she will send the dragons to raze this palace to the ground. Your days are numbered!"

Lady Karth marched across the sparsely populated square and slapped Ondias hard enough to make the girl see stars.

"It doesn't matter what you do to me," Ondias insisted, spitting blood. "You won't get away with this."

Lady Karth only hit her again and began barking orders for the executioner to cover her head.

"Gag her mouth as well. I tire of listening to the traitor."

As the executioner approached, they all heard distant dragoncries and the Dunhams looked visibly shaken by the sound.

"I told you!" Ondias cried victoriously before she was gagged and hooded.

"Shut her up!" Lord Dunham shouted.

"Get her in a noose immediately," Lady Karth yelled, desperate for her orders to be heard over the growing dragon din. "We shall not wait for sundown. Let this treacherous whelp hang now."

The few onlookers began to disperse as the sound of dragoncries grew louder and closer. Ondias fought against the executioner and guards as they dragged her up the stairs. When they tried to hold her steady to secure the noose around her neck, she dropped to the ground and lay there as tense as she could—deadweight with nowhere to hold on to. It took four of them to hoist her back to her feet, and just as they did the deafening dragoncries ceased and the three dragons crested the northern wall and dipped into the square, shooting dragonfire in ahead of them and lighting the wooden support columns of the gallows.

The guards and executioner abandoned their post, but Lady Karth was already up on the platform to ready to knock the flooring out from under Ondias herself, but the pair of dragonesses were already diving while the male continued to shoot fire at anyone who came close. The white dragoness swiped Lady Karth off the edge and grunted in satisfaction when the woman thudded to the stone below, writhing in agony but in too much pain to even shriek. The black dragoness moved like obsidian water, slicing the noose with one hand while plucking Ondias from her doom with the other.

In a single screech of triumph, they swooped out of the square, spiralled into the sky and surveyed their work. The gallows were aflame but the only casualty was Lady Karth who was badly injured but clearly still alive. The white dragoness was satisfied they had sent their intended message without doing enough damage to incite outright war. As she saw it, the score had been settled.

As they flew back toward Reiser's farm, silent now and flying with utmost speed, the black dragoness carefully sliced Ondias's bonds and pulled the hood from her head.

"Many thanks, Mistress," Ondias said, bowing her head appreciatively. "I am forever in your debt."

"Help us find Dionelle and we will consider it repaid."

NEITHER Nandara nor Reiser moved from where they stood in the field, watching and waiting until they saw the shapes of the three dragons returning. Nandara waited on the porch while Reiser stood in the lane, both of them anxiously waiting as the trio of triumphant dragons finally landed with a battered but thankful Ondias in the black dragoness's grip. She carefully set her down and she ran to Reiser, throwing her arms around him and burying her face against his neck, crying softly and in shock.

"Thank you," she whispered.

"Have you got anywhere to hide?"

"Nowhere."

"I'm going to send you to Sharice until the Wizards Guild can protect you. Run and collect your things so our mistress can bring you there and be quick because I have news that I would like to share with everyone."

When Ondias returned, mere minutes later, there was still no sign of Zev so Reiser went on with his revelation.

"Dionelle has always been a mystery to you," he said to the dragons. "And it is a mystery that has been solved. I'm uncertain of how long Dionelle has known the full truth, but she certainly found out shortly before her sister did. Dionelle's father was possessed by a fire demon when she was conceived. Dionelle has known this for perhaps two years at most, but her sister, with the aid of Vozawr, has discovered that Dionelle, in fact, has a shared paternity. Draidel and the fire demon are both her father and she is part demon."

"That's impossible!" Nandara gasped.

Reiser gave her a silencing look, but he could see that Ondias was equally shocked. The dragons, as always, showed little emotion, though their curiosity had certainly piqued.

"Vyranna has always resented Dionelle," Reiser explained. "She was insane with jealousy when my marriage to her sister revealed that Dionelle and I are soulmates. She took up with Vozawr and with his help learned the truth about Dionelle's strangeness. It is clear to everyone that the wicked pair sent the demons after Dionelle, killing Boidossen in the process. I don't know what Vozawr's motives might be, but Vyranna is motivated by spite and her jealousy, which I understand has driven her mad."

"Dionelle is unique," the white dragoness said.

"Yes, she is."

"You are still no closer to finding her though."

"Not on my own, which is why I share this information with you. You are wise and you travel far and see much. I hope that you will find something that can lead us to her whereabouts. Perhaps a demon can be called upon for answers, if the Guild can't wrench them from Vozawr."

"If I may speak..." Nandara interrupted.

"Go ahead," the white dragoness said with an impatient nod.

"The Guild will have to postpone its investigation into Boidossen's murder and Dionelle's disappearance so that we may focus on protecting Ondias. If Dionelle has survived this long, she will likely survive months longer, wherever she may be, and we need to focus on first protecting Ondias and then pressing the king to remove his misguided nephew before the situation in Pasdale can escalate any further. Would the dragons be willing to take up the search for Dionelle until we are able to fully question Vozawr?"

"You are asking us to take on a great responsibility."

"You need Dionelle almost as much as I do," Reiser said. "This is a majestic responsibility best suited for your clever kind. I have no doubts that you can get to the truth of Dionelle's whereabouts quicker than the wizards could even without this distraction. I am ashamed I did not think to seek your wisdom sooner."

"Very well," the white dragoness finally agreed. "We will take Ondias to Sharice Joasera and then I will immediately leave for Golden Hill to speak with the king about his nephew. We will leave you protection against the nobles and do what we can to find Dionelle."

The black dragoness gently took hold of Ondias in her large claws and then the pair of dragonesses headed northward, leaving the grey one to keep Reiser safe.

"It will not take long for the Dunhams to send a troop so I must leave at once, or suffer treason charges as well," Nandara said. "I will meet Zev on the way and explain everything to him. We will leave to assemble the Guild at once and work on seeking protection for Ondias, and then to press the king to remove the Dunhams. I will let the other wizards and sorceresses know about Dionelle's unique situation and see if any of them have any idea what the demons may have done with her."

CHAPTER 11

REISER trudged out to the stables to feed the horses, barely noticing the flight of dragons hovering over his property. There were never less than five of them at any given time and they were guarding him as well as all his livestock and his still-barren fields. They brought him all of his supplies and wouldn't let anyone in at all. The Dunhams had made one unsuccessful attempt to bring him in on grounds of treason, but the guards had given up before any sort of scuffle could even begin, knowing they didn't stand a chance against so many dragons.

The Dunhams risked open war by launching a full-scale attack on the dragons, Reiser and his property, so they were sitting in their castle, quietly scheming. Reiser hoped that those scheming against the nobles came up with something first, but he knew little of what went on beyond his fields as he hadn't left his property since Ondias had been rescued. The dragoness brought him his news, and so far she had little of it. It had been over two weeks, but Ondias was safely away from Sharice's home, long before the Dunhams had gone there looking, and the wizards were now protecting her.

If Reiser had known that the dragons were going to go to such great lengths to protect him, he would have had them leave Ondias with him, for the company if nothing else. The workers wouldn't come near the house and it was unlikely the dragons would let them in if they did. It kept Reiser busy to do all the chores he had once had so much help with, but it was good to be busy or he would go mad. The dragons helped when they could, and it was strangely pleasing to him that they thought enough of him to help him with his chores.

Today was unbearably windy, windy enough that the dragons really could hover, and windy enough that he was relieved to have the silent blue male at his side to help steady him against the unrelenting gale. The dragons caught anything that blew away and secured it again for him. The day before, it had been unbearably cold, and the day before that had been pouring rain—so much so that many areas had flooded. Days that would have normally carried the pleasant warmth of spring were unusually hot, melting the snows at alarming rates and causing more flooding. The weather had been odd since midwinter, but it had been wildly swinging from one extreme to another without relent for over a week now.

A furious cry rang out from the east, and the other dragons in his yard—there were seven of them today—cried out in response. Not long afterward, the black dragoness swooped into the yard, just outside the barn where Reiser was still seeking shelter from the wind, which had started suddenly, with not so much as a gentle breeze as warning—there hadn't been any gentle weather at all in over a week—and it would likely cease just as suddenly.

"Good day, Mistress!" Reiser called over the wind. "You seem troubled."

"The king still denies our petitions for the Dunhams' immediate removal," she growled.

"That is most unwise of him."

"The wizards will not continue their search for Dionelle until the king has replaced his nephew, but will not grant us access to Vozawr as they do not have an adequate dragon whisperer and fear that I will simply tear him apart upon seeing him."

"I had hoped Ondias would have counselled them to the contrary. Surely she can convince them that Vozawr is too valuable in finding Dionelle for you to kill him yet."

"It's likely they won't listen to her. She is simply their ward now and has not apprenticed long enough to be a full sorceress in the Guild. Without membership, she has little sway."

"Humans have some very foolish processes," Reiser agreed. "Has the king explained his decision?"

"He will not remove his nephew until he has an immediate replacement."

"That is extremely foolish. It must anger you that he thinks so little of your opinions."

"My mistress is furious," the dragoness replied. "Our superiors are running out of patience and the problems we have been trying to settle with the Dunhams have only escalated and are now spreading to other kingdoms. The king's other representatives have excellent dragon whisperers, but none who can converse with us here and so the unrest here is spreading."

"Do you share many kingdoms with humans?"

"Nearly all of them."

"With tensions always so high, and sometimes bordering on war, wouldn't it be easier for your kind to have your own kingdom away from the influence of humans?"

"We have lands—our great city is built in a mountain range rarely seen by humans—but they are not abundant enough to sustain our numbers. There is not a space left untouched by human presence that is large enough for my kind to call home. We are left with little choice but to exist in human realms, spread out so that our numbers do not deplete all resources."

"Where do you live then?" Reiser asked, genuinely curious and unable to help himself.

"We have caves and keeps in the highest mountain peaks. Some of us have crafted majestic towers in the more isolated regions that we occupy, but even these pale in comparison to the beauty of our city. We return there frequently, but our numbers cannot be sustained, so we must remain on the edges of human kingdoms in order to survive."

"None of the dragons or dragon whisperers in other lands are capable of negotiating with the king in the name of peace?" Reiser asked, incredulous.

"The king is unmoving and my kin in other lands are growing impatient, viewing the insult and neglect we face here as an insult to all dragons."

"But the king agrees that his nephew cannot do the job?"

"That is correct. However, he will not leave the kingdom leaderless or in the hands of a regent. Instead, he would rather see this land fall to ruin in the hands of a fool and a madwoman!"

"I am sure he simply doesn't understand the dire situation here. Golden Hill is very far from Pasdale, is it not?"

"It is a three-day flight."

"It will take a very long time for information to travel to the king, and all he has is some upset wizards and angry dragons. If the king is like most humans, he mistakenly believes that dragons are always angry. His sources likely have loyalties to the Dunhams and are reluctant to report the true scope of the danger here."

"Do you suggest we double our efforts? Is it time for war?"

"Certainly not. I suggest you keep working at the king. Can you talk to him at all? Directly or through his personal dragon whisperer?"

"There are few who find the task worthy."

"Do you find the task worthy?"

"I will not see this land destroyed. It is Dionelle's home."

"Will your superiors let you talk to the king directly then?"

"I suspect they would disapprove, but would not outright punish me for it."

"Mistress, I think it's a chance worth taking. The sooner we can calm this situation, the sooner we can get back to searching for Dionelle."

REISER stood on his porch, watching miserably as all the seed he had gone through such great lengths to plant in the previous day's scorching heat was washed away by the torrential rains. Two days ago, there had been torrential rains as well as a monstrous gale that had grounded all the dragons. He couldn't see many of them through the rain, but he had no doubts that they were circling in the clouds, still on the watch for any attack from the nobles.

It had been a week since he had last spoken to the dragoness and he hadn't heard any fresh news since. War hadn't broken out, but there had been no resolution to the tensions and watching his hard work wash away to the river left him with a profound sense of hopelessness. Some days he was tempted to send the dragons away and let the Dunhams haul him to the gallows.

The day dragged on with Reiser stuck inside doing chores and only venturing out once to feed the animals. The rain suddenly ceased just after he was finished his dinner and the evening sun peeked out for a few minutes before disappearing behind the hills. Reiser went to bed not long afterward and woke up near midnight, freezing. Sometime after the sun's departure, the temperature had plummeted back to unbearably cold and he trudged downstairs, wrapped in most of his bedding, to prod the fire back to life. He pushed the sofa closer to the hearth and slept there.

Sometime before dawn the dragoness had finally returned and her tapping at his door was what woke him. When he saw her, he didn't even bother with the fire cloak because he almost welcomed the heat of her fire, even if it meant death. But she had news this time and though it was dreadful, it was news.

"Mistress! What brings you at this hour?"

"I was finally granted access to Vozawr and with the help of a powerful, persuasive sorceress, was able to extract the answers we need out of him."

"You know where the demons have taken Dionelle?"

"Because she contains their essence, they have brought her to their fire realm. She is able to survive there due to her fire immunity and a natural ability to convert the energy of their realm into nourishment. Nandara called upon a fire demon after we got answers from Vozawr and we were able to confirm that they have Dionelle."

"How can we get her back?"

"They took her by force, but she stays there by choice," the dragoness said grimly.

"Choice! Why doesn't she want to come home?"

"The demons have made her their empress."

"You jest."

The dragoness gave him a dour look.

"There's nothing we can do?" he demanded.

"The demons are tricksters and Dionelle is novel to them, as she is to us. They will do all they can to keep her in their midst until they grow tired of her."

"How long would that take?"

"Years. And it is likely they might kill her before they will let her go."

Reiser's heart sank. "She is alive, but we will never see her again."

"Not unless she is able to see through their veil of manipulations. She can likely leave on her own at any time, but she must first desire the comforts of home."

"With her sister's jealous madness and my unwillingness to accept dragon whispering as a line of work for her, she's unlikely to want to return. We can't convince the demons?"

"I cannot help you in that respect. The demon realm of fire is the source of dragon power and we would perish without them. Going against the demons in any respect would bring my kind to its end."

"Nandara was able to call on a demon once already, do you think she could do it again? Can I talk to Dionelle directly, or at least try to negotiate with one of them?"

"It is unlikely, but I encourage you to try. Would you like me to bring you to the Guild?"

"Yes, Mistress, but not until the cold lifts."

As the blast furnace of air burned at his face and seared each breath, Reiser almost wished he had chosen to travel to the Guild in the cold. The dragoness was incredibly warm, even apart from the heat of the day, and Reiser hadn't considered that her body—full of fire—would have been enough to keep him warm through the cold. They had left his farm at dawn when the weather swung from freezing to scorching, leaving the other dragons to guard his property. They were nearing the main temple of the Wizards Guild, the dragoness had assured him, but he could see nothing but the rolling plains below them. It had grown overcast very quickly and Reiser was concerned. Minutes later, the temperature dropped to something near normal, but the sky also opened up, dropping sheets of rain on them and turning the world below into an obscure grey curtain.

"This all started around midwinter," the dragoness pointed out.

"When Dionelle went missing," Reiser replied.

"I do not think she belongs in the fire realm."

"We must convince the demons of that."

The dragoness said nothing and spiralled into a dive. Reiser had never flown with dragons before and was feeling a little ill with the height and sudden shifts in direction. The spiralling drop was most terrifying though and he closed his eyes as the muddy ground approached, but the dragoness swooped out of the spiral mere feet from the ground and settled down gently in the mud outside a temple built into the side of a hill. She left him at the human door and flew to the top of the hill to enter the dragon chamber, which was brightly painted since the wizards were no fools when it came to dragons.

Reiser dropped his soggy belongings at the door now that it didn't matter that he had brought an extra change of clothes since everything he brought was as thoroughly drenched as everything he was wearing. A wizard he didn't recognize met him in the entrance and brought him to Nandara and Zev as soon as he explained who he was.

"The dragoness has given you the news then," Nandara said.

"Is there any hope of retrieving her?"

"I'm not sure. One of the other wizards who works exclusively with fire and is what you would call a demon whisperer contacted the demons again to see if he could negotiate Dionelle's release. But the demons insist she is their empress and no prisoner. She is free to leave when she chooses. She refuses to speak with us."

"Mistress has said they are using trickery to keep Dionelle there."

"It's likely. I understand from Ondias that she was vulnerable with problems in her family as well as troubles adjusting to marriage."

"Yes. So they're playing on those concerns to keep her there?" Reiser asked.

"It's likely."

"There must be some way to contact her directly."

Nandara shook her head and shrugged, at a loss.

"Mistress has suggested that the unusual weather is connected to Dionelle's disappearance. The timing certainly matches, and it seems unlikely that it's a coincidence."

"We have been looking into that since we spoke to the dragoness yesterday. We have been studying the phenomenon closely since it began. It started small scale with fires and the warmth of the sun behaving strangely, but has since spread to other elements. We have a theory right now that all of the demon realms are collapsing into our world, giving them greater control over this realm."

"It must be because Dionelle is there."

"That would be the likely cause, though it's hard to say. There has never been a human who was part demon before and it enables her to survive in both realms, but at her core, she is human and not demon and it is throwing the order of nature into chaos. The demons travel in essence and have mere influence over our realm, and Dionelle inherited that ability from them. She has demon essence in her, like she is partially possessed, enabling her to wield fire and causing her to be born immune to the flame and heat. But she is still human and a human in the elemental realm does not appear to be a positive thing."

"Have the demons been made aware of this?"

"It's no consequence of theirs if our world falls to ruin. In essence, they would still survive such a cataclysm."

"She likely wouldn't though. There must be some way to convince her of that. Would bringing her back home, where she belongs, undo what's happening here?"

"It won't make things worse," Nandara said with a helpless shrug. "The damage might be permanent, but I'm sure those of us who can wield the elements can set some of this back into order again."

"We need to get her back," Reiser insisted. "Please, bring me to the dragon chamber. I need to speak with the dragoness."

Nandara led him to the great marble chamber that had been painted with an elaborate night sky scene with the dragon constellation as the centrepiece of the domed ceiling. It seemed to be lit from within, making the stars shine like the true heavens. The dragoness was in there alone with the wizards' dragon whisperer.

"Mistress," Reiser interrupted with a bow. "May I have a word?"

"Of course."

The dragon whisperer was surprised that she was letting an outsider in, but the man bowed out and waited just outside the arched doorway.

Reiser explained what Nandara had said to him about the worlds beginning to collide and that it was unlikely that anything but the demons would survive.

"You still want me to try to reason with the demons," the dragoness grunted.

"Mistress, your kind is doomed either way. Is it not worth the risk to defy the demons in the chance that they will not punish you? We will all perish if we can't bring Dionelle home."

She thought about it as she watched the stars glittering on the dark marble stones. She sighed, a long, grumbling sound—like a teakettle bubbling on the stove—that released a thin tendril of fire and then she finally looked back down at Reiser.

"I will consult the Dragoness Superior and her counsel and see if there is anything we can do. I will bring news to you when they come to a decision."

JOINING the wizards had given Reiser more to look forward to and he was at least able to spend his days in the company of other humans, including Ondias, Zev, and Nandara. Having the company of those he knew brought him small comfort and he was able to cling to the hope that they could still find a way to bring Dionelle home. She had been admitted entrance to the Guild, and so there was increased support in locating her.

Reiser had also discovered that the king was set to execute Vozawr in a month's time and that the king had also given in to the pressure and would remove the Dunhams as soon as he could get a convoy to Pasdale.

There were other nobles—cousins of the king—who would make suitable replacements, though he hadn't yet chosen one. The courts would rule as a collective regent in absence of a proper lord and lady, until the king could send a new representative.

"It's promising, as long as the world doesn't collapse in on itself before then," Ondias muttered, having a hard time keeping an optimistic outlook.

"Once the Dunhams have been removed, we will be able to go home," Reiser said.

"I won't go back until the king's new representative is in place and I have been granted a full pardon," Ondias insisted. "I won't be trapped with a noose around my neck and a dragon as my only hope again."

"The king is fully aware of your situation," Nandara said. "I believe he is sending a pardon for each of you with the convoy heading to remove the Dunhams from power."

"There is still a flight of dragons guarding my home," Reiser said. "I enjoy the company, but would prefer the comfort of home, so I'm going to ask the dragoness to bring me back to Pasdale when she returns with news. Would you like to come with me? The dragons will keep us both safe."

"Let me think on it," Ondias considered. "Do you think they would smuggle Mamma to your house? I haven't seen her since before you left to see Sharice. It seems like an age ago."

"I'm sure we can convince them."

"I will likely take you up on the offer. Ask me again when the dragoness returns."

REISER and Ondias stood idly at one of the balcony doors, closed firmly against the cold, and watched the blizzard unfold. It had been raining, torrential as usual, when the temperature suddenly dropped, turning the mud to ice and the rain to snow. It was fascinating, but frightful in its destructiveness. The gale had only recently burst into the mix, throwing high drifts against the side of the temple.

"Three manifestations at once," Ondias commented. "Air is working overtime and I haven't seen this before."

"Me either," Reiser replied. "It's getting worse."

"We need Dionelle back soon."

"Have you heard anything about how the earth realm is affected by this?"

"There have been earth tremors in some places, only one town so far, but it levels everything and even threatens to bring down mountains. Nandara said the earth demons are the quietest and most relaxed. They spend their energy in bursts and rest for long periods in between. If this increases their activity, the ground will tear itself out from under us."

Reiser said nothing and numbly continued to watch as the snow suddenly quit and the sun broke through the clouds. The heat of it was unbearable and the snow immediately melted, quickly forming a river and causing a large piece of the hillside near the temple to rip away and slide down the valley.

"That's not earth elements at work?" he asked.

"No, that was just water getting its way. Fire and water are probably equally destructive, but water can be much more subtle and often takes ages to make changes like that."

He sighed and said nothing for a long time, but a black spot in the sky caught his attention and though they couldn't hear her cries over the gale, he knew it was the dragoness finally returning. Reiser and Ondias both ran to the dragon chamber to meet her.

"Mistress!" he called, as soon as she came into sight. "What news?"

She landed in front of him, giving him a reproachful look for his over-excitement, but chose to forgive him given the situation.

"Gather your things, we leave now."

"Where are we going? I wish to go home."

"There is no need. We have decided to help you retrieve your wife and request your presence in the Red Mountains immediately."

Ondias gasped and Reiser looked to her, uncertain.

"No human has ever seen their city in the Red Mountains. Few have seen the range at all," Ondias explained softly.

Reiser was unable to mask his excitement. "Mistress! I am not worthy of this honour and I am hard pressed to believe any human is! Ondias would be far more deserving of the honour than me."

"And I'm sure there are many dragon scholars, like my former master, more deserving than I of this tremendous honour," Ondias added, still shocked they were opening their home to a human—a simple rancher.

"It must be you, Reiser. We have decided you and you alone have the greatest chance of success. We considered Sharice, but she is more in Dionelle's past and you are her future. You must do this."

"Why do you need to bring me to the Red Mountains?"

"My kind is gathering there and the power of all of us together is required to enchant you with protection to survive the fire realm."

"Mistress, I don't understand."

"We're sending you there," the dragoness said impatiently. "Dionelle is their empress, so there is no reason why she cannot choose to leave. She simply needs to be convinced that she belongs in this realm."

"Yes!" Ondias exclaimed. "As empress, she can choose to denounce her title and leave, and there is nothing they can do about it. And if she chooses to leave, it's unlikely the demons would punish the dragons for their role in it. They may not even suspect the dragons are behind your presence in their realm," she said to Reiser.

"That is correct," the dragoness replied. "You may stop at your home on the way to the mountains, but I wouldn't advise that you linger. Earth demons are beginning to discover the true extent of their power, and once they awaken fully, there will be little hope for our world."

"How will I get back from the fire realm?"

"You can travel the same way the demons do—through any fire. I would advise you keep a fire burning in the hearth at your home and return through that. If you can convince Dionelle to return, she will know how to bring you back through that portal specifically. If you fail, you may as well remain with her."

"Ondias, do you still wish to return to my home?" Reiser asked.

"Yes. I'll keep a fire in your hearth so you and Dionelle can return safely."

"Mistress, please give us a moment to collect our belongings," Reiser said, as he and Ondias bowed out of the room to gather their things and explain the situation to Nandara.

CHAPTER 12

Reiser stood in his lane, wrapped tightly in his robes despite the sun's scorching heat, knowing he would be cold as soon as they headed skyward again. He was bringing nothing with him except the clothes he wore and he waited as the dragoness gave final instructions to Ondias and the dragons remaining to protect her. Without a word, the dragoness reached out and grabbed him firmly around the torso before taking flight again. Reiser was getting more accustomed to this form of travel, but would be relieved when he could feel the ground beneath his feet. He would be even more relieved to not have to worry about that ground suddenly opening up beneath him to swallow his world.

It was a five-day flight to the centre of the dragon kingdom in the Red Mountains and Reiser was nervous about spending that much time alone in the presence of the dragoness. But she set him at ease by stopping after a couple of hours. It seemed like they had just reached the bitterly cold heights the dragons preferred to fly at, when she began to descend again. As they broke through the cloud deck, Reiser could see that they were over the Great Mountains.

He remained silent, knowing she wouldn't hear him over the rush of wind, and waited to see if she would reveal why she was heading toward the mountains. The saw-tooth peaks here were much higher than he had seen before, snow-capped with sheer cliff faces. As they swooped around the edge of one particularly sheer granite wall, Reiser suddenly saw the deliberate architecture so cleverly built into the stone. From almost all angles, the towers and spires looked like natural mountain crag and valleys, but just as the dragoness angled in for descent, it all became clear. It was her home in the mountains.

Designed to be invisible from the ground, two spires of ice-capped rock towered over a cavern hewn deep into the mountain. It was sheltered on three sides by cliff walls that served as the dragoness's watch-posts. She circled around and landed on the western-facing cliff.

From this angle, Reiser could clearly see how the towers maintained a natural craggy look on almost all sides, and then were smoothed down to gentle curves where they would be obscured from anyone who didn't have wings. At the root of both spires was a large oval opening that disappeared into darkness.

"It continues down to the lake at the heart of the mountain," the dragoness said.

Reiser was saved from asking any embarrassing questions, as movement from inside the cave drew both their attention. The blue dragon who had played dragonsong for Dionelle emerged from the darkness, pleased at first to see the dragoness, but then furious when he realized she had company.

"You dare bring a human here?" he roared.

She hissed out dragonfire in return. The blue dragon dodged the fire and climbed one of the towers to be closer to where they were.

"Mistress, I apologize for speaking out of turn," he said, doing nothing to hide his disdain.

"I'm bringing him to the city," the dragoness explained. "What harm is there in bringing him here as well?"

"To the city? Are you mad?"

"He has been summoned," the dragoness snapped, and Reiser was concerned for a moment by the threatening quality of her tone.

The blue dragon was clearly shocked, but maintained composure and bowed respectfully. "Shall I join you on this journey?"

"I need you to maintain watch of the Pasdale nobles in my stead. The king is sending a replacement, but we must be wary of the Dunhams until they are gone."

"May the winds that carry you be blessed," the dragon said, spreading his wings and drifting back down to the mouth of the cave. The pair of dragons exchanged a nod and then the dragoness lifted off again.

When they stopped again near dusk, the dragoness lit a fire to keep Reiser warm against the fierce cold and so he could roast a pheasant she had managed to catch.

"I hope my presence didn't cause grief at your homestead," Reiser said carefully.

"He gets hot-tempered sometimes, but knows my views regarding tradition are different. He will get over it. He is bound to me, so he has little choice anyway. To abandon me would mean death. Still," she sighed her teakettle sigh, "he will likely put off producing a brood even longer over this. He feels my ways endanger us and will not agree to hatchlings until we are both secure."

Reiser nodded, but said nothing. It had been clear to him almost immediately that their society was matriarchal, but he had heard nothing of their mating customs or the laws that bound them to each other. He wondered if Ondias knew about any of it.

"What can we expect of the journey?" Reiser asked, not wanting to delve into such uncertain waters as her personal life. With no knowledge of what to expect in that regard, he was worried about earning a scorching.

"I will only stop to hunt and to rest," she said. "I prefer not to fly at night, but traversing the sea can be difficult and there will be nowhere to stop, so that day could be longer than others. I will protect you from the weather as best I can, but try to alert me to any problems you are having."

She was kind enough to let Reiser sleep under her wing, where he was protected from the elements and kept comfortable by the considerable heat of her body. Her body heat also helped to protect him from the cold temperatures at the heights dragons preferred to fly at, and she held him close against the obsidian of her chest. She had been forced to fly lower than normal because the thin, cold air was too hard on Reiser, but she still flew as high as she could.

She took them the rest of the way over the towering, craggy slates of the Great Mountains and then stopped at the shore of the Great Sea on the other side of the mountains, but to rest instead of hunt. There were still several hours of daylight left and Reiser was surprised they weren't continuing any farther. He foraged for berries and ate what was left of the previous day's pheasant.

"It takes a full day to reach the other side," the dragoness finally explained. "There are no islands directly in our path and I will not delay our trip with the lengthy detours to islands for rest. We stay on the shore tonight and I will bring us all the way across tomorrow."

It was far too early to sleep, so Reiser tried to enjoy the majesty of his surroundings, realizing he had never been to the Great Sea before. The water stretched on forever, the horizon a perfectly straight line, dazzling orange as it reflected the fire of the setting sun. He heard a strange, eerie cry from the water and the dragoness, who had been dozing idly just below the high tide line, snapped her attention out to sea. She spread her great wings climbing vertically into the air, creating a fierce gale as she pumped her wings, until she was little more than a dot in the twilit sky, circling far out over the water.

Reiser looked on in amazement as she suddenly shot from the sky like an arrow, diving straight into the ocean with a surprisingly small splash. She reappeared not long afterward, just her head above water, and he saw she had something large, black and sleek clutched in her jaws. She swam back to him, enjoying the cool water on her overheated skin and revelling in the chance to cool off. When she trotted back out onto the shore, he saw she was carrying something that looked like a fish, but was larger than a horse.

She devoured its greasy flesh, and then crunched its bones when she was done. Reiser's original fears of dragons always returned when he watched the dragoness eat. By the time she was done, it was growing dark so she dismantled a nearby tree, snapping its mighty branches like kindling, and leaving half of it piled where it had once stood, broken into pieces small enough for Reiser to carry, and lit the rest ablaze just beyond the high tide line.

"The fire will keep you warm," she said. "I shall sleep in the mountains tonight, as the cold air improves my rest. With no prospect of stopping until we reach the shore, I must be well-rested before we leave. With nothing but sand and ocean around you, the fire will not burn out of control, so I believe you will be safe if left alone for one night, so long as the gales do not return."

With that, she retreated to the heights of the mountains behind him.

The journey across the sea was a long one and they set out before dawn. Reiser was amazed by the dazzling, blinding water stretching out as far as he could see in all directions, and in the afternoon was treated to a distant thunderstorm with brilliant and violent lightning. He had been able to see the dark blot of the storm most of the afternoon and could still see it almost until they found the other shore just after dusk.

This new land was a marshy plain, humid and warm with no shortage of biting insects buzzing around his ears. They seemed to be leaving the dragoness alone, but she was miserable in the heat, sleeping directly in a marsh that night. The marshland soon gave way to a gentle rolling plain, much like Dionelle's homeland, before becoming very arid and sandy. The dragoness didn't mind the desert though because she could climb beyond its heat during the day and the nights were frigid.

On the fifth day, when the scorching sun was at its highest peak, the dragoness broke through a cloud deck and the Red Mountains suddenly spread out before them. Reiser was in complete awe of the view— unlike anything he had ever seen before. He had expected the mountains to be the same as the red sandstone formations of the desert they had passed through, but the colour of this mountain range was a colour far less natural than red sandstone and was brilliant, shimmering crimson.

"Ruby dust," the dragoness explained when she noticed his surprise.

"It is truly a majestically fitting landscape for your kind to call home."

"We never tire of its beauty and I long for it when I am in other lands," she admitted.

Reiser imagined that he would do the same, even if he were to succeed in rescuing his wife and return their realm to normalcy and live for another century.

"I might take up painting as a hobby and devote the rest of my days to capturing this beauty."

"That is something we had never considered," the dragoness mused. "Perhaps it would do us well to honour more of your people— particularly your artists—with a view of our mountains. It would please me to no end to see dragon chambers painted with these landscapes. I believe it would make me yearn for them a little less, and make my business with humans more pleasant."

"The dragon chamber in the Wizards Guild was stunning."

"Yes," she replied with a smile. "It is second only to the king's hall in Golden Hill. That one has been painted to resemble these mountains, though I don't know how the artist ever encountered our land. Few humans have."

As Reiser watched the shimmering mountains pass below, he felt a sense of loss—that his people were losing out on one of the world's profound treasures. He hoped the dragoness did bring more humans to the mountains so they could experience it and share it with others. He was beginning to understand why they valued beauty so much.

Less than an hour later, he could see something in the distance outshining the mountains, and thought perhaps it was a glacial lake on a plateau catching the brilliant sunlight, but as they grew nearer it began to take shape and he could see other structures around it as well. The light seemed suspended at dizzying heights above a wide valley, but when a cloud passed in front of the sun, dulling the light, he realized that he was seeing one massive structure spanning across the entire valley. It wasn't exactly one structure, but four arched towers that rose up out of the sheer cliff face of four opposing mountains—one for each direction—intersecting above the centre of the valley and twisting around each other as they spiralled to unimaginable heights.

The east-west towers were made of diamond, giant prisms catching the sunlight and dispersing it throughout the valley and surrounding peaks, and the north-south towers were made of gleaming obsidian, catching the refracted light of their sister towers and reflecting them like the night sky captured in glass. Spires and majestic cupped balconies dotted the hollow towers, licking skyward like one immense flame caught in gemstone. The cliffs of the mountains surrounding the valley were lined with similar but smaller towers, gracefully reaching skyward in blazing sapphire, amethyst, emerald, amber and even more ruby.

Each balcony was an entrance for a different dragon, with low, wide tunnels carved smoothly into the hard surfaces, and each spire a lookout point for the dragons to perch on and take rest while still observing the majestic scene from unfathomable heights. The smaller, coloured towers were homes to different flights and the grand arch was the home of the Dragon Superiors and their counsel where the dragoness was taking him.

"Mistress, you absolutely must bring all the world's artists here. I beg you," he murmured in awe. "If I free Dionelle, will you bring her here?"

"I will," she promised.

"The others won't object?"

"Now that we've broken tradition by bringing you here, I see no reason not to bring others. Your sense of wonder heightens my joy of being home."

"There is so much beauty to see here. How have the other dragons been swayed so quickly in their opinions regarding humans?"

"My influence is limited because I am young and have no hatchlings, but I am respected and in the fifth rank of seven. You are familiar with our circles of rank?"

"Yes, Mistress. Ondias explained to me that you have seven circles with most of your kind in the seventh rank and the superiors in the first."

"That is correct. I was the mistress of the sixth rank until some recent gains with the Dunhams won me entry to the fifth rank. I will not be able to move beyond the fourth rank until I have a brood of hatchlings, but coming as far as I have so quickly has enabled me to earn respect from my superiors."

"That is impressive. Your quick rise through the ranks gained you enough influence to bring a human to your city?"

"Not on its own. The Dragoness Superior was willing to hear my idea based on my rising influence, but the gravity of the situation is what truly swayed her decision to have you brought here. It has become clear that the situation with the elements must be rectified and after discussing many possibilities, the counsel decided that sending you to retrieve your wife was our surest chance of success."

"Because you can't directly challenge the fire demons who are the source of your power."

"That is correct. We cease to exist if we do nothing, but we cease to exist if we cross the demons."

"From what I understand from Ondias, this sense of diplomacy you have is rare among your kind. Do you hope it will carry you to Dragoness Superior one day?"

Reiser saw a spark in her eyes before she answered.

"I have no ambitions to be Dragoness Superior, but I do hope to one day gain entry to the first rank. The rank of superiors is allowed to live in these mountains year round because there are only seven of them and the surrounding forests are bountiful enough to support so few dragons."

She swooped onto one of the large balconies on the northern tower, blending in with the obsidian almost entirely, and slipped into the wide hallway that spiralled around the entire length of the tower. It joined other hallways toward the centre and, as they went farther down, they gathered more halls and the space became larger. It was full of other dragons and eventually opened into their central main chamber, where the counsel was waiting.

The Dragon Superiors were standing in a tight circle in the middle of the vast chamber—four females and three males—while other dragons were entering the chamber from all points and crowding in behind the Superiors according to their circle of rank. The dragoness left Reiser in the centre and joined the other dragons of the fifth rank near the outer edges of the circle. It was hard to tell from where he stood, but there were easily a hundred dragons gathered at the heart of the spiralling towers, and thinking about the size of the suspended dragon city made Reiser's head spin.

The Dragoness Superior, pure white as fresh snow with silvery blue accents on her wings and horns, was the first Superior to address him.

"Human, please forgive our haste, but I'm sure you understand our need to skip formalities and introductions."

"Yes, Mistress, the situation has been explained to me and we lack the time for proper manners."

She nodded, "As long as you understand. We will begin immediately. Do not be alarmed by any of the sensations you experience, though they may be overwhelming. You will likely respond best if you lie down."

Reiser was already dwarfed by the huge creatures and the impossible chamber they occupied and didn't think heeding the advice could make him feel more intimidated than he already was. He spread out on his back on the smooth, cold floor—a swirl of obsidian and diamond—and closed his eyes. The heat of so many dragons gathered in one place made the air of the room stifling and he welcomed the refreshing feel of the cool stone at his back.

The dragons began their spellwork immediately and Reiser could hear a strange, throaty hiss reverberating in the stone and imagined them all with their heads tilted back, breathing their flame at the lofty ceiling— one giant blaze licking at the impossibly perfect ceiling. The heat of the room intensified and washed over Reiser like a summer day, soothing him and bringing him to the fields of his childhood where he would lie and watch the clouds passing.

They suddenly fell silent, the hiss echoing out of existence, but the air continued to hum with the power of their concentration and felt heavy, like he had been submerged in a hot bath. He took a deep, gasping breath, and when he realized he could still breathe unhindered, the fear of drowning and suffocation passed. He felt the vibration of the spell reverberating through the floor beneath him, setting his whole body abuzz in the warmth. It melted through him until he was shrouded in the comforting warmth, like a warm blanket on a winter's day. The heat coursing through him intensified and became dizzying, like the height of a fever, until he felt like the floor was spinning and he would be flung right out of the chamber. He understood now why he had been instructed to lie down. He kept his eyes squeezed shut and concentrated on each slow, deep breath until the dizziness finally subsided.

He didn't even realize the dragon spell had ended until the dragoness spoke to him again.

"Human, you may stand now."

He still felt intensely warm, though not uncomfortably so, and could see nothing different about himself or his surroundings when he opened his eyes and slowly stood again. His body still felt weighed down, like it was trying to sink into the floor, but he wasn't sure if it was plain fatigue or the protection spell still at work.

The black dragoness he was accustomed to was now standing next to the white one and finally spoke to him.

"We are going to send you to the fire realm now," she said. "As empress, your wife will be in the heart of their realm and we can send you there, but not directly to her court. You will stand out, though the demons will be unable to harm you. You can request discourse with the empress and any demons you encounter will be obliged to bring you to her. However, she is not obliged to entertain your request and they may expel you from their realm."

"We will send you now," the Dragoness Superior said. "Be still."

Reiser flinched as she leaned forward to breathe fire on him, engulfing him in flame. The heat of the blaze didn't touch him and all he could feel was the blast of air rushing past him and the unwavering but comfortable heat of the warding spell. He could see nothing but the intense light of the fire and heard nothing over the roar of the flame, but then everything shifted and the light became less intense, giving shape to the flame around him. The very ground beneath his feet had become fire and he realized he was now in the fire realm.

Everything was fire and incessant light, with no shadow to give his surroundings any definition as he cautiously took a few steps forward, trying to gauge distance. He could make little sense out of the scene before him, unsure if he was in some kind of wilderness or in the middle of a demon city. The only movement was the gentle flicker of the surrounding flames that bewildered him with their solid nature. Even the ground beneath his foot appeared as a raging pyre. Shuffling his feet, he continued to move forward, until he finally saw something skulk from behind a nearby blaze and begin hissing at him, like drops of water hitting hot coals.

It took him a moment to realize that the long, low creature—like a small crawling dragon—was a fire demon. He couldn't speak its language or understand anything it was saying, though he recognized the tone as one of warning. He only hoped it would understand him.

"I request the presence of your empress. Please bring me to her."

It hissed something else, and others began to emerge from the flame and light around him.

"I wish to see Dionelle," he insisted.

The demons surrounded him and began to prod at him with their fiery hands, unable to break through the warding spell to actually touch him. They tested him for a moment and then began to move, herding him somewhere. He hoped it was to Dionelle. Even if they couldn't understand him, they must see the resemblance—the human resemblance—he shared with their empress and he hoped they would bring him there as a curiosity if nothing else.

As he slowly walked among them, he began to discern one object from another and the ground from the sky, but only by overall shape, or slight variances in brightness and colour. The intense light of the realm was searing and his head grew heavy from the strain on his eyes, even though he hadn't stopped squinting against it since the Dragoness Superior had lit him ablaze.

He had been able to discern the horizon, as the sky was a much brighter yellow-white than the orange hues of the ground and buildings, and the demons were escorting him to a very large, blazing building that reached skyward and dwarfed everything else he could see. He was relieved to finally enter the building, no matter how imposing it seemed, because despite the heat and brilliance lingering, the inside took on a more solid form than outside. Walls, floors and doorways had definition and burned deep orange and red, rippling like hot coals in a gentle breeze. The halls and chambers the demons took him down formed a massive labyrinth and Reiser hoped they were truly taking him to Dionelle because he would never find his way out on his own.

Finally, they brought him up a twisted staircase that opened into a massive chamber of fire with burning white floors. There was a large ember throne at the opposite end of the room and he saw a white form lounging in it—a human form that could only be Dionelle.

The demons hissed something and she raised her head and swung her long, pale legs off of the armrest to sit upright and receive her guest. Her clothing hadn't benefitted from the dragons' warding spell the way his had, and had burned away the moment she had entered the fire realm. Her eyes were completely amber now, with no hint of the blue flame he had loved so much, and she was still thin, even more so than Reiser remembered, but his eyes were immediately drawn to the swell of her abdomen.

"Dionelle!" he blurted. "You're with child!"

"Am I?" she replied absently, her voice flat and hollow, disinterested. She showed no emotion and little recognition. "My good servants say you were trespassing in my lands, an unwelcome stranger. Tell me who you are and how you came to my world."

Her words knocked all sense of hope from him and he staggered. She had no idea who he was and he had no idea how to make her remember and convince her to come home.

"It's Reiser," he stumbled. "Reiser Ovailen—your husband. The dragons sent me to find you."

"Husband? Dragons?" she replied, confused, contemplating the very meaning of the words.

"Please, Dionelle, you must remember. You have not been gone that long! What have they done to you?"

"I am the Fire Empress and there is no emperor to these lands. You are an imposter."

"I am no emperor," he replied quickly. "I am a simple rancher from Pasdale, here to collect my wife."

"I have not seen your wife," she said, growing apathetic.

"Dionelle, please, listen to me! Hear me and see me! It's Reiser. You know me. We were married nearly a year ago in the temple near the house you grew up in. The day was warm and the temple was refreshingly cool, despite your sister's simmering rage. Do you remember your jealous sister, Vyranna? She is the reason you are here. Will you remain here and let her win this foolish game?"

"My sister will be dead soon," Dionelle said, devoid of all emotion. "Her madness will consume her."

"How can you say that with such wicked calm? You always loved your sister and long defended her despite her malice toward you."

"My family has been ruined by my sister's madness. My mother loves only her son now, having let go of both her daughters."

"That's foolishness! Sharice and Cusec are worried sick about you. They have been pining for your safe return, as have I. After all this time, when everyone else wrote you off as dead, I refused to believe it and continued to search for you. The dragoness helped me. She needs you back in our lands, where you belong."

"I am the Fire Empress, I belong here."

"You are my wife and Pasdale's dragon whisperer. You belong in Pasdale with me where you can hold counsel with the dragoness again. Don't you wish to hear dragonsong again?"

"Dragonsong? It is beautiful, isn't it?" she said, a brief reminiscent smile touching her lips, recognition flashing in her eyes. A flicker of blue passed through her amber irises.

"It was a tremendous honour for them to play it for you. What songs do the demons play for you?"

"They have no use for music. This is a world of light and warmth."

"The light and warmth are empty, Dionelle. There is nothing for you here, please come back with me."

"You don't need me," she snapped, the blue in her eyes becoming constant. Recognition was slowly returning, memory creeping in, and with it came anger. "I won't come back and have you belittle the things I love."

"Dionelle, I have seen the dragon city in the Red Mountains! Do you think they would show that to me if I didn't respect their ways?"

"No human has seen the dragon city. Do not lie to me!"

"How do you think I can survive in this realm? I am purely human and not immune to the flame around us the way you are. The dragons enchanted me to withstand the heat and they needed to bring me to their city to do it. The dragoness promised to bring you there, if you will only return to our world. She would not lie."

"But *you* would," Dionelle said bitterly, her expression darkening.

"I have never lied to you," he insisted.

"You are lying to me as you stand before me! You do not need me and neither do the dragons or my family, so why have you come here?"

"You are my wife and I love you. I need you to come home."

"You do not need me—I have been replaced and forgotten. I have seen it."

"Just think—if that were true I wouldn't be here. No one has replaced you and I don't know why you would think such a thing."

"I have seen it!" she shouted, jumping to her feet in anger.

She hissed something at one of the demons standing nearby and it approached her cautiously, holding out a ball of light. Images began to form in the light and Reiser watched on in amazement as he saw Ondias tending the fire in his house. The image remained of Ondias, but shifted into the past and showed her darting up the stairs of his house to the bedroom and giving Reiser a devious look. Out of context it certainly looked suspicious, but he immediately recognized it as the night Ondias had come to help him sort through Dionelle's life to find clues of her whereabouts.

The image remained that of Ondias, but shifted again to a grey stone hall and her standing before the dragons, speaking with them. It quickly shifted again, still showing Ondias, but this time she was smiling in front of a warm hearth, speaking with Sharice. Finally, it shifted entirely to show Sharice and Cusec in the kitchen, smiling over their chores.

"These are misleading half-truths," Reiser said. "You must see that! Cusec is growing up and helping your mother more as a result. They are content with life as it is, but miss you dearly! That ball of light does not show how thin and grey your mother has become since, or how she lies awake at night wondering if you are dead and where you might be—if she will ever see you again."

"And what about Ondias? Smiling at you over meals at the table we are supposed to share and giving you such playful glances on the way to the bedroom and conversing so comfortably with my mother. She was my best friend!"

"She *is* your best friend and came to the house to help me understand the dragons. I gave her dinner in exchange for her knowledge. She was only in our room once and that was to search for the letters from your mother. She's been helping me try to find you and helped me find the letters from Sharice. That was how I found out about what happened to your father and how you are part demon because of it, and the dragoness used that information to send me here. Ondias is in our house now, keeping a blaze in the hearth so that we can return there together. She was only at your mother's house to hide from Lady Karth's wrath, while she waited for aid from the Wizards Guild."

"And with the dragons?" Dionelle snapped, barely hearing anything he had said and her tone accusatory.

"While I was visiting your mother to get answers from her, Lady Karth kidnapped Ondias to try to force her into dragon whispering. That ball of light doesn't show Ondias inciting the wrath of the dragoness and risking the gallows for refusing to take your place. The dragoness plucked Ondias from death and has been helping to keep her safe from the Dunhams' treachery ever since. The dragons have also pressed the king to remove the Dunhams from power and he has agreed!

"All of this for you and because of you, Dionelle, so do *not* tell me that I am a liar! The dragons have broken most of their conventions in order to see you safely returned. They have spoken at great length with both me and Ondias, have been working in league with the Wizards Guild, have slept in our fields to keep me safe from the Dunhams' treason charges levelled against me, and have even allowed me—a plain, untalented human—into their city! They are even learning patience with our ways, Dionelle—*patience*! And don't you see that I've had to learn their conventions to know just how much they're breaking them? I have learned enough to be able to teach even Ondias, and the black dragoness even brought me to her home in the Great Mountains. You always told me that you were safe with the dragons, and I know now that they are powerful allies."

She watched him carefully, but saw no lies in his expression and she sank thoughtfully back into her throne, suddenly turning away from him, looking distraught.

"They really brought you to their city?" she asked, finally looking at him again. She was confused, but finally sounded normal.

"It was the easiest way they could protect me from the fire and send me here. It took the entire dragon counsel and most of the dragon community to summon the power to both enchant me and send me to this realm."

"They have done so much just to find me."

"Yes. I have met many of the black dragoness's Superiors—right up to the dazzling white Dragoness Superior in the counsel of Dragon Superiors."

"Describe it to me. Tell me what you saw in the mountains."

"The Red Mountains are glittering scarlet and the dragoness tells me they are infused with ruby dust. It's a vast mountain range and the Great Mountains near Boidossen's cabin pale in comparison. The dragon city is at the heart of the mountains, suspended above a wide valley. There are four towers—two each of diamond and obsidian—that intersect above the valley and intertwine as they reach to unfathomable heights far above the clouds. There are no roads and only wings will take you into the towers, which are all balconies and spires for the dragons to perch upon."

She wore an expression of awe and concern and reached out to touch his face.

"Reiser, for someone who has been blessed with such a tremendous honour from the dragons, you look terrible. You're filthy! What's happened to you?"

"I spent five days in the wilderness on the journey from our house to the dragon city. I spent the nights sleeping under dragon wings and ate only what the dragoness could catch for me. I haven't properly slept since midwinter when I saw you last. Please, come home."

"You will let me hold counsel with the dragons? You will let me be a dragon whisperer?"

"Dionelle, I have essentially been the dragon whisperer in your stead! That must mean something. I have come to trust the dragons deeply, especially when they have done so much to help me in your absence. They need you back as much as I do. I see now that any danger you may have faced from the dragons was the fault of Lady Karth, and she will be removed from power very soon, if she hasn't been already."

"I can talk to the dragons without her?"

"Yes. I sincerely hope that the king will find someone a little wiser to represent him. After the Dunhams kidnapped Ondias and tried to force her into dragon whispering when the dragons knew you were still alive, it was just too much. The Dunhams charged Ondias with treason when she refused, and had her at the gallows when the dragons swooped in to save her. It was more cruelty than anyone could bear and the wizards finally united with the dragons in the cause to have the Dunhams removed. They took the campaign to the king and finally made him agree," he explained, and sighed wearily. "I have seen so much since you left and I just want you home where it is safe and quiet."

"It is safe and quiet here," she said. "It is so warm, not like the bitter cold of home. I don't want to leave. Can't you stay with me?"

"I could, at least for a time, but I will not last long, and neither will the rest of the world."

"What do you mean?"

"Dionelle, you are human. You don't belong here."

"I am part demon, this place is part of me and it feels safe and familiar. I do belong here."

"You only survive here because of your fire immunity. It was an enchantment left on you after the demon left your father, but at your core you are human. Your presence here is tearing all the worlds apart and our realm is close to collapse. All of the realms are colliding, and it will be catastrophic, leaving little left alive afterward. I will not survive, nor will any human. You might, at least for a little while, but I'm certain the child you carry will perish."

Her eyes grew wide at his words and her gaze fell to her large belly. She choked back a surprised sob and looked away quickly—tears streaming down her cheeks and sizzling into evaporation before they got far.

"My stars! How long has it been? How long have I been here? When did this happen?"

"Dionelle, you were last with me before midwinter and that was five months ago."

"No!" she cried out desperately, hugging her knees to her chest and weeping openly now.

Reiser moved to her side and took his cloak off, not knowing if it would stay enchanted away from his body, but risking it anyway. He wrapped it around her shoulders, relieved that it didn't burn away, and sat on the arm of her throne so he could hold her close for the first time in many long months. Just to be able to hold her again, he almost didn't care what happened next.

"Please, come home with me. Return our world to its proper balance and help the dragons deal with the nobles."

"Five months," she gasped through her sobs. "I have little memory of what happened before I got here and no memory of the time passing. It's all a blur of warmth and light, but everything seems so much better in that warm blur."

"It's a lot to consider," he agreed. "I know you had hoped to put motherhood off, but you will be okay. It's easy to continue to let yourself be manipulated by this world, to just not think and remain wrapped in its warmth, but there is so much for you in our world."

She leaned into him, still sobbing as she wrapped her arms around her middle, around the swell of a child she had only just noticed. When she leaned against him, her touch ignited a new kind of heat that he sensed over the kiln of the fire realm—a concentrated ball of heat against his chest and he remembered the pendant he had been wearing since finding it as he searched through her things so many weeks ago. He undid the clasp at the back of his neck and pulled the pendant out where she could see it.

"Do you remember the day we were married?" he asked. "Not your sister's hateful ugliness, but how exciting it was? Do you remember how eager you were? Did you realize how nervous I was?"

"Nervous? You looked fine."

"I was always an instant away from running out the door I was so nervous, but every time I thought I would flee, I looked over to you and you were smiling and confident and all of my concerns melted away. Without your confident smile these last months I've just wanted to run, but I have nowhere to go. Do you remember the light?" he asked, holding up the pendant.

"It was so bright."

"It bathed us in its calm warmth and soothed any fears we had left. We danced and ate well into the night. When your sister said all those awful things to you on our wedding night, you came downstairs and we curled up tight on your mother's small sofa. Do you remember how you felt?"

"I was nervous about leaving them, but I felt safe with you."

"It's like our wedding day all over again—full of nervousness, but less uncertainty this time. You know what's waiting for you. A friend and a husband, a career, and the dragons. I have met so many dragons and so many wizards since you've been gone and they're all waiting for you to come back. Even without Boidossen, there are many of your peers left to help you through difficulties."

"Without Boidossen? Has he released me from my duties? Did I gain entry to the Guild?"

Reiser looked away for a moment, uncertain of what to say. "He's gone," he said at last. "Your sister had him murdered the day you were brought here."

She shook her head, denying and remembering at once, and fresh tears began to sizzle on her cheeks.

"I'm sorry, Dionelle. His murderers have been punished, I assure you."

She nodded, but was weeping quietly.

"Before he died, you passed your assessments and your entrance has been accepted. You are a full fledged Guild member now, and you will have many peers to help you master your craft. But you need to come home."

"Reiser, I've lost five months!"

173

"But you haven't lost it—don't you see that? Life has and hasn't gone on without you. From the moment I discovered you were missing, I have put my life on hold and the dragons forgot about their business as they concentrated on finding you. None of them remember a dragon whisperer they were so fond of. Return with me now and the only thing that will have changed is the season and your waistline, I promise you."

She turned away from him, still sinking into despair and her eyes began to fog over with amber—he was losing her again. She had lost so much time to that realm that it would be difficult for her to adjust to the return home, even if everything was waiting just as she had left it. The death of her master and the impending arrival of a child were certainly complicating things and Reiser was desperate to set her mind at ease.

"Your family is sure to come visit us when they find out you are back. I wager they will stay to help with the baby when it arrives and then you will have help and get to see your family again. I'm certain the dragons will welcome our child. Do you know how much they adore children?"

"They do?"

"One night over dinner, Ondias brought up your fear of motherhood and told me you were being ridiculous because the dragons would help you rear a child if you'd let them. Human children are perhaps the biggest mystery of all to dragons and they will watch them play and grow the same as they will watch their treasures sparkle or a beautiful artist at work. Please, my love, at least look at me."

Her gaze had gone inward though and he wasn't certain she heard him anymore. He gently took her chin and turned her head to face him, relieved to see some of the blue flicker in her gaze, even if it was only a brief spark.

"You said when you came back from your winter apprenticing that things would get better, and you were right. I did what you asked of me and even made some new comrades who will be delighted to meet you and exchange knowledge. But you have to go home for it to happen. You've been so uncertain about having a place in the world and I know you wanted to put off children until you had established yourself as a sorceress, but believe me, you are firmly established as Pasdale's dragon whisperer."

"I miss the dragons."

"They need you."

"Do you need me?"

"Finding you has consumed me for five months. I will not leave here without you, even though it would mean my death. It's spring now, but nothing at home has changed and it will be just like you are returning from your apprenticing."

"You know it won't be that easy."

"Things have changed, but not much and you still have lots of time to readjust to home and marriage before you'll be thrust into motherhood. It will be okay. Please, my love, come home."

She shook her head, terrified and uncertain, and tried to look away from him, but he cupped her cheek and kept her from turning away. She couldn't maintain his gaze and looked down, noticing the pendant he still held in his other hand. She reached out to touch it, letting her fingertips graze its dark, glassy surface. The silver light trapped within continued to swirl, but brightened and intensified under her touch, and she could feel its heat as a contrast to the fire of her realm.

"I was nervous too. At the ceremony—I was scared in front of all those people, my whole town. But it was so exciting too and this light was such a thrill. I forgot about it. It was buried under everything else. Under Vyranna's jealous madness, and your meddling, and everyone expecting me to jump into motherhood, and Lady Karth's cruelty, and the dragons' concerns, and the truth about my father."

"Your sister is gone—lost to her madness—and I will not meddle. You have a place among wizards now and I think you will really like Nandara because she wields fire too. Lady Karth will be gone soon and the dragons admire you far too much to let the nobles cause grief for them or you. Remember this light, Dionelle. Do you still love me?"

Her hand fell away from the pendant as she moved, presumably to embrace him, but as soon as she broke contact, her eyes clouded over with amber and she froze for a moment, confused. She sat back on her throne, her expression empty, and demons began to gather around them. He could feel electricity in the air, and realized the demons were working unseen to keep Dionelle clouded in doubt.

"Dionelle? Please, my love! See me. Come home."

She looked around at him, almost like she was seeing him for the first time and Reiser crumbled when he realized all the ground he had gained had been undone in a moment.

"It is time for you to leave my lands. You are trespassing."

"Let me stay," he begged. "I will remain silent at your side, like a jester or pet."

"I have no need for your presence."

"I do not wish to return home without you. Let me remain here. You need not pay me any attention. Please, I beg you, do not send me from your presence."

"If you do not return to your kingdom of origin, I will have you executed!"

Demons closed in around him, pulling him away from her and clearly trying to harm him again, growing infuriated at their failed attempts. Reiser struggled and broke free, rushing back to her side and clutching her shoulder. She pulled away from him angrily, and a swirl of fire spun up around them as she began to hurl spells at him. None of her firecraft could harm him any more than the demons' could. She bared her teeth and hissed, resorting to a different kind of magic—that of her home realm. Reiser felt the pain of it this time, but the memory of alternative magic brought another blue spark to her eyes. The demons were around them again, pulling Reiser away as Dionelle continued her spell assault, sending painful jolts like lightning through his body.

He had one chance left. Clenching the pendant tightly, he lunged, able to break free from the demons and using the momentum to carry him back to her despite her cruel spells. He clasped one of her outstretched hands, the pendant pressed between their palms, and the onslaught of her spells finally ceased. He had little energy left, but pulled her closer to him, finally catching her gaze again. Her eyes flickered from amber to blue—emotions, memories and the demons' deceit warring—but she maintained eye contact this time and with her other hand she reached up to touch his cheek.

She searched his expression for a moment, finally seeing the truth and accepting it despite the difficulties, and she slid her hand behind his head and pulled his face to hers, kissing him with an intensity they had both forgotten. For a brief moment the silver light escaped the pendant and shrouded them both in warmth and familiarity far different from the heat of the fire realm—blanketing them in their love for each other. His hand slid around her back while the other clutched her long white hair. She finally pulled away from him, but only slightly, to rest her head against his chest and wrap her arms around him as the silver light evanesced.

"I can't remain a slave to this empty heat any longer," she said, not looking up, not wavering in her embrace. Reiser heard true strength in her voice for the first time since before midwinter. "I have things to do at home—a child to prepare for and a flight of dragons to tend."

Finally, she eased out of his embrace, standing tall to face the demons gathering in her throne room. Aware of her nudity now, she pulled Reiser's cloak firmly around her and addressed her subjects with a strong resolve Reiser had begun to believe he would never see again. Her eyes were clear, lively blue flames as she spoke.

"I thank you for the honour of elevating me to Empress, but this is a role I must now denounce. I am human and do not belong on the Throne of Fire. You dethroned an Emperor to make way for me and I restore him now."

She stepped away from the throne, pulling Reiser with her as she did. There was confusion and some anger at her words, but little they could do without the new Emperor to give them a command. The pair of humans would be long gone before the Fire Emperor could be summoned back to his throne.

Dionelle pulled flame out of the very air around them and held a small blaze in her hand, concentrating on it until its intensity became blinding.

"Ondias has a fire burning?" she asked Reiser.

"Yes."

"Then it's time to go home."

She threw the radiant ball of flame at their feet and it erupted into a fireball and a portal back to their world. Dionelle pushed him ahead of her and they stumbled over the logs and tripped onto the rug in front of the hearth. Ondias cried out in terror, startled from her slumber—it was the middle of the night.

"Dionelle—your hair!" she gasped, as she realized it was them.

Reiser was shocked to see that Dionelle's hair was the same auburn as her mother's, only streaked with the purest white. Though she was still pale, her skin had a natural tone now and her eyes were still blue, but not as unnaturally vivid and the amber ringing her irises was much less prominent than it had ever been.

"You are a new mystery for the dragons now," Reiser said, baffled by her altered appearance.

He heard another gasp from Ondias and turned to see her staring at Dionelle's pregnant belly, and he gave her a stern look and a subtle but firm shake of his head to keep her quiet. Dionelle was still too busy marvelling over her dark locks and new skin to notice the other two and Reiser didn't want to startle her with a reminder of the baby until she was ready to face reality in full again.

"The rug!" Ondias shouted suddenly, pointing to a log that had spilled from the hearth on their return and began to lick flame at the rug nearby.

Dionelle rushed over to it and grasped the log to throw it back into the hearth, but just as quickly recoiled with a startled cry.

"What is it?" Reiser asked.

"It hurt," she said, puzzled. She looked down at her hands to see that they hadn't been damaged. Despite the pain, she picked up the burning log and placed it back in the fire. Reiser was still protected by the dragon spell and helped her stamp out the charred rug and toss all of the stray embers back into the fireplace.

"Pain, but no damage," Dionelle said, still looking at her hands as if she expected them to be blistered.

"There will be plenty of time in the coming weeks for you to puzzle over this with the dragons and other wizards."

"I bet Nandara will get to the bottom of it," Ondias said.

Reiser nodded and took Dionelle's hands, drawing her attention away from the changes.

"I will run you a hot bath and go find you some fresh clothes."

"You could probably use the same," Dionelle said, running her fingers along the dirty hem of his collar.

"There will be time for that later."

"I'll go let the dragons know that she's back and then help her with the bath. You get some rest," Ondias said to him.

"Can't the dragons wait until morning?"

"There's one sleeping just outside the door, waiting for news of your return so he can bring it to Sharice."

"Very well, let them know."

While Ondias went out to talk to the dragons, Reiser left Dionelle resting on the sofa while he set the cauldron of water on the fire. By the time he had retrieved a couple of buckets of cold water from the outdoor pump, the cauldron was boiling and he dumped it into the bath, mixing in the colder water until the temperature was comfortable. He poured in some cleansing oils and then coaxed Dionelle from her seat and to the hot bath. He met Ondias at the stairs as he was on his way to fetch some clean robes for Dionelle.

"She didn't know she was pregnant until I got there today," Reiser whispered. "She lost a lot of time so try to steer away from talking about any of it. Just let her know how happy you are to have her back, because she almost wouldn't come."

"What did they do to her?"

"I'm not certain, but there was extensive trickery and she's bound to be unsteady for a few days. How long have I been gone?"

"Six days."

He nodded. "Good, that means time was passing the same in the fire realm as it does here. She's still lost a lot of time."

"Sharice will likely be here tomorrow."

"Good, that will help her."

He sent Ondias back to Dionelle and went upstairs, exhausted, but unwilling to rest yet. He decided to just bring Dionelle her bedclothes, and changed into his as well before going back downstairs. The two women were unusually silent when he got back to them, but he didn't know what to say to get the conversation going. He washed his face in leftover water in a basin and felt more refreshed, but the fireproofing enchantment was weighing on him and still made him feel feverish and heavy. He wondered if it was how Dionelle felt all the time.

"Are you all right?" Dionelle asked him, finally breaking the silence.

"Tired. And a little confused," he replied. "I appear to still be enchanted with dragon spell and the sensation is trying my patience. I'm sure everything will look better in the morning when we've had some sleep."

"I've been asleep for five months," she replied. "But I'm still exhausted."

Ondias clearly wanted to talk, to find out what Reiser had seen since leaving his house and to be reassured that Dionelle was all right, but knew she would have to wait for answers. She left them alone and curled up on the sofa again. Away from the energies of the fire realm, Dionelle was incredibly weak and Reiser had to help her out of the tub and to dress. He made sure she ate a bit and took plenty of water before he finally helped her upstairs. He had been guiding her back to the guest room, but she stopped in the hall and shook her head, gesturing toward their room.

"Are you sure?" he asked her.

"Unless you prefer the solitude."

"I've had five months of it and I would prefer to never have you leave my side again."

The blue spark played in her eyes for a moment and she gave him a devious grin.

"I'll cure you of that before long."

He chuckled, relieved beyond belief to know she was largely unchanged by all that had happened.

"Not this time, you won't," he replied, kissing her forehead.

CHAPTER 13

ONDIAS heard the clatter of the wagon in the lane and went out to meet the Joaseras to prepare them for what to expect. Theirs was the first wagon the dragons had let through their guard since Ondias had been charged with treason, and it was likely the last wagon they would let through again until after the Dunhams had been removed. Nandara had assured them all that it would be a matter of days before the king's envoy arrived to remove the Dunhams, and she had also learned that Lady Karth was likely to be tried for treason and for her other crimes of tyranny. The dragoness's testimony about what Lady Karth had done to Dionelle and then to Ondias had gone a long way to sway the king's decision. He was bound to his nephew by blood, but had no loyalties to Lady Karth.

Dionelle was no longer in denial about her pregnancy, but was having a difficult time coming to terms with it and had remained either in bed at Reiser's side or curled up in front of the fire, trying to find her power again. Life had become uncertain for them, and until they could find some routine and normalcy again, it was bound to remain difficult. Nandara had done her best to reassure Dionelle that the loss of power and her new pain sensations when exposed to heat didn't mean that she had lost all her power, but she would likely have to relearn many things.

Dionelle hadn't gone out to talk to the dragons yet either, and that troubled Ondias who had to try to keep the peace with the dragons in Dionelle's stead, reassuring them that Dionelle wasn't snubbing them, but that she was ill and weak from her long ordeal and would need time to recuperate. She was also worried about Reiser. The fireproofing was taking its toll on him and he had almost no energy left, remaining in bed and usually asleep.

Sharice bit her lip at the news, thinking quickly about how to address the situation.

"Cusec, take Fuzzy to see your sister. Soft fur and a cold nose will bring joy to the saddest of souls."

Sharice waited until Cusec was inside before she continued to speak with Ondias.

"It's a lot of change all at once," she said. "She's going to need some time. Have your colleagues had any answers about the change in her appearance or her loss of power?"

"Nandara just left to bring the new information to some other wizards in the Guild. Half the Guild is in the city now, waiting to see if Dionelle returns, and waiting for the lord and lady to be removed from power. Those two still don't know what's in store for them, but I'm glad to know that that horrible woman is going to get what she deserves."

"I can't even imagine what my daughter is going through right now, and I barely know how to approach her."

"Don't treat her differently. Reiser has insisted we carry on as if she's just returned from her apprenticeship—not denying what happened, but downplaying its importance and it seems to be working well enough. But now she's worried about him."

"Did your sorceress friend have any answers about that?"

"It has something to do with the dragon spell, but human wizards know very little about dragon spells. The dragons here had nothing to do with Reiser's enchantment, so we will have to wait for word from the dragon city."

"All right, take me to her. I didn't think I'd ever see her again."

"Mamma! I'm so glad you came!" Dionelle called, springing up from the sofa, leaving Fuzzy and Cusec by the hearth, to embrace her mother. "The puppy is so big now!"

"He's full grown, but still just a silly puppy."

Dionelle was unused to the baby belly getting in the way and it made hugging her mother more awkward than she would have expected. She rubbed her hand over it, both annoyed and fond of it at once, and looked up to Sharice again.

"Looks like you'll get grandbabies after all," she said, trying to be light-hearted, but tears began welling up in her eyes.

"Oh, sweetheart, you'll be okay," she said, stroking Dionelle's newly darkened locks. "And there's certainly no denying you as my daughter now, is there?"

"Vyranna was the only one who ever had any doubts."

"I'm not sure if your sister has any grasp of reality left now, and all she can do is doubt. That awful wizard left her as an empty shell and she's in the king's asylum in Golden Hill right now. That wizard, Vozawr, has been executed, but I don't know what will happen to your sister."

"If she ever regains her sanity, she will likely face grave charges in her role for what happened to me. Murdering a wizard and kidnapping a dragon whisperer are treason."

"Left to rot in an asylum, or a swift death. Neither option seems reasonable," Sharice said with a weary sigh.

"You were always a good mother and Vyranna is responsible for her own actions," Dionelle said.

Sharice nodded, unconvinced. "How is Reiser?"

Dionelle shrugged, "It's hard to say. We're not entirely sure what's wrong. I keep waiting and hoping to hear something from one of the dragons."

"They might be more insightful if you talk to them yourself," Ondias suggested. "You're the rightful dragon whisperer and they have no reason to speak to me in great depth."

"Will they accept me?" Dionelle asked, nervously toying with the ends of her dark hair.

"I've informed them of the change. It doesn't affect your overall beauty and makes you a new mystery for them to solve."

Dionelle nodded and resolutely stepped out into the front yard, waiting there until the dragons noticed her and drew nearer. The blue dragon who had played dragonsong for her was the one to address her.

"We are pleased to see you have returned to us," he said with a small bow.

"It pleases me to be home and to be able to speak with you again. I owe you a countless debt for all that you have done to keep my friends and family safe and to aid them in bringing me home again."

"My mistress seems to believe that it is time we change some of our ways. She has sent a message for you."

"I gladly accept any news you have from her. I have missed her greatly."

"She will be arriving in four days' time to retrieve you and your husband and has asked that you be prepared for the long journey. We informed her of his poor health and it seems he is reacting badly to the enchantment they used to send him to find you. Our kind is unaccustomed to dealing with humans in such a manner and she doesn't believe the spell was properly suited to him. He must rest and take as much water as he can."

"Is there something you can do to help my husband?"

"There are only five of us here, so we lack the power to sway the spell's influence, and without direct knowledge of the enchantment used there is nothing we can do. My mistress will bring him back to the Superiors to remove the enchantment, and she has asked that you be ready for her when she arrives."

"She's bringing me too?" Dionelle's eyes widened in surprise and delight.

"She promised she would. Your husband will need your help during the long journey to the Red Mountains, so now is the time for you to see the dragon city."

"I am not deserving of this honour, but I thank you and am forever in your debt."

"If ever there was a human worthy of our city, it is you. You are always a mystery for us and the Superiors are very curious to hear about your time in the fire realm and to learn what they can of this new change you have experienced."

"IT'S returning to normal," Ondias commented, smiling up at the sun that, for the first time in weeks, wasn't scorching and unbearable.

"How bad did it get?" Dionelle asked, as she watched Fuzzy chase Cusec through the fallow field.

"Not as bad as it could have. The earth demons never really started much mischief before everything started to stabilize again, but the rain and wind and hot and cold would fluctuate worse and worse. Two days before you came home, I felt all four elements at work for the first time. There was a gale and flooding rains, but it was unbearably hot. Then there were ground tremors for a little while. A lot of people thought that the worlds were finally going to tear themselves apart, but it never got any worse than that. And at least it is still early enough in the spring that the planting can be salvaged."

"It must have been terrifying."

"It was for a little while," Ondias admitted. "I think the most frightening prospect was that things wouldn't return to normal once you were back. At least, it was for me. I could accept that it would just escalate and we would all perish before we could truly suffer, but if the weather had continued to swing the way it was, we never would have been able to plant crops and we'd all starve by winter."

"I didn't sense any true malice from the demons when I was there, so it surprises me that they would let everyone perish like that. They must have known what keeping me there was doing. They could have easily lifted the veil of lies, prompting me to head home, or at the very least drive me out on their own."

"You didn't sense a lot of the truth when you were there. I think it would take a great deal of malice to do what they did to Boidossen. I never saw him, but Nandara was at his cabin when they brought him out for his pyre, and Reiser was terribly shaken by it when he found the body. I can't imagine him having to make the three-day journey back here alone with that on his mind plus not knowing what had happened to you."

"I'm thankful to have little memory of that night. It had been normal enough and Boidossen was working on spells in the evening after dinner. I had been in my room getting ready for bed when I heard him scream, but the room was full of demonlight when I got into it and I saw nothing and remember little else until Reiser came to the fire realm."

Dionelle stood and went back into the house to check on Reiser but then she heard Fuzzy barking frantically in the yard. She rushed back out and heard the first of the dragoncries. She was surprised to hear anything as they had been respectful of her requests not to frighten the neighbours anymore, but realized it had been four days since she had spoken to the blue dragon. She glanced around, but couldn't see the dragons approaching yet, though the ones in the yard had begun to respond in kind. She went back inside and up to the bedroom where Reiser was sound asleep despite the noise.

"What's going on?" Sharice asked, wiping his brow with a cold cloth.

"They're here for us. It's time to go so get him up. I will bring our supplies outside and then come back to help you bring him downstairs."

Dionelle had packed two bags—one with some clean clothes and a blanket, and another with some food and cooking supplies. She made sure to keep them small to keep from burdening themselves or the dragons with the extra weight, because she needed to make sure they had all of their waterskins with them to keep Reiser properly hydrated. His temperature continued to climb and when he wasn't asleep he was desperate for water.

"Cusec, bring Fuzzy in and stay inside with Mamma until we've left," she said, setting their bags down. "The dragoness will be impatient and in a hurry when she arrives and may not respond well to Fuzzy's barking."

"The dragons can be so mean," he commented, ushering the dog into the house. "Why do you like to talk to them so much?"

"You just have to learn to ignore them when they're being mean and learn how to talk to them. It's like learning to play music."

"You're a dragon artist then. You work with words instead of paints."

"I guess that's true. It also helps that they can't burn me."

Cusec grinned. "They don't try that anymore though."

"They know better now." She gave him a hug. "And they're being nice to you now anyway because they know they have to keep everyone here safe for now. They are my friends, and when you're friends with someone, it's only polite to be kind to their family."

"But the dragoness will be irritable today. Because of the long journey?"

"Yes. She had to fly for five days to get Reiser to their city only to turn around and fly all the way back, only to make the return journey. That's fifteen days of flying. She's going to be very tired and we're lucky they consider Reiser worthy enough to go through all this trouble for him."

"But it's their fault he's sick."

"Yes, and they understand that. That's why they are helping us. Now come in and help me and Mamma get him outside."

Reiser was awake and alert when Dionelle and Cusec got up to the room, and Sharice was trying to help him stand.

"Five more days, love, and it will be over," Dionelle insisted, draping his arm over her shoulder and pushing into him, pushing him to his feet. Cusec got on the other side of him and Sharice stayed in front of him to help guide him out.

The dragoness had arrived and was pacing outside in the field when they finally reached the front porch. Sharice stayed inside with the dog while Cusec and Ondias helped Dionelle and Reiser out to the dragoness.

"Mistress!" Dionelle called to her. "I am in your debt for all the aid you have provided for us. Is there any way to make this journey easier for you? Will you not stay here and rest while someone else helps us to the city?"

"I have not had the pleasure of your company in far too long, Dionelle, and I will face the exhaustion of this journey to see to it that you arrive there safely. I will have some help, and have found something to make the journey easier on all of us."

The dragoness nodded out into the field where an emerald dragoness with scarlet horns and claws was standing beside what looked like a large basket. It was a wagon that had had the wheels removed and a large, iron carrying handle mounted over top. It would comfortably fit the humans and their possessions.

"My grey and blue companions found the old wagon and made some hasty changes to it so it would be easier to carry you to the Red Mountains and back again. I also have some help to carry it."

"Go in and grab us some cushions and blankets," Dionelle said to Ondias. "We can have a little more comfort after all."

"Bring your own bag, Ondias," the dragoness said. "I believe you have earned the honour of joining us."

Ondias bowed deeply out of respect, but also to hide her shock. "Mistress, I do not deserve this honour."

"If I agreed, I would not have extended the invitation. Now hurry."

DIONELLE and Ondias sat in the wagon, which the dragons had left in a field beside a gentle brook, and watched as the dragons climbed skyward with Reiser. Dionelle was in a panic because Reiser had lost consciousness the day before and hadn't awoken since, so she had been unable to marvel at their surroundings. The dragoness had originally intended to bring all three humans up into the city, but now that Reiser had worsened, they needed to gather the counsel and work on healing him immediately.

"He will be okay," Ondias tried to assure her. "He is very ill, but the dragons are very powerful. Their power increases with their numbers and most of the dragon flights have gathered here to undo the enchantment that has been behind all the problems. That castle above us is full of dragons. Full. Can you imagine? I hope they bring us up there soon!"

"It's so big, I can't believe the sheer size of it," Dionelle replied, finally taking in the scope of the towers, following the arch of one of the obsidian towers as it rose from the mountainside far to their right, disappeared into the clouds and reappeared at the other side of the valley with its foundation in the mountain on that side. She looked behind her and traced the arch of the diamond towers, suddenly feeling insignificant.

Dragoncries were all around them and she could see dragons of every colour of the rainbow streaming from the coloured towers surrounding the valley and heading into the clouds. She had paid little attention to the city as they had approached it because she had been so busy tending to Reiser and was now curious about what it looked like high above them and above the clouds.

The din finally died down and the only sound they could hear was the gentle ripple of the water next to them.

"Are there no animals in this forest at all?" Dionelle asked, growing unnerved by the silence.

"I don't know what would want to live so close to the dragons," Ondias said. "There must be something though. I would expect to see smaller animals as the dragons won't bother to eat those no matter how hungry they get."

Dionelle gave her a sly smile. "I suppose they do have their dignity, but I would rather eat mice than die."

Ondias laughed. "Do you think a dragon could even catch a mouse? Can they even see something that small?"

"It's unlikely. Do you think the stream is safe? Can we drink from it? Or bathe in it? Is the forest safe to forage in? I wish we had thought to bring more food with us."

"I think there's some hare left from last night's dinner. I don't think we should venture too far until we hear back from the dragoness. No human has been here before and there could be countless dangers for us in a place so exotic."

"You're right. The dragoness may not even have the answers."

Dionelle looked up and to the southeast where the full city rose high above them. She was glad that the dragons hadn't left them directly under the towers because it looked so precarious even as it gracefully rose skyward from the mountains. Sitting underneath it, she would have spent the entire time fearing it would collapse at any moment and crush them.

"It's so intimidating," Ondias said, seeing that Dionelle was staring up at the city again.

"Would you expect anything less of a dragon city?"

"I suppose not. Even the mountaintops they choose to call home away from this city are rumoured to be quite spectacular."

"Even the smaller clan towers are huge."

"I wonder if they have any stone structures like these in the Great Mountains, or elsewhere? Do you think you can get the dragoness to open up to you about it?" Ondias asked. "Reiser's description of her home was stunning, but hers is a simple structure and newly built with just the two of them living there. I hope she brings us there on the way home. I wonder how different other towers are. It would be fascinating to learn."

"They seem eager to talk about their culture with anyone who has a genuine interest in learning about them. They keep themselves swathed in mystery but I think it's mostly because very few humans have the sort of genuine interest you have."

"I certainly haven't encountered many dragon scholars who are interested in the dragons beyond keeping them as political allies, or just not offending them enough to provoke a war."

Dionelle picked up a blanket and one of the pillows Ondias had hastily grabbed on her way out the door five days ago, and climbed out of the wagon to lay on the soft, cool grass. She propped the pillow against the side of the modified wagon and sat facing the towers, watching for any sign of the dragons or Reiser. Ondias sat cross-legged beside her, braiding the long grass surrounding them. Dionelle had begun to doze off when a strange vibration rang out from the towers, making them sing out in one clear, high note and the vibration worked down from the towers, into the mountains and across the valley floor.

Dionelle gasped and sat up. "What's going on?"

Ondias was standing now and had taken a few cautious paces towards the city.

"It's strange but calming," Ondias finally said. "I don't think there's anything wrong."

"It's rattling my teeth," Dionelle commented. "And feels so strange in my belly."

"I'm sure they will explain it before long."

She returned to her seat beside Dionelle and the two of them kept staring up at the strange city, in awe of its splendour. They lost all sense of time, but the sun's shadows hadn't moved much when a flurry of dragons rushed out of every entrance and they spotted the black dragoness coming back toward them with Reiser in her clutches. He was still asleep, but his colour had returned to normal and the fever was no longer baking off of him.

"We have removed the enchantment," the dragoness explained, "and applied some of our healing magic to him, but we are not accustomed to healing humans and he will need to rest further in order to recover from the toll his body took while enduring the spell."

"He'll be all right?" Dionelle asked.

"Yes. Let him rest for the afternoon and we will bring you to the city at sunset. I think you will be able to appreciate the glimmer of the towers when the sun is at such a brilliantly coloured angle."

"In these red mountains it must be truly dazzling," Dionelle replied. She was relieved that Reiser would be okay and she was finally able to truly notice their surroundings.

The dragoness helped them flip over the wagon and prop it angled against a tree to give them shelter from any elements they encountered. She made it clear to them that she wouldn't be taking them home until she was rested again and she wanted to make sure they were comfortable for their stay. None of the other dragons were prepared to cater to the humans yet and so she was the only one willing to bring them home.

"Reiser has told me that your kind have made several changes already," Dionelle said. "Will they be more willing to work with our people soon?"

"It will take time still, but they are open to bringing more people like you and Ondias into our city. They're quite eager to have artists here."

"Ondias is very curious about your culture, especially about your city and your homes away from here. Can we see where you live in the Great Mountains?"

The dragoness mulled it over. "If I am not too tired on our trip back to your city, then I will stop to show you my home. For now, I am one of the few still willing to burden myself by aiding you, so you will have to stay here until I am able to make the journey."

"We thank you for your consideration," Dionelle replied. "It is very generous of you to help us during our stay."

"I am not used to being hospitable, but please feel comfortable to make requests of me while you are my guests."

"Mistress, may I speak?" Ondias asked.

"I shall allow it."

"Please tell us about this valley. What creatures live here, and is it safe to forage? If you would be so kind as to enlighten me about your city's history, I would be forever grateful."

The dragoness passed on giving any history, as she was still exhausted and in need of rest, but let the women know about the dangers they might encounter in the forests. The streams were safe and, as Ondias had suspected, they would find only smaller animals in the forest, as anything large enough for dragons to prey on had long ago been driven into extinction. There were some scarlet-coloured berries that they should stay away from and the dragoness discouraged them from eating any roots or grubs, but overall the valley was safe.

ONDIAS and Dionelle stood calmly in the centre of the great hall at the heart of the dragon city, surrounded by the Dragon Superiors. Most of the dragon flights had left for their homes in other ranges spread across the world, but the flight from near Pasdale had stayed behind until the humans were ready to leave. It had been nearly a week since the dragoness had brought the three humans to the city and they were due to go home tomorrow.

It was the second time Ondias and Dionelle had actually been in the towers, with the visit at sunset as their first trek up to the city. That day, they had remained on a balcony with the dragoness until the sun was gone and then she had brought them back to their camp. This was their first time in the great hall before the Superiors, and Reiser, knowing he didn't belong with the dragons as they were his concern only insofar as they were his wife's passion, had stayed behind to rest before the journey home.

The two women were doing their best to maintain a calm demeanour despite how excited and nervous they were. The visit into the city that day had a twofold purpose: the dragons wanted to show them the grandeur of their home, but they also had some answers for Dionelle and they wished to share them with her in the presence of the full counsel.

The black dragoness was nearby, but yielded the floor to her superiors, and the dazzling white Dragoness Superior, sitting on her haunches with her wings folded and her tail curled around the front of her, addressed them instead.

"Ondias, we have heard a great deal about your genuine curiosity and would like to extend another invitation to you to return to our city one day."

"Mistress, I am hardly deserving of such an honour."

"Your curiosity entitles you to that honour, I assure you. We have misjudged your kind as being preoccupied with the mundane aspects of life but it is clear that some of you are more enlightened than we believed. We would like to have more humans like you come to our city to learn our ways. You are a true dragon scholar and deserve only first-hand experience."

"I thank you, Mistress," she said, bowing deeply. "I will do all that I can to help others understand you, as most humans misjudge the dragons as angry and unreasonable beasts. Clearly, you are gracious hosts deserving of respect."

The Dragoness Superior bowed her thanks to Ondias before turning her attention to Dionelle.

"Dionelle, we would like to see you and your husband here again, if you will come."

"I will always accept your invitation," Dionelle replied. "I will not speak for Reiser, as he gets overwhelmed and has certainly delved further into your culture than he ever could have imagined. He is a simple farmer and finds beauty in his family and his work."

"Very well. We have some answers for you at last," the Dragoness Superior said. "We have been able to determine that after your conception, an unusual influence remained of the demon who sired you, as though you were possessed as well. It is the reason your appearance was so extreme and why you were able to survive with child for so long in the fire realm. When you denounced the throne you denounced the lingering effects of your conception, resulting in the dramatic change we see in your appearance. You always had only slight demon in your blood, mixed with the lingering essence, and this is your true form."

She nodded carefully but said nothing so the Dragoness Superior continued.

"We believe that the influence remained because the demon was with your true father for so long. Had anyone realized the truth of your nature sooner, you could have been restored to the proper form we see now. Because of the circumstance of your conception, you were always destined to exhibit some of the demons' traits and that is what we see now, but the lingering effects were left behind in that realm when you returned with your husband. You are still immune to fire and your powers, though diminished since your return, are still quite strong."

"That is a relief to me, Mistress, and I thank you for sharing that information with me. I am forever grateful that you took the time to find the truth."

"You know that we love a mystery because it is a challenge in finding the truth. Solving a mystery is the greatest thing about an enigma in the first place. You will be able to continue to practice your craft and we will see if we can find out any more about the lasting effects. Your child may have some lingering effects as well and we would like to examine the baby."

"I would be honoured to raise my child in your presence so that he or she may grow up knowing about your ways."

"We send you home tomorrow, but understand that circumstances there will improve soon. Once a proper lord or lady has been restored to Pasdale, we will continue our business with the humans."

"I look forward to holding counsel with you," she said with a bow.

EPILOGUE

DIONELLE stood with Ondias for a moment as they watched the painter work his magic on the newly installed marble. The dragons had brought a few ruby slabs from the Red Mountains to decorate the hall and Ondias had done her best to describe the mountain range to the painter.

"What do you think, Mistress?" Dionelle asked.

"I believe Ondias has been doing justice to our kind. We will be certain to bring the young painter to our city to see its beauty firsthand before he puts the finishing touches on the mural."

Dionelle noticed that the artist was grinning wildly, but he remained respectfully silent.

"He would be honoured," she said. "Anyone who appreciates the world's beauty would be honoured by the invitation."

"No one appreciates life's beauty quite like an artist," the dragoness replied. "This lad is a fine artist for his kind."

"Our lady has been carefully choosing her counsel," Dionelle said.

"Lady Zyx has been proving her worth as a representative of the king," the dragoness admitted.

Dionelle glanced at the lady to see her smiling, pleased, but she also said nothing.

"She has quickly agreed with you that Ondias makes an excellent dragon consultant," Dionelle said. "We will have this hall shining alongside the Wizards Guild and Golden Hill. And Ondias is finding work with the Guild and with dragon whisperers and members of foreign courts. She's quite busy."

Lady Zyx, the king's cousin, stood quietly at the edge of the room to oversee the refurbishing of the dragon chamber, and to let Ondias guide the artist, and to let Dionelle do her job talking to the dragons. Lady Zyx had removed the distasteful fireproof glass barrier that the Dunhams had insisted on conducting business from behind. That gesture in itself had helped the new noble set the dragons at ease, but she also consulted with Dionelle separately before she met with the dragons so that Dionelle was fully prepared to represent the nobles without any interference from Lady Zyx. She often wasn't present in the chamber at all when Dionelle met with the dragons.

"I have a dragon whisperer for a reason," she had explained to the dragoness on the only occasion she had spoken to them directly. She preferred to let Dionelle do her job.

Lady Zyx had been installed as the king's representative in Pasdale a mere week after Dionelle, Ondias and Reiser had returned from the dragon city. Lord Dunham was stripped of his titles and exiled long before her arrival and Lady Karth had been executed in Golden Hill for treason shortly after Lady Zyx had begun her reign in Pasdale.

Before ever holding counsel with the dragons, Lady Zyx had been wise enough to gather her advisors and see what changes needed to be made to the existing policies in order to make the dragons more comfortable with her presence. That was how Dionelle brought Ondias into the court, at the insistence of Zev and Nandara, who were impressed with Ondias's dragon knowledge even before she had begun to learn more from the Dragon Superiors directly. Lady Zyx came to Pasdale with only basic knowledge of dragon customs and Ondias had done a great deal to educate the noblewoman since her arrival. In the last month, Ondias had been making regular trips to the Wizards Guild to meet with various wizards and sorceresses, as well as foreign dragon whisperers, to share what she was learning in the dragon city.

Removing the ugly grey stone from the dragon chamber had been Lady Zyx's top priority and today was the first time they had brought the dragons to the palace to see the changes firsthand. They had been holding counsel at Dionelle and Reiser's home and would continue to do so until the chamber was ready to be unveiled. Lady Zyx, a shocking contrast to Lady Karth—with long blonde hair that she kept neatly and ornately plaited, and she preferred simple robes in soft colours over Karth's preference for harsh blacks—insisted on keeping Dionelle informed of the court's wishes, but otherwise let her conduct business with the dragons as she saw fit and Dionelle and the dragons were relieved by their new lady's unintrusive approach.

"Ondias herself did an excellent job reporting the changes to the Dragon Superiors on her last visit," the dragoness said. "I don't expect to return to the city until winter, but they would like to play host to you again soon."

"I'm afraid I will have to decline the invitation until the baby has arrived and is strong enough for travel or to be left with Reiser," Dionelle replied. "I'm sure you understand it would be unwise of me to risk birth in the wilderness or the unfamiliar setting of your city."

Dionelle was reclining in a large, soft chair that had been brought in for her, as she was due to give birth in a matter of days. She sat with her hands on her cumbersome belly and did her best to remain comfortable while talking with the dragoness. She often sat to talk to the dragons now, and they were as eager as she was for the birth of her child.

"You will bring the child to our city?" the dragoness asked.

"I couldn't think of a greater honour. When we're fit for such a long journey, we will come to your city. Has the dragon counsel considered my suggestion?"

"They are considering it, and so far haven't objected to the camp Ondias has set up in the meadow under the city, but it will take some time before they will be willing to accept a permanent human settlement. We will not allow roads in our mountains and few dragons are willing to help ferry in humans. In time, as interest among humans grows and understanding between dragons and humans is strengthened, the camp Ondias has set up will expand."

"Lady Zyx and several of the wizards have expressed interest in nurturing these new bonds between humans and dragons. You have proven powerful allies and we feel in your debt already, but are eager to learn more. The patience you and some of the other dragons have exhibited is truly appreciated by those of us who understand the sacrifices you have made."

The dragoness snorted a thin wisp of flame and grinned a mouthful of teeth in a rare display of emotion.

"I am not sacrificing much, and the curious new friends I have gained certainly make the effort worthwhile. We dragons are beginning to learn the extent of our conceit and that there is beauty and joy in unexpected places. I have every confidence that the others, in time, will learn just how much we have to gain by continuing to allow humans into our world. This very hall is a perfect example of how much joy humans have to offer. The others will learn that we sacrifice very little for the joys of friendship we gain in return."

"Mistress, if you are satisfied with the hall's progress, I believe it's time for me to return home," Dionelle said. "Ondias and Nandara have insisted on inviting minstrels over to send me into motherhood through celebration and I insist that, along with my family, all of my friends be present. Will you do me the honour of joining us this evening? Perhaps you can teach the minstrels something about dragonsong."

"I would like that."

ACKNOWLEDGEMENTS

A lot of people have helped to make this book possible, and a lot of them are listed on the Contributors page. I think it's easiest for me to thank people in chronological order; that way I'm less likely to forget anyone (and no one should get too miffed about not appearing here sooner).

First, I need to thank my family for forgiving my oddball writerly inclinations as I was growing up. I want to thank my husband for his patience, especially during NaNoWriMo, when I tend to disappear for the entire month. And then there's NaNoWriMo itself (nanowrimo.org, if you're curious)! I owe a lot to Chris Baty and all the good folks at the Office of Letters and Light—I owe them six books' worth, actually. I think that this event is a tremendous opportunity for writers and aspiring writers, and *Dragon Whisperer* was written during the insane NaNoWriMo of 2009.

The event also led me to a fantastic writing group whose feedback helped me shape this book into what it has become. So a big thank-you to Alex, Alex, Doug, Matt, Meredith, Miroki and Susan. Thanks to Greg for giving the dragon a chance, and to everyone at Iguana for their hard work and guidance: Jane, Emily, Kathleen, Mehreen, Maya, and Meghan. Extra thanks to Stephanie for a stellar proofread, and to Beth for helping get the word out. And of course, thanks to Laura for being my second set of eyes.

Finally, a special thank-you to the top three contributors to the Indiegogo campaign: Louie Ricci, Sue Ricci, and Rick Thode.

CONTRIBUTORS

Joanna Anderson
Kathryn Anthony
Danielle Arbuckle
Kendra Berni
Alistair Bleeck
Tammy Burns
Jessica Chivers
JoAnn Cleaver
Anna Cologna
Jessica Cowan
Daphne Davey
Gerry Ecker
Abby Egerter
Laura Foster
Jennie Fuller
Marg Gilks
Shelley Goretzki
Rosemary Gretton
Sara Groves
Karen Hardy
Daniella Harrington
Dustin Harrington
Rosa & Kirk Harrington
Jane Hegney
Meredith Heitner
Maxine Henry
Dawn Hunter
Joanne Kasaboski
Karen Kawawada
Eric Klimstra
Amy Knapp
Wen Li
Cat London
Patricia MacDonald
Janet MacMillan

Laura Magalas
Tina McFarlane
Jeanne McKane
Ben & Irene Parkes
Benjamin Parkes
Susan Parkes
Rhonda Parrish
Denise Penney
Tony Reccia
Giuseppina "nonna" Ricci
Louie Ricci
Susanne Ricci
Tano Ricci
Bruno Riccia & Nancy Langlais
Olivia Riccia
Stefauna Riccia
Tina Riddell
Sam Sabko
Troy Sabko
Amber Shaw
Amanda Spakowski
Gael Spivak
Jack & Charlotte Thode
Janice Thode
Mike Thode
Rick Thode
Garret Tracey
Jeremy & Elaine Tracey
Nolan Tracey
Reid Tracey
Ken Turner
Christina Vasilevski
Sharilyn Wardrop
Michael Zonta

Excerpt from

BLUESHIFT

The first book in the Blueshift trilogy

CHAPTER 1
TRIAL AND ERROR

SUMMER climbed into the tree house with a heavy heart after finally breaking things off with Trevor, but she also felt lighter than she had since before losing contact with Aurora and Ben. It had been a nightmare of a year without them and she realized now just how much Trevor had been bringing her down—and just how much she'd been letting him do it. She'd stayed with him to punish herself, she realized—first for being a lousy mother in the first place, but then for being lousy enough to completely lose track of her daughter—and she couldn't believe how much freer she felt now that he was gone.

Summer pulled the rope ladder up over the edge of the balcony and then flung herself down on the musty old mattress, gathering her ratty blankets around her to ward off the autumn chill. She pulled out the card the Earthlings had given her when she first had met them, almost a week ago now. She didn't look at it, but mulled everything over as she rotated the card in her fingers. The recruitment drive would start that afternoon, and now that she had dumped Trevor like the pile of abusive garbage he was, she knew it was only the beginning of changes for her.

She had decided upon meeting the pair of Earthlings—the Luccio brothers with their mesmerizing fighting abilities—that she would go to the recruitment. As she sat in the tree house—the dingy and haphazard board structure that had been her only refuge for so long—contemplating that bizarre first meeting, she decided if she wasn't accepted in the brothers' recruitment today, that she would use what she would learn from the trials to enlist for the regular military. It was the way out of poverty that had eluded her for so long, and it would give her the opportunity to cultivate her inherent but untested potential as a mage.

It would also be an opportunity to exact some revenge and help see justice served after living so many years on the streets and having to dodge Kasma raids and the destruction wrought by the Blood Knights gang. The

Knights had begun centuries ago as a brotherhood meant as a counterbalance to the monarchy, but quickly became corrupt, now controlling all major illegal markets, particularly when it came to insurance fraud and drugs. The Knights were based on Qiran, but their sphere of influence waxed and waned throughout the solar system as they roamed through it, looking for new vulnerabilities. They had only recently returned their focus to Zandrosa, but Summer already longed for the days when she could feel even remotely safe on the streets. The streets were all she had left and the gang was slowly chiselling away her freedom.

Becoming a soldier was perfect.

With the resources that would be made available to her as a soldier, she could finally resume her search for Aurora. Whispers on the streets had led her to nothing but more heartache. It had been a brutal year and Summer didn't want to think about the winter solstice just over a month away—of spending another of her daughter's birthdays alone. The first one had been smothering in its loneliness.

The recruitment didn't start until the afternoon, so she had a few hours still. She tucked the card back into her pocket and pulled back a false cover on the wall next to her where she kept her stash of pictures. She found the one of her and Aurora hanging from the monkey bars in the park. She wiped away an errant tear, but grinned at the memory of how happy they had been that day.

It wouldn't be long now and they could finally be reunited. Summer would be a soldier—she'd be a *somebody*—and she'd finally feel worthy of the little girl's adoration. Summer was twenty now and it was high time she got her life in order. Until today, she had shuddered at the thought of the girl really seeing who and what her mother was—of the girl going down the same faulty paths that Summer's life had been lost on for so long. But no more.

She traced her fingers over her daughter's likeness, imagining the feel of the girl's soft, shining tresses under her fingers. Aurora had the same golden ringlets as her father, Ben; she had her mother's captivating blue eyes.

Summer sighed wearily, wishing not for the first nor last time that she had loved Ben with even a fraction of the intensity that she had loved Trevor. Maybe things would have been different.

"It *will* be different," she murmured, using her index finger to place a kiss on Aurora's cheek before returning the photos to their hiding spot.

Orchid and Shemmer were the only ones who knew how to find her in the tree house, but Orchid didn't know about Aurora, and Summer didn't know how to tell her. Especially now that Aurora was lost, it was a secret Summer couldn't share. She didn't know how to talk about it at all and Shemmer only knew because she'd been at Summer's side throughout the whole thing. Summer could go a year without seeing Orchid, depending on the amount of danger the monarchy faced. These days it seemed like the threats were severe and constant.

Orchid was a princess of the Low Thrones, the court that served the planet's High Throne, currently occupied by High King Seth, and it was a rare occasion when her path crossed Summer's. There was plenty of correspondence between them—all of it sent through Shemmer, who lived with her aunt. But there was only so much you could say in a letter and sometimes it seemed like Orchid was from a different universe.

If Summer was recruited today, she'd become a part of that universe and she was certainly nervous about the prospect. She'd heard a little bit about these Earthlings from Orchid. Orchid had been there the day the high king had hired them and she had seen some of what they could do—had watched them train the king's army.

Summer had known for a long time that she could both take and land a punch. She was a survivor and she hoped that transferred well into work as a soldier.

"I'm here!" Shemmer's voice rang out, cutting into Summer's thoughts.

Summer went to the balcony to see her small friend standing alone on the forest floor far below. She unfurled the rope ladder so that Shemmer could join her. The woman was dark and tiny, like the shadow of a bird on the fields, with playful brown eyes and an expression that always seemed set in a watchful, knowing smirk.

"You up here brooding, then," Shemmer commented once she had joined Summer on the balcony.

"There's a big change coming our way," Summer replied. "Mine especially."

"You're thinking about Aurora."

"That's like saying I'm breathing. But it would certainly help me find her, wouldn't it? I'm going to enlist if I don't get recruited for this. If those guys thought I had a chance at this elite group of theirs, then I must have a good chance of being a normal soldier."

3

"Yeah, that's true. I don't know why you thought I should try this too," Shemmer said. "I can't fight worth a damn."

"But you don't know that! You've never *had* to fight."

"I'm perfectly happy to let you keep fighting for me."

"They'll teach you. And you're stealthy. The king's army is full of giants—you've heard it from Orchid. Don't you think you'd be able to bring something different to it?"

Shemmer shrugged. "Only one way to find out."

The small woman stood only ten and a half hands tall, but was considered tall among her race, the Lyteltinians. They were renowned for their timid personalities and their stealth. They weren't renowned for their bravery, though they were certainly courageous when challenged. Shemmer had an untapped well of bravery, and Summer knew she wasn't coming to the trials solely to show her support. When Shemmer had been a young child, she had lost her parents and brother to a Kasma raid. She wanted to do something about it—about the treachery the Kasmas brought.

The massive, leather-skinned, winged race of Kasmas, frightening both in their similarities and differences to the human races of the solar system, hailed from the tumultuous planet of Xira and were ruthless in their pursuit to colonize all the planets. They were met with resistance at all points, but the power of the Zandrosan monarchy had been their biggest perceived threat and became the primary target of their brutality. Of the many Kasma clans, there were two that frequented Zandrosa— both ranging in the millions—one led by Draeve and the other by his cousin Sowb. They often struck at random, slaughtering all races that got in their way, and were notorious for their cruelty. They lived in squalor in their valley and frequently sent out raiding parties to scavenge supplies and bring back slaves. It was during one of these many raids that Shemmer had been orphaned.

Enough was enough. The two women were ready to fight back.

Summer had crouched to talk to Shemmer—eye to eye the way they both preferred—but when she stood again to look thoughtfully out into the trees, Shemmer was barely more than half Summer's height. There were the giants at one end of the spectrum—standing around twenty-four hands in height and hailing from the island nation of Vistyz—and Lyteltinians at the other, but most of the humans of their planet, Zandrosa, were somewhere in between.

4

With a resigned sigh, Summer began plaiting her long dark hair, preparing for the battles she would face that afternoon.

"Should I braid mine?" Shemmer asked, watching Summer's fingers deftly work through her hair.

"It's easier to fight without it getting in your eyes."

Shemmer's raven tresses were shoulder-length, but still long enough to distract her. When Summer was done with her own hair, she plaited Shemmer's into two braids running down the sides of her head.

"Have we got time to eat?" Shemmer said.

"You know there's no food here."

"I've got some money for sandwiches."

"Yeah, we should grab something then."

They both climbed down out of the tree and out into the city of Queen's Bay, the planet's capital.

"Did you talk to Trevor?" Shemmer asked as they hiked the chilly streets to a deli.

"Yeah. Wasn't as hard as I thought it would be. Not after everything that's gone on this week."

"Did he admit to it?"

"Yes. That hurt, but sure made it easier. It's over and about time."

Shemmer nodded, but said nothing. She had long suspected that Summer's on-again off-again boyfriend had been unfaithful right along with being abusive and a general creep. Summer hadn't wanted to see it, but had been over him on a subconscious level for months, and it was a good enough reason to end a relationship that never should have begun in the first place.

"You doing okay?" Shemmer finally asked.

"Better than I thought I would. I guess there's too much to think about to worry about him. He's a loser. It's time to do better."

They ate in silence, both starting to feel nervous and tense. Summer had learned where to find the brothers—at the house the king had recently given them out at the southern edge of the city—and she led the way there. It was down the highway on the outskirts of the city where there wasn't a bus to take and they walked the whole way, arriving earlier than they anticipated.

The house was just off the highway about a mile from the city, yet it seemed to be in the middle of nowhere. The city spanned a good length east-west along the seaside, but stopped abruptly on its south side. The city of Queen's Bay itself was on the shore of the Rimba Ocean and was the planet's busiest seaport. It had an airport, a space station and an expansive portalhouse but only two major highways leading in or out. One road led east, between Thunder Mountain and the ocean, and later between the ocean and the volcanic Holocaust Mountain Range, while the other highway went south—the highway that the house was only a short distance from.

The house was on a short cul de sac that it shared with only one other home across the street, and that was a vacation home. It was a two-storey, four room house (and had plenty of room for expansion) with Hybrid Forest at the eastern edge of the large yard and Glass Lake's shore serving as the south part of the yard. Glass Lake, and the house itself, was almost completely surrounded by trees. The driveway was almost non-existent leading up to the small front porch, and there was a deck out back, facing the lake.

There were several soldiers on the property and there was a table set up in the driveway where participants could sign up. Summer spotted the Earthlings—Nero and Ouija—standing just to the side of the table, speaking with a giant. The pair was dwarfed by the giant despite being average height for their kind. Nero, who was two years older than his brother, was also a half-hand shorter. Ouija, whose real name was Antonio, was a gifted telepath who always kept a neatly groomed appearance. Today, he had a knit cap pulled over his short, black hair while Nero was oblivious to his shoulder length black hair whipping around his face in the cold autumn wind. If the Zandrosan women had known anything about Earth, they would have recognized the brothers' Mediterranean good looks, but Italy was a word that meant nothing to them. Shemmer's anxiety overtook her and she shrank behind Summer as she followed the woman to the table.

"You came!" Ouija greeted, a wide grin spreading across his face. He immediately held a hand out, palm up, to his brother and Nero begrudgingly slapped a ten credit in his hand.

"You bet against a telepath?" Summer said to him, astounded.

"He really didn't think you'd come after you were so resistant to help," Ouija said. "Sometimes I wonder if he'll ever learn to trust my instincts."

"You've got to be wrong one of these days," Nero muttered before turning his attention to Summer. "Anyway, go ahead and fill out the forms. We'll start some training in the back yard—as long as the weather holds—and then we'll get to the trials."

"What if it rains?" Shemmer asked timidly, speaking for the first time.

"We have a training room in the house. It's not ideal, but it will do."

"This is the friend you were talking about?" Ouija asked Summer.

"Yes, this is Shem. I'm sure you understand she's nervous, and all the giants aren't making it any easier for her."

"They take some getting used to," Ouija sympathized. "Did you bring the card we gave you?"

Summer nodded and took it out of her pocket. It was an invitation—the way in—as well as having the necessary information on it. Ouija traded her a pair of digital tablets in exchange for the card, and she and Shemmer sat against the side of the house and punched their information into the screens.

As more participants arrived, Summer realized that she and Shemmer were the only women present, except for one giant who was part of the king's counsel. That woman was standing away from everyone else, just observing. There were a fair number of giants and Shemmer was the only one of her kind there.

As the sun finally peeked from behind the clouds and helped take the edge off the chill, Nero stood forward and called everything to order, giving them a verbal itinerary of the day.

"We'll start with some training first. It's just the basics, though it will seem extensive to some of you. The training will take most of the time, as we're more interested in how receptive you are to learning it than we are about how well you're able to use it. You will get the chance to show off what you learn and what you already know, but that will be later this afternoon."

He led them out onto the expansive lawn near the lakeshore and brought them through the paces learning some kicks and punches, impressing most of them with just how many of the hand's surfaces could be used for striking and how a simple change in stance could result in vastly different kicks. They learned to deliver blows with knees and elbows, and then how to roll forward and backward from standing, primarily as a means of dodging an attack to regroup. The sun was inching toward the horizon when they partnered up—each recruit with one of the dozen trained soldiers who were in attendance to help, protect, and observe—to learn throws and blocks. Tiny Shemmer was too mismatched with everyone there, so Nero partnered her with Ouija, who took her aside to train her on some weapons.

"You'll never win hand to hand combat against anyone other than your kin," Ouija said to her. "Let me show you a few things that will help even it out."

He had done well to learn about Lyteltinians since hearing about them from Summer, and he taught Shemmer how to throw stars and knives at a target on the shore. The others would learn a little of this as well, but as Ouija suspected, this was where Shemmer's talents shone through.

"I've always been good at throwing things," Shemmer said. "Whenever I get mad and pick up a rock, Summer knows I mean business."

"Good," Ouija said with a grin, genuinely pleased. "Look, Shemmer, I want you to use the talents you've got—to do what you're good at when the trials start, okay? Don't try to compete with everyone else at their level. Show me what you can do that no one else can, all right?"

Shemmer was relieved. "You got it!"

"And you don't have to be so afraid, you know. You're not going to get tossed in a dungeon if you don't pass here."

"I'm more worried about Summer," Shemmer admitted. "She needs this change."

"The change has already happened," Ouija insisted. "We'll see what she's made of today, but even if she isn't made for this, she's made to fight and she'll get her place in the army one way or another."

"I hope so."

Shemmer looked down at the line of knives spread out before her and tentatively picked one up.

"It's easy enough to throw these at a burlap sack," she said, driving one into the bull's-eye, "but I just don't know if I could throw one at a person."

"That just makes you human," Ouija said. "I still don't know if I could throw one of those at a person. I haven't faced that test yet. I keep hearing that battle is different—that when you're faced with hurting others or being killed, that it's easier to make that decision."

"I hope I never have to find out."

"There's more courage in you than you think," he assured her. "You can't be friends with someone like Summer for as long as you have and not have a bit of that rub off on you."

8

"Oh man, you don't know the half of it!" Shemmer replied with a grin. She glanced over to where Summer was learning to roll and fall properly, executing each move with inherent grace. Shemmer finally turned back to the row of daggers and resumed pitching them at the target drawn on the sack, each blade hitting remarkably close to the bull's-eye.

As the afternoon waned and the air grew colder in anticipation of the coming night, Nero called everyone back to the centre of the lawn to begin the trials.

"We're going to give you two different tests. Right now, we want you to spar with whoever you were partnered with earlier. You don't necessarily have to win—that will help, but it's not necessary. Again, we just want to see how well you've received what we've taught you today."

Shemmer had been practicing with real blades, but Ouija gave her some wooden replicas to use now. Even though she was terrified with Nero and a couple of giants watching on, she was still able to send every weapon she had sailing for Ouija's face when he pretended he was going to attack her. Even when he did his best to dodge them, flipping and rolling to keep out of her way, she still managed to hit him in the head, face or near vital organs—anticipating the way he moved and landing the blades where she wanted them.

"I'm going to be covered in bruises," Ouija said, wincing. "You've got a good arm!"

She managed to be both pleased and ashamed, grinning while staring guiltily at the ground in front of her, exceeding her own expectations and revelling in a new talent to cultivate. She sat back to watch Summer spar with a soldier nearly as tall as she was.

Summer felt ridiculous attacking someone who wasn't a threat and she was also self-conscious, knowing she hadn't absorbed enough of what the Earthlings had taught to really hold her own for long. She could only confidently remember two of the many kicks, and decided to test her partner with a quick and simple front snap kick aimed at his hip. He deflected her with one forearm while the other swung for her chest. She managed to get her forearm up to block, but the force of the blow knocked her backward. She had the presence of mind to use the momentum to propel herself into a backward roll and came up on her feet, ready to fight again.

She came back into the fray, more determined this time, and swept a low roundhouse kick at her partner's shin. He leaned back, putting his weight on his rear leg and didn't lose his balance after the hit. She came at him quickly, but missed with a hook, her fist sailing over him, and he sprang up behind her, driving her to the ground and twisting her arm up and behind her, placing pressure on her shoulder. She hissed out a groan through clenched teeth but refused to tap out, despite an increase to the pressure on her shoulder.

Nero finally stepped in, encouraging the soldier to break the hold.

Summer joined Shemmer and sat on the edge of the lawn, breathing deeply through her aches, and watched the last few pairs finish up. Everyone was given a few minutes to catch their second wind before Nero divided them into two groups of five and a group of four. There were three soldier giants spread out evenly along the lawn and Nero assigned each group to a giant.

"This is the final trial," he said. "I want you to knock the giants down."

The giants were all trained masters and the participants all grew doubtful. Shemmer let out a low whistle and hung back tentatively with Summer as the other two in their group slowly stepped up to the giant. As the two men in their group advanced, Summer managed to call them back.

"Don't you think we should attack at the same time?" she said to them.

"Who put you in charge?" one of them challenged her.

"No one, but it kind of makes sense, don't you think? I mean, anyone who gets accepted here is going to have to work as a team anyway. We should try to surround him, that way it's harder for him to get at any of us."

The others shrugged and moved in quickly, but Shemmer still hung back, knowing Ouija was right—she didn't stand a chance in close combat. She watched curiously as the other three moved in quickly toward the giant and Summer suddenly cut to the right and darted around him, out of his reach. He went to the other two, easily knocking one aside. The other man ducked and dodged the giant, but it was difficult to get in close. While the two men had been in front of the giant, distracting him, Summer had circled in behind him, looking for an opening. None of the other groups were having much luck either.

Shemmer circled around to the giant's left and stayed to his side, just out of his sight and waited to see if Summer could get close enough. While the two men charged from the front, Summer came in and hit the big man with a roundhouse to the back of his leg, hitting him just above the knee. His leg buckled, but she didn't time it well enough for the other two to capitalize from it. The giant recovered his balance and threw an elbow backward at Summer, which she had to drop straight to the ground to avoid. He tossed the two men aside and turned, kicking her away from him before she could get up. Summer rolled across the lawn and right back to her feet and charged the giant again.

The other two men were down and one of them wasn't even bothering to get back up. The giant was watching them and didn't realize that Summer had already recovered and was charging up behind him. Still on the fringes, Shemmer seized the opportunity and assailed the man with the pocketful of stones she had been collecting while she watched. All of them hit him in the head or face, but one of them got him squarely in the eye.

The giant roared in agony and Summer saw he'd narrowed his stance and his knees had buckled, so she hit him with another roundhouse, sweeping this one much lower than the last and catching him just above the right ankle. He cried out in surprise, but still wasn't going down, shifting his weight to the other leg, but without fully regaining his balance. So Summer grabbed the back of his uniform with both hands and lunged backward while he was still off-balance from her kick. She dived and rolled out of the way to avoid having the big man land on her. Shemmer came running from the edge of the battle as soon as she saw that Summer's blow had put him off balance, and before he could even think of getting up, Shemmer pounced onto his chest and held the point of one of her wooden blades under his chin.

"Gotcha!" she cried triumphantly, grinning broadly and enjoying the moment. She doubted she'd ever get to knock a giant down again.

"What the hell?" he gasped. "Where did you even come from?"

Shemmer hopped away and quickly joined Summer at the edge of the lawn where she was watching on.

"I think that was the greatest thing I've ever done!" Shemmer cheered.

"That was awesome," Summer agreed.

They watched on, seeing that the other two groups weren't having much luck, with many of the recruits in retreat or injured. It didn't take long for the giants to overpower the ones that were left.

The Earthlings congratulated everyone on their efforts, and a healer was on hand now to help with any significant injuries. More help had shown up to dish out large bowls of stew and fresh bread for all of the would-be warriors.

"Sweet! They're even going to feed us!" Summer said, relieved and eager.

While they all stood or sat on the lawn to eat, Nero addressed them all a final time.

"We hope to make our decision within the week and will reach all of you at the contact points you've provided. As you may already know, we're only taking two or three recruits right now, but everyone here has shown promise and I encourage you to apply for the standing army if you aren't chosen by us."

Shemmer had begun to grow nervous again, the rush of defeating the giant had subsided, and she and Summer left again as soon as they were done their meal.

"I'm not sure what was better—beating the giant or that stew!" Summer declared.

"You need to get out more," Shemmer said, rolling her eyes.

"No, just fed more. I'm going to go out of my mind waiting to hear back from them. Do you think I should just go apply as a general recruit right now anyway? That way I've got things in motion while I wait?"

"Just wait. I doubt it will actually take them that long to decide. Didn't you see? Half those guys just gave up against the giants. I don't think it was actually about knocking them down—I'm sure it was more a test of courage than skill. The first bout was a test of skill."

"I really didn't do very well with that first one."

"You did fine. And then you took down a giant—I think that cancels out slipping up the first time around."

Summer shrugged. "Well, it was my determination they noticed when I met them, and I'm sure that's the talent they hoped to draw on."

"You've always got plenty of that to go around."

Iguana Books

iguanabooks.com

If you enjoyed *Dragon Whisperer*...
Look for other books coming soon from Iguana Books! Subscribe to our blog
for updates as they happen.

iguanabooks.com/blog/

You can also learn more about Vanessa Ricci-Thode and her upcoming work on
her blog.

vanessariccithode.iguanabooks.com/blog/

If you're a writer ...
Iguana Books is always looking for great new writers, in every genre. We
produce primarily ebooks but, as you can see, we do the occasional print book as
well. Visit us at iguanabooks.com to see what Iguana Books has to offer both
emerging and established authors.

iguanabooks.com/publishing-with-iguana/

If you're looking for another good book ...
All Iguana Books books are available on our website. We pride ourselves on
making sure that every Iguana book is a great read.

iguanabooks.com/bookstore/

Visit our bookstore today and support your favourite author.

IGUANA

CPSIA information can be obtained at www.ICGtesting.com
Printed in the USA
LVOW07s1040030615

440980LV00002B/23/P